FREE TO LOVE

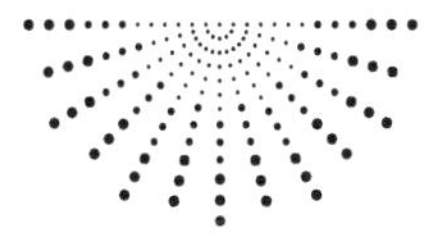

SUZETTA PERKINS

For information:
Suzetta Perkins Productions
P. O. Box 64424
Fayetteville, NC 28306

Cover design by Rebecca Pau.

ACKNOWLEDGMENTS

It's been a true blessing in continuing to bring you the stories that find their way to my pen—stories that are suspenseful and yet leave a message of hope, trust, faith, peace, and redemption. *Free to Love* is no different and is the long-awaited sequel to *Betrayed.* I promised and am happy to deliver this novel to my wonderful readers.

My family has been the mainstay of my writing career. Their love and support sustains me, and I appreciate them from the bottom of my heart. JR, I appreciate your constant and ever ready assistance in all I do; I couldn't make it without you. Love to my sisters, Jennifer and Gloria for always loving me.

Writing is a gift from God, and he's allowed wonderful friends, book clubs, and other readers to advance my career. First my book club, Sistahs Book Club—Tara, Bridget, Valerie, Bianco, Donna, Melody and Bianca, thank you for being my rock. Sister Circle Book Club, The Girlfriends of the Carolinas, Sisters Unlimited, Words with Friends, Black Pearls Book Club, New Visions Writers, and DRR, I can't thank you all enough for repeatedly sponsoring me at your book club meetings, retreats, celebrations, and anniversaries. It has meant the world.

To my agent, Maxine Thompson, you're still my number one girl. I can't thank you enough for giving me access to your radio show, "ArtistFirst." To Norma McLauchlin and Patricia Davis of Chosen Pen, thank you for the opportunity to mentor aspiring authors. There's nothing like giving back. To Jacquelin Thomas, my heart and soul, I love you for who you are and your undying support in my endeavors. And to Troy Johnson of AALBC, thank you for showcasing me on your website amongst all the literary giants.

Just want to shout out a few names that I haven't always acknowledged but have been in my corner since day one with their undying support—Cousins Wanda Washington and Virgina Moss-Jones, LaWanda Miller, Yolanda Bonnett, Tanya Ortiz, Patricia Mendinghall, Mary Evans, Pamela Farmer, Jessie McNeil, Edithe McLean, Nadine Hutton, Sandra Prewitt, Sheila McKoy, Alice Williams, Syrana (Diva) Smith, Janice Robinson, Deborah (Angelou Book Club), LaSheera Lee, Angela Reid, Pat Flanigan, Jennifer Jennings, Thal Morris, Carlitta Moore, Margot Pittman, and Dr. James Anderson. And to my BFF's Mary Farmer and Deborah Miller, thank you for always going the extra mile to support a sister. You all ROCK!

May God's love continue to shine on all of you.

DEDICATION

To all my beautiful friends,
who recognize that there's no greater love than God's love.

FREE TO LOVE
By: Suzetta Perkins

I've watched my life float by
like a tumbleweed in the wind,
Mirrors reflecting how my life wasn't
supposed to be...and then again
Secrets had me bound
But there was no one around...
that I could tell, I could tell.

I never thought the hurt and the pain
of that day would ever go away
I hadn't realized how many people
I had betrayed along the way
Because I refused to share the
dark secret that would've set me free
Free to love my man
Free to love my best friend
Free to love the best of myself
Free to put the shame to rest
But when I did, I was free to love

And now I'm free to love; I'm free to love;
Yes, I am free to love, I'm free to love
Free to love my man
Free to love my best friend
Free to love myself
Free to put the shame to rest
Yes, I'm free; I'm free to love

CHAPTER ONE

A death sentence was unacceptable. Breathing heavily, she willed herself to move from the safety of her car to tread across the black-tar-topped parking lot —it's pavement a crisscross of coordinated white lines to keep motor vehicles in check. Light snow blanketed the ground that would soon evaporate once the sun was able to push from behind the fast-moving clouds according to the latest weather forecast.

Brenda Christianson, wrapped in a heavy wool scarf, a bronze-colored midi-coat, large designer sunglasses, and brown-leather Cole Hahn boots, moved swiftly from her Lexus SUV that she parked on the grounds of the imposing medical clinic. Her head roved from one side to the other, as she assessed her surroundings before entering the safety of the building.

Once inside, Brenda's eyes scanned the interior of the lobby making a mental note of the persons who'd already occupied seats in the waiting room. Medical literature was scattered in an organized fashion throughout and a small, flat-screen television was mounted up high in a corner for easy viewing. The interior walls were painted a soft, matte-yellow color that gave a calming…soothing effect. Satisfied that there was no one she recognized, Brenda pulled off her shades and moved toward the reception desk.

As Brenda approached the blonde-haired receptionist, she caught a glimpse of a woman seated in the first row of chairs, whose eyes were obviously checking her out. When Brenda turned to get a better look, the woman quickly turned her head, her neck making a creaking sound as if she needed some oil. The woman's face, as much as Brenda could see, appeared hard and hollow, while her eyes were almost vacant. She wore a short haircut that was in bad need of a perm. Dressed in a wrinkled black-and-white-striped jumpsuit, the woman sat slouched down in her seat, but refused to make further eye contact. Brenda smirked, although an uncomfortable feeling came over her.

"May I help you?" the receptionist asked, causing Brenda to jerk her head around.

"Yes," Brenda whispered as she cowered over the counter. "I called earlier about taking an HIV test."

With her index finger, the blonde-haired receptionist scrolled down a piece of lined paper. "Are you Brenda Christianson?"

Brenda threw up her finger to quiet the receptionist and then looked around to see if anyone was listening. However, when she looked in the direction of the lady in the jumpsuit, the woman stared back deep into Brenda's prying eyes, seemingly unafraid of Brenda's imposing figure. In fact, she met Brenda's eyes head on, giving her a once over and sat up straight in her seat. The woman rolled her eyes in contempt and made a movement like she was about to get up but thought better of it. Brenda cocked her head and sneered at the woman, unable to comprehend the woman's apparent interest in her.

"Mrs. Christianson," the receptionist said, "you may have a seat in the lobby. The lab technician will call when he's ready for you."

"Thank you." Brenda sighed and took a seat two rows behind the inquisitive woman. There was something alarming about the woman, but Brenda still couldn't put her finger on it. She reached into her brain's library for a hopeful reference but for the life of her came up blank.

This was the last place Brenda wanted to be, but before she was able to move forward and go on with her life, she needed one crucial question answered. All the fornicating and trifling disrespect her late husband Victor had inflicted on their marriage had led to this moment. Married for over twenty years, he had slept with many women, laying his seed all over town. And to think, he had raped her best friend, Mimi, when they were in college and had sired a child that looked so much like her own. But it wasn't until his untimely death did she find out the other truth about the great Victor Christianson. He was HIV positive.

In bold and blaring headlines for all the world to see were the words that had scorched her body and soul—*The late Victor Christianson, Director of Admissions at North Carolina Central University, Infected Several Women with the HIV Virus to Include His Longtime Secretary.* Although she and Victor hadn't been sexually active for some time before he died, to calm her nerves and curiosity, Brenda needed to know if a death sentence had been passed on to her; she needed to know if she was HIV positive.

Thirty minutes passed before her name was called. Brenda looked up in time to see the haggard woman who had been staring at her exit from one of the examining rooms. She lowered her gaze right before the woman passed her. Then she felt it and then looked up in alarm and disgust. The woman had spit on her.

"What the hell?" Brenda jumped up from her seat and pointed at the woman who had now exited the building. In alarm, Brenda ran to the reception desk to report what happened.

"Here's a tissue," the receptionist said. "You may need to keep the contents in the tissue to show the doctor. No damage was done, so long as it doesn't get into your pores."

Brenda hunched her shoulders. "What are you talking about?"

"The woman who spit on you has full-blown Aids. She doesn't have insurance to go to the hospital, so she always comes to the clinic hoping the doctor will give her samples."

Brenda's mouth flew open. "I'll be damned."

CHAPTER TWO

The trip to the clinic was a small inconvenience. If it meant learning that she wasn't infected by Victor's poison, the trip was more than worthwhile. She prayed that the questions in the back of her mind—the anxiety attacks she'd experienced on the regular and the constant fear in which she lived her life—would soon be resolved, the results negative, and she could go on with her life. However, if the results weren't favorable, new fears, questions and anxiety attacks would take control—how long would she have to live?

Brenda was beside herself; her heart was strangled with fear. A woman she didn't even know had taken the liberty to thrust her Aids-laden spit in her face. But why? She hadn't done anything to her; hell, she had no idea who the woman could be. The staff was unwilling to give her the woman's name.

She'd let it go for now until the tests results confirmed what her spirit believed—that she was HIV negative. There was a bigger fish to fry—one that consumed her every other thought. Her baby...her Trevor was locked up in prison for killing his father. There was no way that Trevor should've been behind bars. It was justifiable homicide; Victor had provoked Trevor to pull the trigger. And if she'd been put in the position, she might have blown Victor's brains out too.

Saving Trevor was her priority. If it meant spending every red cent she had, she was going to do everything within her power to get Trevor released from prison. Brenda had connections with some power hitters, and she'd already hired the best representation for her child.

Brenda sighed. Silence now occupied her now empty home and she felt the loneliness that covered her like a thick blanket. Even Beyoncé, her faithful cat, stayed balled up in the confines of Brenda's bedroom, opting to still away from the quiet that enveloped the home that was once so full of life. Brenda's daughter, Asia, was finishing up her first year in college but made rare trips home, although only twenty minutes max separated them in distance.

Asia and her half-sister, Afrika, had become rather close after learning the truth that her father was also Afrika's. It wasn't until Afrika wanted to attend college at North Carolina Central University in Durham did anyone find out what Victor had done—that he'd raped Afrika's mother. In fact, it was his demise.

Brenda looked around her tri-level dwelling with its wall-to-wall hardwood floors that were covered with expensive Chinese rugs. The funk she was in was getting the best of her. She sighed again and looked up at the cathedral ceiling with its balcony that connected some of the second-story rooms. The loneliness continued to haunt her. Brenda moved from the couch where she sat in the family room and walked into the kitchen to get her purse. She took out her iPhone and called Mimi.

"Hey, Mimi, this is Brenda? How are you? It's been awhile."

"Hey, Brenda, I apologize for not being the attentive friend. Raphael left for Afghanistan two days ago now that Afrika is doing well and back in school. I miss him so much."

"I'm sure it was hard to see him go. That is a fine hunk of a man you have there. You and Raphael seem so happy."

"I can truthfully say, Brenda, we're at a wonderful place in our marriage, although the events this past year almost had a devastating effect on us. I made a lot of not so wise decisions, but I'd do it again not see the people I love hurt. I certainly had no intentions of being the catalyst for tearing your family...my family apart." Mimi sighed.

"Look, don't beat yourself up about it, Mimi. Victor's sins were going to find him out anyway. Honestly, while I didn't wish death upon Victor, I'm glad that he won't hurt any more people. I mean...can you believe he infected other women with the HIV virus?"

"Have you been tested?" Mimi asked slowly.

"Yeah." Brenda sighed. "I went to the clinic this morning and took a blood test. I should have the results soon. Victor and I didn't have a sexual marriage in months. I'm not sure when he contracted the disease, but I feel more confident now, talking to you, that I'll get a clean bill of health."

"That's the spirit."

"Look, if you aren't busy, how about meeting me for lunch? I need a friend right now. Besides the possible HIV scare, something strange happened at the clinic today. It really frightened me."

"What happened?"

"I don't want to talk about it on the phone. It was eerie, but I'll tell you all about it when I see you."

"I'm here for you, Brenda."

"Thanks, Mimi. So much is going on with me. Trevor's incarceration is weighing heavy on my mind. I can't let my son rot in that horrible prison, but I've got the best working on his case. While Victor may have deserved what he got, Trevor is only guilty of trying to protect all of us, even Freddie's mom, from a low-down, dirty, adulterous rapist and attempted-murderer of a father, who should've been put out of his misery."

"I pray for Trevor's safety every day. I'm not sure what kind of characters he's up against in that prison, but from the things I've heard, life isn't safe for a young man Trevor's age. I'll meet you at the Macaroni Grill in an hour, if that's okay. We've got to talk."

"Okay, I'll see you then." Brenda ended the phone call and exhaled. She needed Mimi more than she could say.

BRENDA GRABBED her bronze-colored midi-coat and headed for the door. She needed Mimi like a carpenter needed a hammer...like an addict needed his cocaine. One couldn't live without the other and together they offered a kind of high one needed to get the job done. Although the sun had come out, it was still bitter cold outside, and Brenda rushed upstairs to get her gloves. Even Beyoncé raised her head to see what all the rush was about.

As Brenda descended the stairs, the doorbell rang.

"Who could that be?" Brenda wondered out loud. "I'm coming," she shouted when the doorbell rang for the fourth time.

Finally, at the bottom of the stairs, Brenda rushed to open the door. It never occurred to her to peek out of the peephole. She snatched the door open, and standing on the doorstep was a wonderful surprise. Brenda stared without saying a word.

"Well, are you going to let me in? It's cold outside."

A smile washed over Brenda's face. She swung her arm in a half-circle. "Come in. I was on my way out to meet Mimi, but I... I think I can spare a minute. So, what brings you by?" Brenda watched as John Carroll entered her house, smelling like paradise. She closed her eyes for a second and inhaled his intoxicating scent. Brenda didn't know what wind blew him in her direction, but she wanted to shake her head and lick her lips. The man who stood before her was divine.

John wore a grey wool overcoat that was draped with a plaid, black, red, and white wool scarf. He peeled off his grey, wool fedora with the black band that circled the base of the hat, and Brenda nearly swooned when he exposed his shiny bald head. She had no right fawning over John; after all he was Mimi's ex and they still seemed close. But that was years ago, and anyway, Mimi had a husband who was a smart and gorgeous hunk of a man.

Coming back to her senses, Brenda offered John a seat in the family room. "Would you like some tea or coffee?"

"No," John said absently. "I was in the neighborhood and thought I'd drop by to see how you were doing and to offer assistance if you should happen to need it."

"I'm flattered, John." A broad smile lit up Brenda's face. "Wow, I appreciate the thought. While I can't think of anything I need assistance with now, I certainly am going to take a rain check on your offer. You never know what might come up."

"Well, okay. It's good to see you again. You're looking well. I don't want to keep you from your date with Mimi."

"Sure thing. Raphael left a few days ago for Afghanistan."

"Oh?"

So, he's still mildly interested in Mimi, Brenda observed. "We both need each other's company, so we're going to meet for lunch. Would you like to join us?"

"Not today, but maybe I'll take a rain check and meet you on a day that you're free. I was thinking about Trevor the other day, and I told myself that Brenda may need some assistance in getting his legal defense together."

Eyebrows arched toward heaven upon hearing that she had been in John's thoughts. Brenda was now very interested. "Gosh, John, how could you've known that Trevor's defense was weighing heavy on me? It's almost as if you have ESP. To tell the truth, I've got a great defense attorney working on Trevor's behalf. He's looking for loopholes since Trevor all but admitted that he shot Victor in cold blood. The lawyer is trying to ascertain what prompted Trevor to do it, which could lead to a ruling of emotional distress or self-defense. The trouble is, Trevor hasn't been very cooperative. He hates where he is and doesn't want to talk to anybody. Anyway, why don't I call you later in the week to set up a time to do lunch and talk? I may be able to use your assistance after all."

"Sounds perfect, Brenda. Well, I'll let you get to your lunch with Mimi. Give her my regards."

"I will."

Brenda noticed that John allowed his eyes to linger on

her a little longer than expected. She didn't want to read anything into it, but she felt a tingle in her spine, in her stomach, and between her legs. Damn, she hadn't gotten the results of the HIV test yet, and now that a handsome man had suddenly appeared before her like an apparition, although he was very much in the flesh, her body wanted to read more into the friendly gesture. She squeezed her legs tight and the lust for him out of her mind. She followed John to the door, closed it behind him, and exhaled.

CHAPTER THREE

Days turned into weeks and weeks into months since Trevor's incarceration. Trevor's attitude hadn't changed much since he arrived at Central Prison. He had lots and lots of time to reflect on what had gotten him thrown in the slammer in the first place, and the more he thought about it, his heart wouldn't allow him to feel bad about killing his father, although he wasn't sure that he had. At any rate, Victor deserved what he got.

Prison life had worn thin on Trevor. He should've been on the court shooting some basketball or thinking about where he would be going to college. If he had any regrets about shooting his father, it was that his life, such as it was, was truly over. No lawyer was going to be able to save his ass regardless of how much his mother believed in his freedom. Freedom, what a thought. A small pool of water filled Trevor's eyes.

Trevor sat up on his cot when he heard the automatic locks on the cell release, which meant it was time for lunch. Lunch had been a lonely affair, as Trevor felt no loyalty to no one and preferred not to mingle. In some ways, Trevor felt he was better than the other prisoners he'd labeled scum, although his crime had put him in the same category. The only thing Trevor could hope for was a light sentence when his case came to trial.

Entering the chow hall, Trevor moved toward the chow line, ignoring the stares of some of his fellow inmates. Out of the corner of his eye, he saw Hammer, the self-proclaimed godfather of their cell block, dressed as the others in his orange jumpsuit, watching him like a hawk. Black prisoners followed Hammer like he was the Pied Piper of Hamelin, bidding to do his dirty work. So far, Hammer had left Trevor alone after their first, brief encounter, but Trevor knew that it would only be a matter of time before he'd be approached again.

There was tension between the blacks and Hispanics—a drug bust that had gone sour on the outside. Hammer had solicited men for a potential shakedown, but Trevor wanted no part of it. He wasn't a criminal by his thinking.

Trevor moved forward and received the slop that was put on his plate. As he moved to find a seat, Hammer suddenly appeared in front of him, blocking his freedom, as limited as it was for an inmate. Holding tight the edges of his food tray, Trevor stared straight through Hammer's soul, letting him know that he may be a young brother, but he wasn't one to be messed with.

Hammer crossed his arms over his chest and gave Trevor a half smile. "Yo, you wanna be a tough brother, huh? Can't fault you for that, but like I told you some time ago, this my turf, and to play here, you gotta pay."

"Whatever," Trevor said, shrugging his shoulders. "Now if you would move out of my way, I'd appreciate it."

The faint smile that covered Hammer's face moments earlier was now replaced with a scowl. Hammer pointed his finger in Trevor's face, narrowly missing the bridge of his nose. "Nigga, yo get-out-of-jail-free card has expired. And as I told you befo', I'm the daddy in this here joint, and you've got to play by my rules."

"I play by nobody's rules but my own," Trevor spat out. "Now move out of my way."

Hammer stepped aside and held up a hand, as Hammer's crew eased out of their seats to come to his defense. "You will bow down, nigga. Know dat!" Hammer stuck his finger in Trevor's chest. "In the meantime, watch yo back."

Still holding his tray, Trevor stared straight through Hammer. Moving his head in a semi-circle, Trevor scanned the room and watched as Hammer's crew sat back down in their seats. Trevor looked back at Hammer. "Nigga, I ain't scared of you." Then he proceeded to an empty seat. Inmates who already occupied the table, picked up their trays and moved to another.

BRENDA WAS EXCITED about meeting Mimi today. It had been awhile since they had spent some girl-bonding time together. But her excitement had scaled up a notch, and John Carroll had something to do with it. Brenda couldn't shake the feeling their brief encounter this morning had caused.

Driving through the maze of traffic, Brenda still had John on the brain. She wanted to tell somebody how she felt, but like the red light that loomed ahead of her, a flag in her subconscious made her put on brakes. Talking about John to Mimi might not be a good idea. After all, Brenda had conjured up all these thoughts about John who hadn't indicated one way or another that his strange visit to her home was anything but a friendly visit to see about a friend. So why was she feeling this way? It was settled in her mind. She wouldn't say anything to Mimi.

Brenda turned into the parking lot of the Macaroni Grill and waved to Mimi who had arrived at the same time. She exited her SUV and tried to act natural, imploring her excited soul to keep her secret. She and Mimi met on the sidewalk outside of the restaurant and hugged each other for a minute before entering.

"Girl, you look so good," Mimi said, giving Brenda a once over. "If I didn't know any better, I'd say that whatever was weighing you down earlier is now sitting on the back burner. You actually look happy."

"Do I?" Brenda asked, hoping that her excitement about seeing John wasn't leaking out of her pores. "I feel good; my only wish is to be able to move on with my life. Let's go in."

"I'm following you."

The ladies cackled as the waitress showed them to their seats. They pulled off their coats and scarves and sat across from each other, basking in the knowledge that they were best friends again and that they had moved past the uncomfortable part of their lives. Although Brenda had forgiven Mimi for not telling her that Victor had raped her years ago, reminders of the fact cropped up every now and then, like a sharp pain that came out of nowhere. They were in a good place with each other, and in time, the old wounds would completely heal.

"So, what happened in the hour or two since we spoke on the phone this morning that has you beaming?" Mimi asked. "Are you hiding something from me, girl?"

Was she that transparent? She had been in John's presence all of fifteen minutes, and here was Mimi telling her she had a sudden glow about her...that she was hiding something from her. As much as she wished she could blurt out the magical feeling she was now experiencing, there was no way she could tell Mimi. First, it was premature—maybe a desperate desire to be wanted that made her conjure up the idea that John might have been flirting with her in the first place. Would Mimi get jealous if she told her about John? Hell, yes, she would.

"Mimi, I don't know what you're talking about. I'm only happy to see you. We're kindred spirits, and maybe I was a little jealous that you were over there at your place cuddling up with your husband."

"Come on, Brenda. Yes, Raf and I enjoyed every minute of the time he spent at home. You were always in my thoughts and prayers, although, I might have been a little selfish for wanting Raf all to myself."

"I don't blame you, girl. Once upon a time, Victor and I enjoyed our marriage, but while I wasn't certain then, I'm sure that even then Victor was scandalizing our name."

"Well, don't think about it. It's all water under the bridge now. You have two beautiful children. How is Trevor?"

"Mimi, his state of mind is not good, but I'm going to do everything in my power to get my son released. His father was an evil man. He tried to kill Raphael and then went after Trevor's friend, Freddie's mother. You know, Mimi, I don't blame Freddie's mother for being with Victor. She didn't know any better."

"But what about those other women Victor played around with? Do you forgive them, too?"

Brenda looked thoughtfully at Mimi and then

dropped her head. Brenda sighed and then looked up at Mimi. Victor is the person I blame. I can't help that those women didn't have morals and when he dangled his sorry ass dick in their faces, they jumped at the bait. I wonder how many of them contracted the HIV virus..." Brenda's brows arched.

"What's wrong, Brenda? Are you okay?"

"Mimi." Brenda paused, turned her head to contemplate something, and finally brought her hand to her mouth. "I don't remember if I told you that when I was at the clinic this morning, a woman kept staring at me."

"No, you didn't mention it."

"Damn, she kept glaring at me and when the receptionist called out my name, the woman stared at me as if I had done something to her. I don't know what Freddie's mother looks like, but it was as if there was some recognition when she heard my name. This woman was crazy, though, and on her way out of the clinic the hussy spit on me."

"She did what?"

"You heard me, Mimi. And guess what the receptionist told me?"

"I haven't a clue."

"How about...the woman had Aids?"

"Damn, what does it mean? Wasn't Asia's boyfriend Freddie's brother?"

"Yes."

"Maybe Asia can find out from him."

Brenda let out a long sigh. "Asia doesn't like coming home, Mimi. She hates to be reminded about her father's death and the fact that Trevor is in jail. Home is a bad place in her book, and she doesn't call as often as she used to. Many times, my calls to her go straight to voicemail."

"She'll have to come home soon. Summer will be here before you know it...if we can ever get rid of this snow."

"Yeah, who would've thought we'd have snow at the end of March? Crazy weather. "Look, why don't I talk to Afrika and see what she can find out?"

"Would you do that? But I don't want Asia to know that I'm the one inquiring."

"Okay, I'll talk to Afrika, and you should stop worrying about those other women. We're going to pray that your test turns out negative."

"You're right. But I do have a task I need to handle."

"What is it?"

"Kicking Victor's secretary, Sheila, out of the condo she thought he bought for her. I have the deed, and girlfriend is about to be evicted."

"Doesn't she have HIV?"

"Yes, she's got HIV and she's getting ready to get FUHA."

"What in the hell is FUHA, Brenda?"

"Foot up her ass." The ladies broke out in laughter. "I hate to be the executioner, but I'm terminating her right to live in that condo. I'm going to sell it. I'm getting rid of all memories of Victor and his fornicating ways." Brenda shook her head. "Nasty."

"It's going to be all right. You've got your friend here to assist however you may need me. Speaking of friends, have you seen or heard from John?"

Brenda froze in her seat. Mimi was steadily stepping on the nerve she was trying to keep in check. "John who?"

"John Carroll. Who else would I be talking about?"

"Girl, of course, John. He slipped my mind. Don't tell me you're going to dig him up now that Raphael is across the ocean."

Mimi smiled. "John was good company when Raf was away...and not in a physical way. He made me laugh and it was good to know that a good friend was nearby. And Lord, that man is still fine after all of these years."

Brenda bunched her lips together and thought about what she'd say. "No, I haven't seen him," she lied. "He's been a good friend to you, Mimi, but be careful. Loneliness can make a woman slip, especially when their special someone is so far away."

"I would never have a physical relationship with John. Raphael is my heart, my life. I hurt Raphael terribly when he found out that Victor had raped me and that Afrika wasn't his biological daughter. Thank God for time that heals wounds. We were able to work through all of that betrayal, and I'll be damned if I'm going to jeopardize my marriage now. John is just a good friend; that's all."

"Okay, I believe you. Here's our food; let's eat."

CHAPTER FOUR

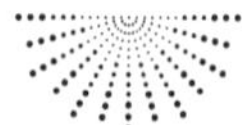

Mimi pulled her car into the garage and sat for a moment. She smiled and thought about her lunch with Brenda. Mimi was thrilled that Brenda was back in her life and that the secret she'd kept from her for more than nineteen years was out in the open and hadn't torn their friendship to shreds as she first believed it might. Although Brenda had a lot on her mind, their conversation had been pleasant and light even with her worrying about Trevor being in prison and the thought that she could possibly have the Aids virus.

Mimi dragged herself out of the car and entered her townhouse. She sifted through the mail she'd pulled out of the mailbox earlier and then decided to pour herself a glass of Moscato. She poured and sipped.

Her daughter, Afrika, and Brenda's daughter, Asia, were now joined at the hip and enjoyed their new-found status as sisters. Afrika had fully recovered from the gunshot wound that Victor Christianson had inflicted on her in his quest to get rid of the evidence of the rape he committed against Mimi. However, the revelation of the rape had torn Mimi's and Brenda's families apart for a moment—Raphael finding out that Afrika wasn't his biological daughter and the Christianson children (Asia and Trevor) finding out that Afrika was their sister. In the end, however, Victor was the one who found the bullet that silenced him forever. Mimi smiled.

Now that Raphael had gone to Afghanistan, she had too much time on her hands. A job was what she needed to keep her from going crazy. A job would also keep her from worrying about Raphael's well-being. She prayed every night that God would bring her husband home in one piece and he would retire out of Uncle Sam's Army.

Mimi took another sip of her Moscato and reached for her purse. She pulled out her Smartphone and, as if she had the numbers memorized, punched in John's number.

While the phone rang, Mimi thought about Brenda's reaction to her asking about John. It was almost as if Brenda was passing judgment on her—as if she inferred that Mimi was going to play up to John while her husband was gone, even with Brenda going as far as to say *be careful...loneliness can make a woman slip, especially when their special someone is so far away.*

Mimi thought about it. Maybe Brenda hadn't gotten over the rape incident and still blamed Mimi, although many years had passed since it happened. Mimi hated Victor, and if she could turn back the hands of time, she probably would've had him arrested. Even at that, Brenda couldn't possibly think that she would lead John on and play with his emotions. She was in love with her husband. Mimi smiled and banked her previous thoughts when she heard John's voice at the other end of the line.

"Hey, John, this is Mimi? How are you doing?"

"I'm fine. How's Raphael? Is he still in Durham?" John

asked even though Brenda had already given him the four-one-one.

"Raphael is doing fine. He's in Afghanistan. I hated to see him go and I pray he'll be all right."

"I'll be praying for him, too. So, what do I owe for the pleasure of this phone call?"

"Nothing, I…I was sitting here sipping on a glass of wine and you crossed my mind."

"Oh, really? I haven't heard from you in weeks and I suddenly came across your mind?"

Mimi chuckled. "Well, Brenda and I had lunch today and your name came up."

"Oh, really?"

"Is *oh really* the only thing you can say?"

John chuckled. "Okay, Mimi, I'm flattered. So, what did you say about me?"

"Nothing really." They both laughed. "Actually, I'm the one who brought up your name. I asked Brenda if she had heard from you, but she said she hadn't."

"Ummm."

"But Brenda seemed a little irked when I asked about you. Basically, she said that I was a married woman and I should be careful."

"Careful about what?"

"Exactly my point. However, Brenda went there and said to me with a straight face *be careful because loneliness can make a woman slip, especially when their special someone is so far away.*"

"And what did you tell her?"

"I told her that I love my husband. What else would I have said? You were there when I needed a friend, and I believe that friends should be able to talk to each other or have a meal together every now and then. What I feel in my gut, John, is that Brenda hasn't gotten over the fact that Victor raped me. In a way, I feel she blames me for it. If I didn't know any better, I'd almost say that she was jealous of our relationship."

"Brenda's been through a lot."

"She went to the clinic today and took the HIV test."

"We have to be there for her, Mimi. And she's probably worried sick about Trevor being locked up in prison."

"You're right. Anyway, getting a job is in my immediate future, but I'm going to take some time out for Brenda before I decide to go back into the work force. So, what are you doing tomorrow? Do you have time for lunch?"

"Gosh, tomorrow is tight. I have several meetings, and I'm not sure I can get away."

"Well, why don't you stop by after work? I'll fix you a delicious meal."

"Look, Mimi. You've got a good husband and I don't want anyone running back to Raphael telling him that I've been spending time with his wife. The man trusts me now, but I'm not sure that I can trust myself with you, especially knowing that your husband is thousands of miles away, taking heat for our country in the Afghan desert."

"Now you sound like Brenda. I love my husband, John. Sometimes it gets a little lonely around here, and talking with an old and dear friend is what the doctor ordered."

"Mimi, you're not naïve and don't play me for a fool. Honey, if I'm anywhere close to you, you're going to set the warning bells off and then set my soul on fire, and I can't promise that I'll behave myself. I've given you fair warning and I'm quite sure that I'm not what the doctor ordered."

There was silence for longer than a minute. Mimi looked at the phone and let what John said sink into her subconscious. She loved Raphael, and if she was straight up and honest with herself, it would be a dangerous liaison if she and John were together. Her mind said that all she wanted was a friend but having such a handsome man in her midst to remind her of what she was missing wasn't a clever idea. Her body could easily succumb to the likes of John.

"Even though I hate to admit it, you've made a valid point. I love myself some Raf, and my husband wouldn't take too kindly to me hanging out with you all the time." Mimi laughed in spite of herself.

"Exactly my point," John stated matter-of-fact. Your loyalty lies elsewhere, so there's no reason to lead me on because that's exactly what you'd be doing. I shouldn't be saying this, but I'm going to go there. I've always wanted you and when I saw you again, I had high hopes that one day I'd get to enjoy the essence of you—your sweet lips, your sweet nectar..."

"Okay, John, I get the picture."

"I don't think you do, Mimi. When I saw you in the park a year ago and we exchanged that innocent kiss, the blood rushed to every part of my body, especially between my legs. Our little lunches started out innocent enough and I believe that I would've been in your bed if Afrika hadn't been shot and Raphael hadn't come home."

"John, that simply isn't true."

"You calling me a liar? Tell me that I'm lying and I'll drop this whole conversation."

"Well..."

"Well? Come on, Mimi. You and I both know it's true; we have history. We were under each other's spell and you were crawling under my skin, which was the reason I couldn't stay away from you. But Raphael wasn't going to sit by and let some other dude rub up on his wife. I respect your husband. He knows what he's got and will do whatever to protect what's his."

"You've made your point."

"You still haven't admitted that you wanted me, too." John sucked his teeth. "My crystal ball says you were itching to find out what you missed by kicking John Carroll to the side of the road all those years ago. I know you wanted to feel my arms around you, my fingers crawl through your hair, and my lips all over your body."

"All right, maybe I did want to know, but I also knew that Raphael Bailey is the only man I would ever love. You're right and maybe Brenda is right as well. It's best that I distance myself from you." Mimi smacked her lips and sighed. "Thanks for putting me on blast and allowing me to see myself. I won't say that I'm proud of what I confessed, but if you're feeling the way you are, I'm not going to be the honey to lead you to the nest. Take care of yourself, John. I'll see you around."

"If that's what you want."

"That's what I want. Take care of yourself."

"I'll do that, Mimi. Love you."

Mimi clicked the OFF button and stared at the phone. John all but accused her of leading him on, and maybe he was right. She had been playful, excited about seeing him after nineteen years. Again, Brenda's words came to her *—one thing leads to another.*

CHAPTER FIVE

Three days had passed since Brenda had gone to the clinic to take the HIV test. All the waiting for the results had Brenda on edge. She couldn't move on until she had the verdict, whether good or bad. But there was a small matter she was going to take care of today, come hell or high water. Ms. Sheila, Victor's secretary, was getting ready to be evicted from the domicile that had hers and Victor's name on it.

As she grabbed her coat, for a fleeting moment she thought about John. He had pricked her interest, but now she was glad she hadn't acted on it. He hadn't called or come by since she last saw him, which more than proved that what she perceived was only a figment of her imagination. John was still in love with Mimi; it didn't take a rocket scientist to figure it out. She saw the way John looked when she told him that Raphael had left the country. There was a whimsical look in his eyes that betrayed him. Brenda brushed her hands against the air, picked up her purse, and headed into the garage. John was now a blur.

As Brenda exited the driveway, she almost collided with a slow-moving, beat up sedan. Before Brenda could pull completely from the driveway, the car sped off, even if it wasn't at lightning speed. Brenda wished she had gotten the license plate, but it was probably nobody. Everything seemed to have her a little jumpy these days.

Exiting the neighborhood, Brenda sped toward Interstate 40 and the condos where Sheila lived, which wasn't far from the Streets at Southpoint Mall. She hadn't thought about what she would do if Sheila wasn't home. It was the middle of the day, and Sheila might be at work. Before Brenda could talk herself out of it, she drove on. She might need to get her a new bag after she finished her dirty work.

When Brenda came to the condos and followed the instructions of her navigator, she bunched up her lips. She wondered what kind of money Victor had dropped for this secret hiding place. It only made sense, as Victor thought he deserved the best—money he'd taken from the pockets and mouths of his children. Well, Brenda, thought, *he paid his dues.*

Brenda turned off the ignition and took a deep breath. She looked out of her window toward the door that she'd soon be knocking on. While the deed had to be done, it was going to take a lot more energy than Brenda had at the moment. Damn, she wished she had a Red Bull. She could plow a field like a mule when she drank an eight ounce.

The trip to the front door seemed to take a month. Brenda dragged her feet, but finally stood in front of the place where her husband had kept his whore, the one who was now infected with the Aids virus. It was a beautiful collection of condos that stood three stories high. The brownish siding that looked like brick and the white, wrap-around balconies that were planted on the end units gave it an upscale look. It wasn't far from the university where Sheila and Victor worked, making it a convenient location for cohabitating with a skanky side-piece.

Brenda stood a moment, contemplating how she would handle it, willing her anger to quiet itself right on down. Now composed, she lifted her hand to knock on the door. Before she touched the door, an elderly woman's high-pitched voice shouted at her.

"She's not there," the woman hollered from her balcony. "Her husband took her to the hospital; she's sick."

"Husband?" Brenda remarked almost as if trying to convince herself of what the lady said as opposed to it being a question."

"Yeah, she got married right after that other feller died —the one she used to date that got himself killed some months back. He must have been some kind of bad guy 'cuz I remember the day Sheila waved a gun at him. Heard she shot up her condo. She must not have been that good a shot; I heard she left holes all over the wall. That boyfriend was lucky to be alive.

"He was a meanie, though. Sometimes when he'd come around, he treated Sheila bad. I could hear her sometimes beg for him to stop. Now, I don't rightly know why she was asking him to stop, but she seemed like she was in terrible pain. Anyway, I don't mean to take up your time, but since you must know Sheila, I thought you should know that she was a good girl. No one should have to go through what she's going through. That Aids stuff is nasty. It come down on her real quick."

"Well, thank you, Ms...."

"My name is Ms. Pomeroy. I'm the self-appointed neighborhood watch for this community. They say I'm nosey, but these tenants are glad I am. Even for an upscale place, I've interrupted some near robbery attempts and kept a few of these fast-tail women from getting their behinds beat to the ground. Oh, yes, sister, I've seen it all from my perch. Ask Sheila when you talk to her. Old eagle-eye don't miss a thing." Ms. Pomeroy pointed at her eye. "I'm sure you don't engage in crazy criminal activity like I described. You look respectable."

Brenda laughed, unsure if this woman had all her marbles, but she was probably right on about Sheila and Victor. "To tell you the truth, Ms. Pomeroy, that nasty man Sheila shot at was my husband. And I can't imagine that all you say happens in this nice neighborhood really does occur."

"Ohhhhhhhhhhhh, is that right?" Ms. Pomeroy said, swinging her head around like she was a spinning top and truly crazy. "What do you know? I live here and what I say goes on in my neighborhood is the truth. You're the one who should've kept your man out of other women's beds. If you had satisfied him in your neighborhood, maybe he wouldn't have gotten himself killed."

"Yes, he got himself killed, but when you do wrong, you pay for your sins. And my husband is no different but he certainly wasn't any business of yours."

"Hmph. So, if I may ask, since I'm the neighborhood watch, what did you want to see Sheila about?"

"You may be the neighborhood watch...and I don't take that from you since you seem to be a darn good one, but my business with Sheila is none of your business."

"Oh, I see. Well, Missy, I've got to get back to my game shows. They done took all of my favorite soaps off the air—a crying shame it is." Ms. Pomeroy turned to go back into her house. As if a last-minute thought occurred to her, Ms. Pomeroy turned back around. "Ahh, Miss…I didn't catch your name." Brenda looked at her without answering.

"Well," Ms. Pomeroy said with annoyance, "Ms. Whatever-Your-Name-Is, surely you didn't come here for any good. Ms. Sheila is in a bad way, and if you've come to make her situation worst, you better think on it. I'm going to be watching out for you and that fancy Lexus you got."

"A word to the wise is sufficient, Ms. Pomeroy." Brenda rolled her eyes, shook her head, and proceeded to her car. As she hit the remote to unlock the car door, a nicely dressed gentleman stopped her in her tracks. Brenda hadn't heard him approach.

He was of average height and weight, nothing you would stop for initially. Upon close examination, Brenda noticed that his large, brown round eyes were offset by long, thick black eyelashes. His complexion was medium brown and his thick lips were imposing in a nice kind of way—a way you couldn't ignore. His lips reminded Brenda of those women who had been over injected with Botox, but this man's lips were inviting and probably satisfied anything he touched with them.

Brenda came to her senses when his baritone voice broke the silence. "May I help you? You seem lost."

Brenda was about to speak when she saw Ms. Pomeroy sneak back to the balcony. "I was looking for Ms. Sheila Atkins, but I understand she's married now."

Jamal ran his eyes over Brenda and immediately went

on the defensive. "My name is Jamal Billops and I'm Sheila's husband. And who might you be?"

"Is there somewhere we can talk, at least away from the prying eyes of that nosey woman?"

Jamal chuckled and relaxed his face for a minute. He looked at Ms. Pomeroy who sneered at Brenda. "I may need her to be a witness."

"I don't trust that one, Mr. Billops," Ms. Pomeroy said as she leaned over the bannister.

"I've got this, Ms. Pomeroy. Thanks for watching out."

"Okay, sonny. Call if you need me." Jamal nodded his head and waved at Ms. Pomeroy.

Jamal bunched his lips and turned in Brenda's direction. "How may I help you?"

"My name is Brenda Christianson. Victor Christianson was my husband."

"Oh," Jamal said. He pointed toward the steps that led to one of the condos. "This is my residence. Why don't you come inside? My wife is very ill. In fact, she's in the hospital, and I ran home to get some papers."

Brenda sighed. This was going to be tougher than she thought. "I won't take up much of your time."

"Come in."

Brenda followed Jamal into the well-furnished and decorated condo. The colors were warm and inviting. African masks and wood carvings tastefully littered the room, and throughout the room were yellow, orange and green candles in numerous sizes in ornately-styled candleholders. An overstuffed green chair sat next to a plush green sofa. The coziness of the room put a damper on what she was about to do and sent a chill up her spine.

She sat in the overstuffed green chair that Jamal indicated with his hand, while Jamal took a seat on the couch. Brenda wondered if Victor had sat in the very same chair that she now sat. It was a moot point, and there was no reason to allow the question to linger in her mind a minute longer.

"So, Mrs. Christianson, what can I do for you?"

"Mr. Billops…"

"Jamal."

"Jamal, this is hard for me, especially now."

The thick eyebrows on Jamal's face became animated as he anticipated Brenda's intention for being there. "I'm listening," he finally said after a moment of silence.

"I'm not sure if you're aware, but my husband bought the condo in which you now reside. I'm not sure if Sheila believed that Victor had purchased the property for her or not, but to cut to the chase, he didn't. The deed is in my possession, and my name, along with Victor's is on it. Of course, when he passed away, the property became mine."

"I see. And your point?"

"Maybe Victor had a premonition that his life, as he knew it, would somehow be different. He paid the property off and taxes became due, which I've paid off. Not to prolong this conversation, as I suppose you need to get back to your wife, I'm going to need you both to vacate the premises as soon as possible—the sooner, the better. I have a potential buyer for it," Brenda lied.

Jamal stared at Brenda, which made her shudder. He stood up from where he was sitting and walked close to where Brenda sat. "Mrs. Christianson, I don't mean any disrespect, but my wife is dying from a disease your husband inflicted on her." Brenda flinched. "Right now, you're taking time away from me taking care of business as it concerns my wife and the disease she's battling. It seems that you're physically fit and the Aids virus hasn't caught up with you. While I understand your concern, I don't have time for this right now."

"Well, I'm going to have to throw your asses out," Brenda heard herself say. She couldn't believe that she could be so cold and callous.

"As a refined woman that you appear to be, you lack tact. Look it up; it's in your etiquette books as well as the dictionary." Brenda looked at Jamal a little closer. "Yeah, I know what you're thinking—that I'm a boy from the hood who doesn't have any idea what the hell he's talking about. So that you know, I have an undergrad and graduate degree in business with a minor in accounting. So, don't blow your smoke in my direction."

"As educated as you are, surely you know that two plus two doesn't equal free rent or a free ride. Now I'm the one who's appalled. With your self-righteous indignation, the last laugh is on you. The ball is in your court, and if you don't take my request seriously, I'll see you in a court of law."

"It's time for you to leave, Mrs. Christianson. You've made your point, and so that you are aware, I understood every word you said. I didn't go to Walmart University... rather Morehouse College, where I excelled in my studies. But while you're checking yourself, be looking out for a lawsuit against the estate of Victor Christianson for medical expenses on behalf of my wife. There's no getting around it; her death sentence was announced in the local and national media. Now, have a good day, Mrs. Christianson. I'll see you in court."

Brenda proceeded through the door that Jamal held open and immediately felt ringing in her ears as he slammed it after her. Things certainly hadn't gone the way she intended. This setback was sure to put her further into a funk, but now she had to arm for battle. She hadn't been ready for the well-educated husband who was as well-prepared to fight on his wife's behalf. Damn, double damn.

She sat slumped over the wheel of her car, contemplating her next move. She didn't want to come off being the asshole, but HIV or not, it was time for Sheila to bounce. Her daddy always told her that if you lived by the sword, you died by the sword. While death wasn't the sentence Brenda would've given Sheila for sleeping with her husband, kicking her out of the condo would be revenge enough. But even she wasn't the kind of person who'd kick a person when they were down, especially as down and out as Sheila was at that moment.

SWEAT POURED from the brow of the feeble woman who lay balled up in her bed with the covers pulled high. The heat on the thermostat registered seventy-five degrees, and even at the beginning of spring, that was hot. She needed medicine to get her through the month, but her welfare checks and small amount of Medicaid weren't enough to pay for the medicine she needed along with her living expenses. Even her aged mother had closed the door in her face.

If only she could get up enough nerve to approach the woman who held the key to her survival. There she was sitting up in that great, big fancy house in Chapel Hill without a care in the world. It ate at Evelyn Slater's soul. Here she was suffering from Aids, while Victor Christianson, her baby's daddy, had a wife who had reaped all the benefits of his passing. Evelyn had given a lot of years to that scum bag, and now the few extra dollars she did receive from him had evaporated. Somehow, she had to make Victor's family pay for what he'd done to her, although she was the one who'd given him Aids.

CHAPTER SIX

"Hey there, pretty boy," the shirtless high-yellow man, who appeared to be in his middle thirties said as he approached Trevor while he showered. "I'll be glad to dry you off. I promise to be gentle."

Trevor ignored him and continued to let the water flow over his body. Feeling the presence of the man behind him, Trevor turned off the water, grabbed his towel, and wrapped it tight around his waist. When he looked up, the man stared him down, taking liberties to let a roving eye envelop Trevor's body that soon became glued to the area of his genitalia. Although Trevor had completely covered up, the green-eyed monster continued to stare, as if his eyes were lasers and could penetrate beneath the towel.

Rolling his eyes, Trevor tried to mask his anger. While the high-yellow man stood guard at the entrance to the shower, he licked his tongue out at Trevor and made a hissing noise before fondling himself in a grotesque manner.

"I know you want this, pretty boy. I can make your gray skies blue."

"You better get from in front of me you stupid pervert, if you don't want me to make your gray skies black. There isn't anything about you that I want."

"Oh, you're going to get this, lover boy. They don't call me Easy Rider for nothing."

"It's none of my business what they call you, but you're barking up the wrong tree. I don't want a confrontation; I just want to be left alone."

Easy Rider covered the entrance to the shower with his buffed body, leaning with his right arm on one side of the wall, while stretching his body and blocking the exit with the left. Trevor tried to rush past, but Easy Rider pushed him gently back with his hand, letting it gently slide down the length of his chest.

Trevor grabbed Easy's left arm and twisted it until Easy Rider squealed in pain. "I'm going to kick your ass, bitch."

Trevor kicked Easy in his chins; Easy dropped to the floor. As Trevor prepared to leave, Hammer mysteriously appeared with a couple members of his crew.

"Take Easy to his cell," Hammer said as he motioned to his flunkies. "I'll take care of the kid. He's got a lesson to learn."

"Look," Trevor said, putting up his hand and for the first time showing some signs of uneasiness, "I don't want any trouble; I don't have a beef with you. I was minding my own business."

"I hear you, blood, but you ain't got the message yet. Sooner or later you're going to have to choose a side; you ain't going to make it in this here joint all by your lonesome."

"I don't need any friends."

"I ain't talking about being your friend. I'm talking about preparing for war inside these concrete walls. You gonna be my foot soldier." Hammer stuck his forefinger in Trevor's flesh. "Now Easy Rider is a little sweet, and every now and then I must give him a few treats so that he'll be ready to handle some inside stuff, since he has the liberty to go lots of places in here...you know with him being high-yallow and all."

"Whatever; your fight isn't my fight."

Before Trevor could turn and walk away, he felt the weight of Hammer's fist to his mid-section. Trevor bent over and grunted, still holding onto the towel. Hammer snatched the towel from around Trevor and beat him about his head and body until he began to bleed from his nose. Trevor squirmed and fell to the floor. Hammer kicked Trevor in the buttocks and threw the towel on top of him, and then he was gone.

Ten minutes passed. A Hispanic inmate on his way to his cell came across Trevor lying in a pool of blood. He called out to one of his partners in Spanish, and they picked Trevor up and dropped him off at the infirmary.

"Hector, this is Hammer's work," the other inmate said. "What you going to do?"

"I've got something for Hammer, but the time is not now. The thing with the kid is Hammer's business, but I know it was meant for me. I'll let the others know when the showdown begins." The two exchanged fist bumps.

CHAPTER SEVEN

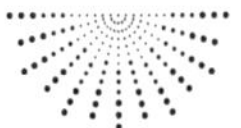

Brenda's stomach was tied up in knots. She pushed the pedal to the metal and sped toward home. The more she thought about Jamal's arrogance in her attempt to get him and his sick wife out of the condo that didn't belong to them, the madder she got. She hit the steering wheel hard with both hands and screamed. Why was she on this bumpy road? A honk from the car in the next lane brought her back to the now, and she pulled the car back into her lane to avoid an accident.

"Victor, you son-of-a-bitch, you haven't won. You may have made a mess of our lives, but I'm going to win. Be glad that you're already six feet under, and I hope and pray that I don't have to stomp your ass another two feet down."

Tears began to fall from Brenda's eyes but wiped them with her free hand. Brenda felt ridiculous but was determined not to let all the crap that was a direct result of the hell Victor had inflicted on their family while he was on earth cave in on her. She eased off the interstate and headed toward home.

As Brenda pulled into the circular driveway, a call came through the Bluetooth embedded in her car. She pulled up her iPhone and smiled for the first time that day. Without another thought, she touched the button to answer the Bluetooth.

"Hey, John. What a pleasant surprise."

"I was thinking about you. It's been a few days since I spoke to you last, but you weren't far from my mind."

"Oh," Brenda said with a smile as she pulled her car into the garage and let the garage door down.

"It's the truth. Have you eaten lunch yet?"

"Well, I only pulled into my driveway two minutes ago, but I'm game for lunch since I have eaten anything today."

"Good. We can talk about strategies to help Trevor."

Brenda sat and listened. This was too good to be true. The last time anyone cared about her needs…well, she couldn't even remember. "John, where do you want to meet?"

"How about the Cheesecake Factory at Southpoint?"

"Uhm."

"Is something wrong? It was only a suggestion. We can go anywhere you like."

"The Cheesecake Factory is fine. I... I was near there about twenty minutes ago is all."

"Really, Brenda, we can go somewhere else. My thought was to suggest a place that wasn't too far for you to drive."

"It's fine, John. In fact, I'll tell you all about it when I see you. Is twenty minutes okay?"

"I'll be there."

"Okay, I'll see you in twenty." Brenda was in a daze. John calling her was so strange and made her feel out-ofsorts. What did he really want? A wicked smile crossed her face. "Mimi," Brenda said out loud, "your man wants me." Brenda laughed. After letting up the garage door, she pulled out onto the street and headed for the Cheesecake Factory.

PULLING her collar up around her ears, Brenda exited the car and gave the keys to the young man to valet park. She entered the restaurant and saw John sitting on one of the benches with an electronic reservation beeper in his hands. His dress was casual, topped off by a heavy, fur-lined suede jacket. He appeared to be checking his email. Brenda moved forward and tapped him on the shoulder.

John jumped up from his seat, kissed Brenda on the cheek, and offered her his seat. Brenda smiled, sat down, unbuttoned and took off her coat.

"How are you doing, beautiful?" John asked. His voice was sexy but sincere.

Brenda couldn't contain her smile. "Fine, now that I'm here." She wanted to say more, but she thought better of it.

The electronic reservation beeper vibrated in John's hand. "They're ready for us. Your timing was impeccable." John extended his hand to Brenda. She took it and they went to the reservation desk and waited to be seated.

The restaurant was noisy with friendly chatter. Anxious waiters carried trays of hot food to their waiting parties, while others carried bags of different flavored cheesecakes in to-go boxes for their filled-to-the gill customers.

The waitress seated John and Brenda and handed them

each a menu. "I'll be back in a moment to get your drink order."

"Thank you," John said, eyeing Brenda over the top of his menu. "What's good on the menu, Brenda?"

"You tell me; this was your choice."

"I'm famished and I've already decided on the chicken marsala."

"I'm going to have the chicken club sandwich with guacamole."

"Didn't take you long to decide."

Brenda laughed. "It's one of my favorites when I come here. And I'd like to finish it off with their delicious raspberry lemonade."

"My favorite, too. I think we're ready to order when the waitress returns."

John smiled at her. Brenda returned the smile. Her female instinct wanted to grab his hand and hold it tight, however, the refined side of her made her sit up tall and admire him.

"So, what had you under the weather today? You seemed to be bothered by something when I called."

"Long story short, I attempted to throw Victor's concubine out of the condo she's living in…where they had their trysts, except that Sheila is in the hospital."

"What's up with her?"

"She has the HIV virus...that she got from Victor. I met her husband at the condo..."

"Husband? Do you mean she was cheating on her husband with Victor? Damn. He probably has the virus too."

"No, he married Sheila after Victor was killed, but I assume they were having a relationship; it's only been eight months since Victor's death."

"And we've got winter in March."

"How about that? But Sheila's husband, Jamal, was pleasant until I told him why I was there. That's when he showed me the door. I made it clear that I wanted him and Sheila to immediately vacate the premises they didn't even own. He had the nerve to get bent out of shape, although they hadn't paid one red cent to stay there. And on top of that, he had the nerve to tell me he was going to sue me for medical bills that Sheila incurred since Victor gave her the disease."

"Now I understand. Coming here only drudged up what you'd been dealing with earlier in the day."

"Yes, however, now that I'm having lunch with a friendly face, I can move on from that experience. At least for now."

"I'm glad that I called. I want to be of help to you—with the Sheila situation if needed and by supporting you with whatever you need for Trevor's defense."

"What did I do to deserve your friendship?" Brenda asked with innocent curiosity.

"Well..."

"May I get your drink order?" the waitress asked, interrupting John's explanation.

"Yes, two raspberry lemonades, please, and we are also ready to place our order."

The waitress took their orders and was on her way. Brenda willed herself to look into John's eyes. "You never finished your answer."

"You are a smart, beautiful, and classy woman. I loved the way you took control of things after all the chaos that surrounded Victor's death. You didn't get ugly or mean; you handled it in style...with dignity—all alone."

"My family was a rock. I couldn't have gone through

all that I had to go through—Victor's death and Trevor being incarcerated for killing him—without my sisters. But I thank you for noticing.

"To tell you the truth, John, the days have been lonely since then. Asia hates coming to the house and spends all her weekends at school. At least she has Afrika, but I miss her a lot."

"Why don't you plan a little spring party and invite, Mimi and the girls? Asia has gone through a lot as well, especially finding out that her best friend is her half-sister. This will break the ice for Asia and will be good for you too. Ask Mimi to help you plan it."

"John, you are a heart fixer."

"Well, I hope you'll let Dr. John give you check-ups from time to time." Brenda looked surprised. "That didn't sound exactly right, did it?" John said.

Brenda laughed. "You are so cute with that bald head of yours. I had forgotten what true laughter was all about."

John smiled. "I hope I can make you laugh a lot."

Just then, their food arrived. The next fifteen minutes were spent chewing their food and licking their fingers. *It was what the doctor ordered* Brenda thought to herself. And she was beginning to like the doctor a lot.

"Ready for a slice of cheesecake?" John asked as he wiped his mouth with a napkin. "They've got more than fifty-nine assorted flavors. Uhmmm."

I can't do the cheesecake as much as I'd like to have a piece," Brenda said, rubbing her stomach with her hand. "Don't want to stress my waistline, especially since I haven't been to the gym in a while."

"From my vantage point, all of your curves are doing fine and are in all the right places."

"Is that what you tell Mimi?"

"What?" A puzzled looked clouded John's face. "Where did that come from?"

"Why the sudden interest in my needs, John?"

John seemed taken aback by the question. "Brenda, I'm not sure how to say this, but you've been on my mind a lot. The night we all went to your home after Victor died, I watched how you handled things—so meticulous even in your grief. My heart went out to you, and I believe that on that very evening, I told myself that I'm going to help Brenda any way I can."

Brenda smiled. "Wow."

"And, I'm very interested in helping you move toward fulfillment and contentment."

"Strange choice of words."

"Okay, Brenda, I won't mince words. You are a first-class lady."

"What about Mimi?"

"What about Mimi? She's a married woman who's in love with her husband. And Raphael is in love with her. Those two are destined for family-of-the-year. Furthermore, I'm nobody's home-wrecker. But let's be clear, Mimi is my past."

Brenda attempted a smile. She knew that if Mimi wasn't anchored to the hip with Raphael, John would be with her at that very moment, telling Mimi the lies he was telling her…or so she believed. "Let's change the subject."

"I already have. If you don't mind, I'm going to get myself a slice of chocolate mousse truffle cheesecake to go."

"I've changed my mind. I'm going to have a slice of the fresh banana crème cheesecake…to go. And…if you want to take it back to my house, I'll fix us a cup of flavored coffee to go with."

John stared at Brenda. "Only if you're comfortable, but I'd like that. Let's get our cheesecake and be on our way. Lunch is on me."

"Thank you, John. Thank you for being a good friend."

John's eyes sparkled. "I hope I can be much more."

CHAPTER EIGHT

Mimi busied herself about her townhouse while she sang "No Other Love" along with Estelle. It felt good to belt out tunes that made her feel frisky and wild. Her voice was still crisp and alluring, and the old spark that was there years ago had come rushing back. Mimi had shunned the spotlight for years, but now she felt ready to come from behind the shadows and allow her other self to rise.

"No other love, no other touch," Mimi sang along with Estelle. "Gimme, gimme, oh so much." Mimi cleared her throat. "Sing it, girl."

Mimi became lost in her wonderful mood, allowing the song to carry her through her chores, that consisted of washing the few dishes that stood hostage in the sink and wiping down her appliances. Life was grand; she only wished that Raphael could be with her and out of harm's way.

She stopped singing when she heard the familiar ring on her Smartphone. A smile formed on her face when she answered.

"Hey, baby girl. This is a pleasant surprise."

"Hey, Mommy, I called to see how you were doing since Daddy left."

"I'm doing fine, Afrika. In fact, I was in a singing mood. Maybe I'm getting my chops ready for something to come."

"You go, Mommy. It's about time you let loose and go for yours. This would be an exciting time to get your singing career started."

"I don't know; I'm too old now."

"Hmph, remember that lady on the British version of *American Idol*? She's not mad that she waited so long to rake in the cash. She got rid of that homely look and is rocking some new threads and a new house somewhere."

"Well, I'm not trying to be Beyoncé or Mariah Carey."

"Just do you, Mommy. If you want, I'll be one of your background singers." Mimi and Afrika shared a laugh.

"We'll see. While I have you on the phone, I need you to do something for me. How's Asia?"

"She's fine. We're done cheering now that basketball season is over. We're doing other stuff."

"I trust that "other stuff" means you're hitting the books. I don't have any money to waste. But I know you're going to be successful in whatever you end up doing."

"Stockbroker."

"Okay. But listen, between you and me, Brenda is a little worried about Asia. She rarely goes home or calls. It's been a tough few months on all of us, but since you two have gotten closer, maybe you can talk to her about going to see her mother."

"She hates the thought of going home. She lost both her father and Trevor at the same time, and the house holds nothing but bad memories for her."

"How are you feeling?"

"I'm doing fine. There was no love lost when Victor died. He was already dead to me when I found out he was my biological father. And after all that he did to me, you...I'm glad he's dead."

"What a horrible thing to say."

"Admit it, Mommy. You're glad that asshole is dead, too."

"I will admit that I'm glad he's out of our lives. He was evil through and through—hurt a lot of good people. Having said that, do you know if Asia still talks to...to... what was her boyfriend's name?"

"Zavion. No, they haven't spoken to each other since he walked out of her house after finding out that Victor was Asia's father."

"Brenda wanted to know how his mother was doing. I'm sure Freddie hasn't communicated with Trevor since he went to prison; the only other link was Zavion."

"Oh, now I understand why you're asking. Zavion and Freddie's mother may have contracted Aids from Victor. Mommy, I'm sure Asia doesn't know anything since she hasn't spoken to Zavion, but I'll approach her about it."

"Remember, her mother doesn't want Asia to know that she's the one inquiring."

"I've got your back, Mommy. Now tune up those vocal chords so we can get a recording contract."

"Girl, I'm not trying to get into the industry. I'd like to be able to sing every now and then at special functions."

"I'm so proud of you. It's going to happen."

"So, when are you coming home to see your mother?"

"I'll stop by this weekend so we can do the mommy/daughter thing—lunch and spa?"

"Sounds like a wonderful mother/daughter outing. Love you, baby."

"Love you, too, Mommy. Bye."

A broad smiled crossed Mimi's face. Afrika was her heart, and she'd do anything to help her succeed. Now that Victor was a minor detail in their life, there was no doubt in Mimi's mind that life was looking up.

Pleased with her telephone conversation with Afrika, Mimi looked around the house to see if there was anything else she needed to do. She put her hands on her hips and nodded in approval that everything was tidy and in its place. Catching a glimpse of herself in one of the mirrors, Mimi shook her head. She needed to get back on a health regime. However, getting a job was at the top of the list.

Mimi raced upstairs to her bedroom and pulled out a warm jogging outfit. It was cold outside, but she'd be warm inside and out after a good jog. Mechanically, she reached for her purse and pulled out her cell. Memories of the time she went jogging at Lake Johnson upon her return to Durham came rushing back to her. It reminded her of the day she ran into John.

Straight to voicemail her call went. Maybe Mimi had punched in the wrong number, however, his face and number sat next to the button with his name on it. She dialed once more. Again, the call went to voicemail.

"Hmph," Mimi said out loud. "He must be in a meeting. I'll catch up with him later." Mimi hummed as she traded her street clothes for jogging attire. Then she headed out the door.

CHAPTER NINE

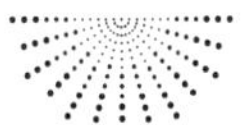

They were like old friends who'd never been apart, sitting next to each other on the white leather couch, letting their inhibitions fly out of the window. They shared a joke or two and other pleasant conversation that had Brenda giggling or John roaring with laughter. They passed smiles back and forth like they were playing table tennis, and every now and then Brenda would bat her eyes seductively. They sipped the piping hot coffee that Brenda made although they barely touched their cheesecake that together cost the sum of one hearty lunch.

"This coffee is so good, Brenda. Just what I needed to warm up my body."

Not immediately responding, Brenda smiled and took a sip of her coffee. "I'm feeling a little toasty, too."

Without further hesitation, John took Brenda's chin in one hand while the other found its way on her thigh. "Let's not waste another moment with meaningless chatter. I want to kiss you."

Words didn't part Brenda's lips, and John found hers.

Before Brenda could protest, they found themselves in a lover's embrace. Their kisses were long and sensual. John caressed Brenda's face and allowed his free hand to move to her back. Without being forced, Brenda wrapped her arms around John's shoulders and she melted into him.

For the next twenty minutes, the two lovers explored the contours of each other's mouth, catching their breath and coming up for air ever so often. John held Brenda as if his life depended on it, and Brenda refused to let go. And finally, their lips parted and they gazed at each other for the longest time.

"Do you want to take it further?" John asked gently, not wanting his desire for her to be misconstrued for lust although there was no other name for it.

Brenda smiled. "I don't think so...at least not today."

"So, there's a possibility of an encore."

"Maybe." Brenda sat up, the white leather of the couch a nice contrast to her beautiful, caramel-colored complexion. Look, John, I'm not sure what you felt, but I felt something when I kissed you. I could say yes and have sex with you, and that's all it would be—sex. If this should become more than what we have today, I want my first time with you to be more than a lust-filled meeting of two bodies. When I give of myself, I'm totally committed to the act, and I want it to be a beautiful thing.

"Something you may not know about me is that I'm a very passionate person, and when I finally make love to you, which I'm praying will be part of our journey since I've made a major step by getting on deck, I want there to be fireworks, an explosion, a thrill of a lifetime that I never want to end."

John was dumbfounded at the honest and soul stirring explanation of her feelings. He grabbed his chest for emphasis and then burst into soft laughter. "Brenda, you're so poetic, and it turns me on. But I want you to know that I heard you loud and clear, and I believe your admission of how you feel is what endears me to you more than I can say. I won't deny that I wanted you this very minute and the explosion would've come, but knowing that you're anticipating whatever this is between us and see a future in it, I'm willing to wait for however long it takes. I've been with quite a few women, and it wasn't hard to get the goodies. But you are special, and as I said earlier, I'd like to see what we've experienced here today grow...blossom into something much bigger."

"Now who's being poetic?" They both laughed.

"I want to kiss you again," John said. And his lips grazed Brenda's lightly. He took the time to taste them and add his own flavor to hers. She reciprocated in a way that was so sensual it felt as though they were in heaven.

They stayed in each other's embrace for more than an hour. "I'd better go home before I become a bad boy." John put his lips to hers and kissed her passionately.

Brenda smiled, but it evaporated from her face as fast as it had appeared. "John, I don't want to put a damper on things, but you know I haven't received the results of my HIV test yet. However, that wouldn't have changed my answer of *no* to your earlier proposal, even if the situation was different. I have a responsibility to myself and any other person I encounter to be up front and truthful. Today was beautiful, and if this is all I'll have with you, I want this time to remain special. I hope you understand."

John rose from his seat as he prepared to leave. "Brenda, it had slipped my mind, but it doesn't change how I feel about you. I'm praying, as I'm sure you are, that everything is going to be all right. Now don't forget to call Mimi so you can plan that coming out party." He kissed her on the tip of her nose.

Brenda smiled. She hadn't been this happy in a long time. "I won't, John. Thank you for a glorious afternoon."

"The pleasure was all mine."

After John departed, Brenda sat down on the couch and hugged herself for the longest time. Happiness became her and no one was going to take it away.

CHAPTER TEN

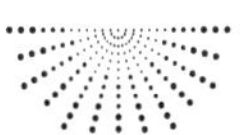

When Trevor awakened, he was back in his cell. He had no idea how long he'd been there. The last thing he remembered was Hammer's fist hitting his mid-section and several punches later the memory faded.

"Ugh," he said as he tried to sit up on his bunk. He lay back down and closed his eyes. He saw Hammer coming toward him and out of nowhere a knife materialized in Trevor's hand. With one quick swoosh, he sliced Hammer across the throat and he fell to the floor, blood oozing out of him like a river flooding its banks.

Trevor shook and opened his eyes, only to find that he was still in his cell with no Hammer in sight. For that he was grateful. He lay there a few minutes longer, assessing the dream. Was he a cold-hearted killer who lashed out without giving the consequences a second thought? Trevor closed his eyes and saw his mother bending over him. She kissed his cheek and disappeared.

"No," Trevor cried out. "No, I'm not a cold-blooded killer. Mama, I need you." And then he was still.

A second later, he felt the presence of someone at his open cell. Trevor opened his eyes and saw Hammer standing on the other side of the bar.

"You for-tu-nut this time, little nigga, but your black ass won't be so lucky next time. That little booty whipping you got will give you time to think about my offer. And the next time Easy Rider ease up on you, apologize and give him what he want."

Trevor lay on the bed but didn't utter a sound. He tried unsuccessfully to hold back the tears.

"Easy Rider is the sissy. Now act like a man." Hammer hit the bars that separated the two men and walked away. Trevor was left alone to weep.

BRENDA FLITTED around the house and felt that at any minute she'd dance her way into the starry night. In fact, she was on cloud ten...no cloud twenty-five. No one could tell her a thing. A bud in her life had burst through her sorrow and sprouted something new.

Remembering that she'd left her unfinished cheesecake in the family room, she headed that way. She sat down, picked it up, and took tiny bites and wallowed in the memory of what led to her having the cheesecake in the first place. Lunch was perfect, their conversation wonderful, and his lips were divine. Smiling, Brenda knew that she couldn't wait to see John again.

"Oh," Brenda said out loud, "I've got to call Mimi and tell her about the party I want to plan for the girls." Brenda reached for her phone and selected Mimi's number. The phone rang and rang, and just as Brenda was about to hang up, she heard Mimi's voice."

"Hey, Brenda, what's up?"

"You sound all out of breath."

"Yeah, I went jogging on one of the trails near my house. I needed to tighten up the muscles. If I'm going to begin my singing career, I've got to look my best."

"Oh, so you've decided that you're going to start a singing career?"

"I've thought about it for some time, and now that...that I'm not fearful of anyone finding me, I want to follow a dream I had long ago."

"Good for you. In fact, you can showcase your talent at the spring party I'm having. You and the girls will be my guests, in fact, my only guests."

"That sounds wonderful, Brenda. Your mood has definitely stepped up a notch."

"Pity parties are no longer allowed. I've got to move forward. Trevor's trial will be coming up in a few months, and I've got to be strong for my son. So, the party is a way to begin the process. It'll be small, but I'm taking baby steps to get to where I need to be."

"Sounds like you've got it all figured out."

"Not quite; I need you to help me plan it."

"I would be delighted, Brenda. Let me know when you want to start."

"Tomorrow if that's okay with you."

"That sounds good. I'm going to go jogging in the morning and then I'll be over. I'm going to Lake Johnson; that's where I ran into John after all those years. I think he's avoiding me, though."

"How so?" Brenda asked.

"I asked him about lunch the other day, and he said he was busy. He is a busy man, however, when I called him today to see if he wanted to go jogging, my call went straight to voicemail."

"The man does have a job and was probably giving a presentation of some kind."

"You're right. It wasn't a big deal, only a feeling. Oh, I spoke with Afrika, and she said she'll try to talk with Asia about Freddie's mother. But like you said, Afrika said that as far as she knew, Asia hasn't had any contact with Zavion. I'll let you know what she finds out, if anything."

"Thanks, Mimi. I appreciate you looking out. So, I'll see you tomorrow at what time?"

"Is eleven okay?"

"It's fine, and I'll prepare lunch."

"I'll see you then."

Brenda ended the call and hugged her Smartphone to her chest. *Oh, won't Mimi be upset if she knew that John was interested in her.* Brenda chuckled to herself. Now she had a secret.

CHAPTER ELEVEN

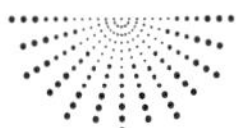

A hint of sunshine began to creep from behind the array of clouds that cluttered the sky. It was a brisk morning, but nothing would cloud Brenda's mood. In fact, she felt like the day it was—a little chilled at the thought of pretending in front of Mimi but sunny on the inside because she knew that John had begun the thaw that would eventually melt her hardened core that had consumed her body and spirit for a long time. To be honest, she smiled at the thought that she and John might have more than a friendly relationship and what had recently transpired was just the beginning.

Reminiscing about her day with John, Brenda jumped when the doorbell rang. She tried to push the wide smile to the inside, but she was having the hardest time doing so. Brenda felt like a school girl who'd been wowed by the captain of the football team—the ultimate catch-of-the day. Oh, John was so in her system, and she was losing the fight to shut it down before she answered the door.

Brenda peeped through the peephole and saw Mimi standing on the other side. Brenda grabbed her mid-section to try and suppress the feeling of ecstasy that had enveloped her. The doorbell rang again, and Brenda pulled her lips straight and answered the door.

"Hey, Brenda," Mimi said, as she stood on the porch.

"Hey, Mimi, come on in. You're looking good girl."

Brenda stood aside and let Mimi pass. She followed Mimi into her family room, and they sat down for a sister-girlfriend chat like old times. Brenda knew why John had been mesmerized by Mimi. She was still gorgeous at thirty-nine. It was evident that Mimi worked out on the regular. Her curves were all in the right place and could still generate head turners.

Mimi crossed her legs. "Thanks, Brenda. I ran this morning and I feel rejuvenated. Now I feel as if I could conquer the world."

"Weren't you cold?"

"Yeah, a little. Once I started running, my body warmed up on the inside. I like running in this weather. Thank goodness, the temperature wasn't as low as it was last week. So, what's on the agenda?"

Brenda looked at Mimi thoughtfully. Mimi hadn't seen the glow in her face. She'd concealed it better than she realized. "Well, I thought a small tea party with me and Asia, you and Afrika, would help mend whatever broken fences Victor's death caused."

"We're okay, aren't we?"

"Yeah, yeah, but Asia has been so distant. My hope is that with this party, it will help Asia to get beyond all Victor did that interrupted our family togetherness. It only seems appropriate that you and Afrika are a part of this, since Asia and Afrika seem to have accepted each other as step-sisters and best friends as you and I are. You're frowning. What's on your mind?"

"I think it's a wonderful idea, Brenda. May I ask you a question?"

Puzzled, Brenda looked at Mimi thoughtfully, not sure of the path Mimi was taking her. "Sure, what is it?"

"How are you doing since Victor's death? Have you been to counseling?"

Brenda looked away from Mimi and gave her question some thought. "Mimi, I'm fine. As much as I hate to admit this out loud, I'm glad Victor is out of my life. I didn't have enough courage to walk away from our marriage when he was alive. He did me a favor by dying, and I'm over it...over him."

"Wow. Are you sure?"

"I'm a psychologist for heaven's sake."

"I'm not implying that you need to see someone, but if you haven't truly gotten over Victor's death...after all, you were married for..."

"Stop, Mimi. I'm fine. The purpose of having this party is to define a new timeline—I'm moving forward with my life."

"You need a man in your life," Mimi said lightheartedly, trying to make a joke of it.

Brenda watched Mimi—her excitement about being with John eating her up inside. She wanted to tell Mimi that a new man had already knocked on her door, but she came to her senses and refrained from letting the cat out of the bag. "A man doesn't define me, girlfriend. I'm bad all by myself." Brenda and Mimi shared a laugh, although Brenda noticed that Mimi still wore concern on her face.

"Come on, lighten up, Mimi. I didn't call you over here to bring me down. We're getting ready to plan a party —for us and our girls."

"Well, I'm ready to start planning this shindig,

Brenda. I think it's a great idea. But we need to go out. You need to meet somebody."

Umph, Brenda thought to herself. *If Mimi only knew.*

The ladies hammered out plans for the small, intimate get-together. It would be a "white" party and they decided it would take place on Brenda's terrace—the first weekend in May. It would be catered, allowing the four of them to be free to bond. Everything was coming together.

"Your cell is ringing," Mimi called out to Brenda, who'd walked to the bathroom.

Like a lightning rod, Brenda rushed back into the room and scooped up her iPhone. What if John was calling and Mimi saw his name pop up on the screen? Brenda couldn't afford that kind of slip up.

Out of breath, Brenda answered the phone. She noticed the puzzled look on Mimi's face but ignored it. "Hello."

"Is this Brenda Christianson?"

"Yes, it is. You called my cell number."

"Whatever," the voice retorted.

"Who's this?"

"This is Sheila Billops. I understand that you stopped by my house the other day."

"You mean my house. Yes, I came by to serve you an eviction notice. If you're unclear about the details, the property that you and your husband live in belongs to me, and I'm getting ready to sell it. I need you out of there by the end of the month or sooner. Your freeloading days are over."

"I won't pretend that I like you Mrs. Christianson, but here's the deal. I'm a very sick woman because of your husband."

"And whose fault, is it? Certainly not mine. You got

what you deserve for having sex with another woman's husband. There's a consequence for everything we do in this life. Remember that."

"I thought you were a different kind of person, according to media pieces I've seen about you."

"Oh, you can read."

"You are a mean and spiteful woman, Mrs. Christianson. Say what you will, even if you are right; I don't have the strength to fight back at this moment. But I'm asking you to give us some more time. As I said, I don't have the energy to move. You see, my HIV status has changed. I've got full-blown Aids."

Brenda clutched the phone tight. She could hear Mimi in the background asking her if everything was all right. Brenda began to sob and then pulled the phone back to her mouth. "At the end of the month. That's it and not a minute longer." Brenda shut the phone off without giving Sheila a chance to respond.

"What is it, Brenda?" Mimi asked, coming up behind Brenda and rubbing her back. "Is everything all right?"

Brenda's eyes bulged from their sockets. She turned around and looked at Mimi whose hands were outstretched. "Am I, all right? Hell no, I'm not all right. Damn, Victor is still threatening me from the grave."

Mimi enveloped Brenda with her arms and held her. They were silent for a minute. Mimi unwrapped her arms and pulled Brenda down to the leather couch. "Is it something I can help you with?" Mimi asked.

Tears flowed down Brenda's face. She looked at Mimi and then wiped the tears from her eyes. "That was Sheila, Victor's mistress/secretary on the line." Brenda sighed and took in a deep breath. "It was headline news that she contracted the HIV virus from Victor. Now...now, she has full-blown Aids."

"Oh my God, Brenda." Mimi grabbed her chest. "Oh my God." Mimi sat back in her seat not sure what to do.

"The other day, I went to the condo that Victor bought for his and Sheila's booty calls. Sheila believed that Victor had bought the place for her. Going through Victor's papers, I found the deed. That bastard had the gall to purchase the property in both of our names."

"He probably had to purchase it."

"I never signed anything, but that's water on the bridge now. Sheila is married and living in the condo rent free. Anyway, I went over there to evict them. I met Sheila's husband, Jamal. He's a very nice gentleman. You could tell he's in love with Sheila. He told me that he took Sheila to the hospital that very day and that she was ill."

"So, what are you going to do?"

"Didn't you hear me? I was mean and hateful. That's so uncharacteristic of me. When Sheila said she had full-blown Aids, I tripped. I told her to get out of the condo by the end of the month, ignoring what she'd said. So, cold and callous."

"You didn't mean to be, Brenda. It was the hurt talking."

"What am I going to do, Mimi? What if I have HIV? The thought that I could have the disease scares me to death. I hate you Victor Christianson," Brenda roared. She sobbed uncontrollably. She thanked God that Mimi was there to give her solace.

CHAPTER TWELVE

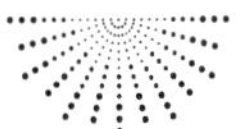

Attorney Reynaldo Aziza closed the case study he'd been pouring over the past few days. He shook his head at the road ahead in his defense for the young kid, Trevor Christianson. Aziza had read over forty self-defense cases, looking for a loophole in which to drop through in getting an acquittal for Trevor or at least a manslaughter conviction. Trevor wouldn't survive long in a cell block dedicated to cold-hearted killers because he wasn't one. A victim of circumstance brought him to the moment Aziza knew Trevor regretted, but the cold, hard fact was that Victor Christianson was dead—plain and simple.

He picked up his cup of coffee and sipped. He spit the cold coffee back in the cup and wiped his mouth with the back of his hand. He needed to talk again with the detectives who'd worked the Victor Christianson case to go over details prior to Victor's demise. Maybe there was something...a small piece of evidence in all that fact finding that he could use for Trevor's defense.

Aziza looked up in time to see the well-dressed

gentleman pass his door. He wasn't aware that his partner Jonathan Locke had taken on another case. They were a two-person law office. Reynaldo and Jonathan liked the idea of having their own practice and the leeway to practice law the way they saw fit, all while abiding by every legal limit of the law.

Reynaldo was suave, handsome, with jet-black hair that he wore behind his ears and that fell to the nape of his neck. He wore three-piece Italian suits and loved a gator on his feet regardless of the cost. His mixed Puerto Rican and African-American heritage looked good on him. Jonathan on the other hand was a short, white runt of a man who stood at five-feet-five, who'd met Reynaldo at Harvard where they both received their law degrees. The only attribute Jonathan had that caused some women to take a second look was his emerald-green eyes. They sparkled like diamonds, and Jonathan could bat those eyes and talk a woman out of her bra and panties in under a minute flat.

Reynaldo got up from his seat. He was famished and a good meal would do him good. He put on a trench coat and headed toward Jonathan's office to let him know he was going out. He stopped short of the open door when he heard Brenda Christianson's name. Reynaldo's eyebrows shot up, and he squinted his eyes, his ears on radar alert. *What did Brenda Christianson have to do with the new client?* That was a question Reynaldo needed an answer to. He had scheduled a meeting with her for early next week, but he wasn't ready for any more complications than what he already faced.

Reynaldo decided to forego telling Jonathan he was out for lunch. He'd get with him later. Curiosity was getting the best of him, but it was better that Jonathan have something to tell him upon his return.

SHEILA LAY IN BED, looking up toward the ceiling. Her hair was twisted in braids and she wore a colorful scarf around it. Sheila pulled the down-feathered comforter up to her chin in an effort to keep her body warm. The thought that her days were numbered—not knowing the number and how she would endure the pain along with the lesions that had appeared on her skin were catastrophic to her well-being. Many people who'd already contracted the virus had been able to live a long life with drugs. Magic Johnson was a testament, the poster image—the proof of what medicine and the money to be able to afford it could do. Magic had lived well over two decades with the virus. What Sheila didn't understand was why she didn't have any knowledge or symptoms of the virus, but in a matter of six months, she'd already taken a turn for the worst?

Already thin, she'd lost close to thirty pounds. The last time she looked in the mirror, her face was sallow and hard for even her to look at. Sheila allowed herself a smile, although brief. God had honored her prayer by sending a man that would love her for who she was. There was no way to describe that miracle from God. The only thing Sheila regretted was that she and Jamal hadn't consummated the marriage, even with a condom. Sheila didn't blame Jamal. She was happy to have him by her side.

She willed herself to move past this day. Today wasn't one of her better days, but she prayed it wouldn't be her last. Sheila had only enough strength to call and beg

Brenda Christianson to give her some time, but Brenda had been a bitch about it. How could she have thought she'd be different from Victor?

Jamal had heard the whole commotion and left the house to *do something about it.* Those were his exact words, and Sheila had begged him not to do anything stupid that would put them in jeopardy. But Jamal was adamant about pursuing what his mind had perceived as getting back or doing something about it, and out of the door he went.

Lying on her back had allowed Sheila to think about the error of her ways. God, why had she been pronounced with this sentence? Many women had slept with married men and committed the sin of adultery without her consequence. She couldn't fathom why her name had come up on the good Lord's roster. And to think that there were other women out there who Victor may have infected with the virus. Were they now walking around with Aids? Someone gave the virus to Victor, but whom? Sheila knew he was a whore, but Victor was a good-looking, professional, upstanding, good money manager, and a good family kind of whore who was immaculate and almost OCD about himself. Who would've thought?

The doorbell startled Sheila. She was barely able to move. Jamal had a key, so who in the world would be knocking on her door? Her good friend Phyllis hadn't darkened her door since before Victor's funeral.

Whoever it was wouldn't go away. They rang the doorbell as if it was a new toy, and it was driving Sheila crazy. She gathered up enough strength to make it to the door. With every ounce of her being, Sheila opened it. Her mouth gaped open and she stared with contempt when she recognized the inconsiderate intruder.

The woman standing on the porch also stared back and seemed horrified at Sheila's countenance. Sheila could tell that she wanted to turn around or admit that it was a mistake to have come there. Then the woman opened her mouth, a mouth that was nasty and vile only hours before, but Sheila didn't have the strength to cuss her back.

"Sheila?" the woman asked.

"Mrs. Christianson," Sheila retorted. "I'm surprised to see you here." Brenda stood there without saying a word. "Would you like to come in?" Sheila asked in slow, painstaking breaths. "You can't get Aids from looking at me...that is unless you already have the virus."

Brenda frowned but refrained from ushering out the words that were now caught in her throat. "Yes, I'd like to come in."

Brenda eased by Sheila who seemed too feeble to stand up. "I'm sorry to have barged in on you like this. I... I came to apologize for my harsh words earlier today."

"You could've saved yourself a trip and said what you needed to say on the phone. It would've kept me from struggling to get to the door."

"I'm sorry. Where's your husband?"

"He's out at the moment. Let's cut through the pleasantries and tell me why you're here. I got your message loud and clear."

Brenda looked around the room. She'd been there only a few days ago, but now looking at Sheila, the room was different. It seemed cold and sickly. Brenda hated that she'd been such a bitch. "Sheila, I've done some thinking in the past few hours. I'm not used to talking to my husband's ..."

"Is whore the word you're looking for?"

"Not necessarily, but close."

Sheila took a deep breath and sank into the overstuffed chair. “Mrs. Christianson, it's brave of you to come here. Right now, I'm not feeling well, and I'd like to lie down.”

“Can I assist you?”

Sheila had a crazy look on her face. “Okay, Mrs. Christianson...”

“Brenda.”

“Mrs. Christianson...Brenda. I don't know what you have up your sleeve. If you've come to stick the knife in deeper, save your energy; I'm dying anyway. Say it; I'm getting what I deserve.”

“Sheila, please be quiet. I want to help you. You and your husband can stay here as long as you like. If you need to go to the hospital, I can assist. Right now, I need someone to talk to. I need to know what the symptoms are and your coping mechanism.”

Sheila stared at Brenda in disbelief. As feeble as she was, Sheila couldn't wrap her mind around the likes of this woman—her ex-dead lover's wife. What in the hell did she want from her? She had access to the internet and was a clinician herself. Maybe she was afraid of being alone to do the research. “Do you have the virus, Brenda?”

“I... I don't know.”

“You need to get tested right away.”

“I've already been tested but haven't received the results yet.”

“I didn't have any symptoms, at least none that I recognized. The piece of paper with the words HIV positive typed on it was the first inkling I had that my life was about to change. I must have contracted it awhile back because I can't believe that in the six months after I found out that I now have full-blown Aids.”

"Did you take the medicine...the AZT or whatever it's called?"

"At first I didn't. I was in denial. I looked like you do now except I had the results in my hand. I had no earthly idea that I was a walking time bomb. Why don't you have a seat?"

Brenda moved to the couch that sat next to the chair where Sheila sat. Brenda sat down and stared at Sheila, unable to remove her eyes from her. "You've lost a lot of weight."

"That's a sure sign that something is wrong. I'm tired and sometimes it's difficult to breathe."

"How's your husband taking all of this? I understand he married you even after he found out about the HIV."

The nerve of this woman, Sheila thought. *How in the hell do you think he's taking it? They hadn't even had sex since Jamal proposed.* "He's handling it as best as could be possible under the circumstances." Sheila looked thoughtfully at Brenda, dropped her hollow eyes and then brought her head back up. She turned her head then opened her mouth. "Jamal hasn't made love to me at all. Sometimes I wonder why he married me knowing that I was carrying the virus. Maybe it was out of pity, but on the other hand I'm grateful to have him by my side. I wished I was well; he's the kind of man every woman deserves."

"So...so what made you resort to sleeping with my husband?"

Sheila tried to sit up straight but was unable to. She couldn't believe that this woman had the audacity to come up in her space talking about what she and Victor had done. Brenda had already placed the knife in her heart by saying that she'd gotten what she deserved. And now she wanted to know why she slept with her husband? Maybe it was to ease her conscience.

"I'm sorry," Brenda began after Sheila's prolonged silence, "I'm sure you weren't expecting that question. I'm not sure why I asked."

"Do you really want to know, Mrs. Christianson...Brenda?"

Brenda shook her head. "I think I do."

"I wasn't Victor's only lover. He used and manipulated people, and I was one of those people who allowed him to use me to do his bidding. At first, all his sexual advances and presents were cute and inviting. I was aware that he was seeing other women after he'd been with me. Although I knew he was married, I had a crush on him… and I liked the attention.

"One day, I caught him changing some files, and I guess the only way to shut me up and keep me quiet was to put me up. He used me; I used him, but I was there for him until I met Jamal. But I had to keep it a secret; I had this fabulous place that I didn't have to pay for." Sheila dropped her head again. "I wished I had been smarter...hadn't fallen into Victor's trap. But I guess that's easy to say now that I've been hit with this death sentence."

No one said anything for a few moments. "While I want to blame you, Sheila, Victor has been a whore his whole life. He raped my best friend when we were in college. She tried to talk me out of marrying him, but I did anyway. I guess that's easy for me to say now that Victor is dead."

"I'm sorry, Brenda. I don't know what else to say. I appreciate you coming by and giving Jamal and I a reprieve. I'm really tired and need to lie down."

"May I assist you?"
"You want to assist me?"
"That's the least I can do, Sheila."
"Thank you."
"You're welcome."

CHAPTER THIRTEEN

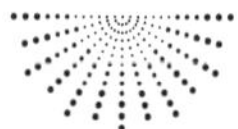

Brenda breathed a sigh of relief when she closed the car door behind her. She sat a moment, going over in her mind the exchange she had with Sheila. The side of her brain that generated charitable deeds felt great about what she had done for Sheila and Jamal. Brenda wanted Sheila to know that even after all the crap she went through with Victor's lying and cheating ways that she was a decent and compassionate person. However, the side of Brenda's brain that bore bad, malicious, and evil thoughts, wanted to put the other side in check. Brenda was the victim. Sheila and Jamal should've been kicked out of the condo with their belongings thrown on the sidewalk for everyone to see.

Sitting a moment longer, it seemed that all of Victor's transgressions, at least those she was aware of, flooded Brenda's memory bank. And who could forget all the media attention and shame he brought on the family when the world found out he had tried to kill his daughter who was the result of a rape—the rape of her best friend, Mimi?

Shaking her head, Brenda released the bad thoughts and whispered a prayer. She didn't care what anyone else thought about how she handled this situation, she was a bigger and better person, and in the end, God would reward her for being obedient to him. Yeah, Brenda got a good tongue lashing from God about how she'd treated Sheila during her illness. Sheila was paying the price. Would she?

Brenda pulled away from the condo and headed home. Right now, she wished John was somewhere near. He electrified her, made her feel something she hadn't felt in years —needed, wanted, appreciated, and important. Brenda picked up her phone, but then thought better of it. She didn't want to become the possessive and desperate woman she'd easily could become and run John away. Brenda believed something had blossomed between her and John, and she was going to put it on slow and let it simmer into a nice, thick stew. And when the time was right to taste the luscious concoction, she'd be ripe for the sipping as well as the picking. A thought came to Brenda. If her HIV test turned out to be positive, all this day-dreaming would be for nothing.

Red, yellow, or green, Brenda wasn't sure what the traffic light emitted until she heard the full blast of a horn. She put on brakes and they squealed, just in time to avoid a collision. God had brought her through the last accident she had when she was on her way to have lunch with Mimi almost a year ago, but it would've been her fault this time, and she couldn't afford to not be around for her children. That's when the reality of Trevor set in.

Brenda had an appointment on next week with the attorney she had acquired to represent Trevor. So many details to work out and everyone needed her attention.

And then there was the waiting on the verdict that would either give her a new lease on life or condemn her to the pit of hell. When would it all end?

Her house was in view. Brenda sighed as she pulled into her circular driveway and into the garage. She felt the slight onset of a headache coming on, but she was going to get through this day. The urge to call John was calling again, however, she resisted with every fiber of her being.

Beyoncé bounded down the stairs as if she was happy to see Brenda. Brenda rubbed her furry friend and checked her food container. No wonder Beyoncé was eager to see her. Her bowl had been wiped clean and it was well past lunch time.

Reaching down to get the Tasty Choice, Beyoncé's favorite, Brenda stood up when she heard her phone ring. She grabbed it and then frowned when she looked at the phone number that occupied space in her screen. With an upturned mouth, Brenda winced again, but decided to answer the call.

"I have a collect call from Mr. Trevor Christianson. Will you accept?"

"Yes," Brenda hollered into the phone. Even before the operator put the call through, Brenda was hollering Trevor's name. "Hey, baby, how are you doing?"

"How do you think I'm doing? You've got to get me out of her, Mom. I can't take it."

"What happened, Trevor? Did someone do something to you?"

"I was almost molested..."

"What? Did you tell the authorities? When did this happen?"

"Calm down, Mom."

"Don't tell me to calm down. My nerves are about to

get the best of me. All my life I've tried to protect you, Trevor, and when you need me most, I can't do a damn thing. Damn, damn, damn."

Trevor sighed. "Mom, listen to me. I beat up a faggot, but he...he is part of a group of dudes that's trying to start something up in here. The leader of the group, a dude named Hammer, beat me up."

"God, Trevor, did he hurt you?"

"Yeah. Hammer may have kicked my butt, but he didn't take away my spirit. I may have killed Dad..."

"Be careful what you say on the phone, Trevor. You can't go blurting out the truth if you expect us to get you out of that hell-hole."

"Listen, Mom, I want out. These thugs don't care nothing about you. They're trying to teach me a lesson because I'm not down with the crowd. Thing is, I don't know how much longer I'll be able to last. I should be out with my boys shooting some hoops."

"Hang in there, Trevor. Mama is going to get you out come hell or high water. Reynaldo Aziza is a top-notch attorney, and if anybody can get you out on a technicality, he's our guy."

"Tell him to hurry up."

"I have a meeting with him next week. In the meantime, you do your best to hang in there. I'll come and see you after Reynaldo and I meet."

Get off the damn phone Brenda heard in the background.

"Wait your damn turn," Trevor hollered back.

"Please be careful, baby. Let's get off so someone else can use the phone."

"I ain't scared, Mom; my fear is for my life." And the phone clicked in Brenda's ear.

Brenda cradled the phone in her hand, too afraid to let go, too afraid that she'd loose connection with Trevor if she did so. Without notice, the tears began to fall and before she realized it, she was dialing John's number.

"What's wrong, Brenda?" she heard John say at the end of the line.

"I need you."

"I'll be right over."

CHAPTER FOURTEEN

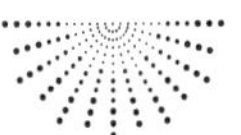

Mimi sashayed about the room, fluffing pillows and straightening up the few magazines that were scattered across the coffee table. Before Raphael went back overseas, he purchased a beautiful cream and gold chaise lounge for her to enjoy one of her pastimes, which was reading an enjoyable book. On the wall behind the chaise, hung a large beveled mirror encased in an antique white frame with flecks of gold dust sprinkled throughout. It enhanced the chaise lounge and made Mimi look like royalty when she stretched out on it, especially in the white flowing lingerie and gold bracelet and earrings from Tiffany's that he lavished on her.

She was in a good mood, and before she knew it, Mimi was warming up the pipes. "Do, re, me, fa, so, la, te, do," she belted out. Her lungs were clear. She still had the velvet voice.

Walking to the stereo system, Mimi flicked on the CD player and Toni Braxton's voice floated through the air. Mimi sang in chorus with Toni, at times overtaking Toni's sultry voice with her own. It felt good to belt out tunes to her heart's content, and for the first time in a long time, she knew what her destiny was to be. She'd mouthed the words on several occasions, had even told Brenda that she was going to sing; but today and at this moment, she knew that it was truly meant to be.

Mimi looked at her watch. The noon-day sun, what little of it could peak from behind the cloudy sky, was heading due west. It felt good to lounge around with no inhibitions, although Mimi missed her some Raphael like crazy. Her fervent prayer always was for God to bring him home safe.

Sitting down on the chaise, Mimi picked up the book she'd been reading, Toni Morrison's, *Love.* As she read, Mimi's life flashed by and the vision that she thought had been buried with Victor's death came rushing back. Mimi threw the book down and held herself tight. Although it was late afternoon, suddenly she felt afraid or maybe it was loneliness that had set in.

Mimi picked up her phone and called John without any luck. Ever since Raphael had come home to be with Afrika, John seemed distant. Raphael was a little rough on John, but as soon as she made it clear that John was her past life, Raphael eased up.

Since John wasn't available, Mimi headed upstairs to change. She needed a change of scenery, and since she and Brenda hadn't finalized their plans for their tea party, a surprise trip to Brenda's would be in order. She put on a pair of off-white wool slacks and a rose-colored knit top that grabbed all her curves.

Mimi sang her heart out, and in under twenty minutes, she was ready to go and be around civilization. Her white, wool coat hung in the hall closet. She put it on and wrapped her neck with a long, eggshell-colored scarf.

Now dressed for the weather, she headed to the garage. After her car was involved with Victor's murder, Mimi couldn't stand to see the red Lexus she used to own. She opted for a black Mercedes Sports Coupe.

Off to Brenda's, Mimi turned on her car stereo and sang along with Estelle, a fairly new recording diva, who was fast becoming one of Mimi's favorites. After a few bars of the sing-a-long, Mimi's mood escalated and she felt fresh like the winter's breeze that oozed through the small crack in the window that Mimi had partially let down.

Mimi was excited about the tea party that Brenda was hosting for her and the girls. While Mimi was sure that Brenda needed something to perk her up after all that she'd been through with Victor's death, Mimi felt that this was also an attempt to solidify their friendship that had been tattered at the beginning of their reunion.

Enjoying the music, Mimi eased down Interstate 40 and when she approached the exit for Chapel Hill, she jerked the wheel to the right and exited the freeway. Mimi loved Chapel Hill, the typical college town with its quaint shops and small-town feel with expensive taste wrapped around it.

The sun peeked from behind the clouds and offered up a hint of what the day could've been like if it hadn't been so overcast, although now it was heading due west with a promise to vanish from sight in the next couple of hours. Mimi went several long blocks and at the next major intersection made a right turn.

Still tuning up the vocals, Mimi hummed, her good mood expanding in her lungs as she belted out another song that floated through the airways. She could already taste success as she allowed her subconscious to visualize the moments—her excepting her Grammy and American

Music Award before a crowd who gave her thunderous applauses along with a standing ovation. Mimi snickered in spite of herself.

Slowing to a crawl, Mimi made a series of lefts and rights until she was on Brenda's street. Another tune was crawling through her windpipe when she came upon Brenda's residence. Mimi slowed and abruptly caught her throat with her free hand. Her good mood went to a slow melt until it evaporated into thin air. She gawked then assessed the situation, not sure how her mind wanted to entertain it. There was no mistaking whose car sat a few yards in front of hers; she'd seen it enough times. What was John Carroll doing at Brenda's house? Hell, was he there when she tried to call him not less than an hour ago?

Mimi pulled her Mercedes forward in the circular driveway and turned off the ignition. She sat a moment, not sure that she wanted to get out. What if something was going on and she walked into the middle of it? Mimi shook her head.

Getting out of the car, Mimi dragged her feet to the front door, her radar on alert and her nerves on edge. The only way to find out what was going on was to knock on the door and face the two. But whatever was going on wasn't her business; it surprised her that Brenda hadn't been forthcoming with the information.

Mimi rang the doorbell and waited. After a moment, she rang it again and put her ear to the door. As she was about to pull away, the door swung open and Brenda stood with a broad smile on her face.

"Hey, Mimi, what a pleasant surprise."

"I'm sure that I am. How are you? I was in the neighborhood and thought we could work on finalizing the tea party."

"Well come on in. John is here. He stopped by to give me advice on how to proceed with Trevor's case."

Mimi walked in the door and looked around. "I thought you had obtained a lawyer...what's his name...to handle the case."

"Yes, Reynaldo Aziza is handling it."

Mimi followed Brenda into the family room. John got up as Mimi entered, looking good in an off-white cashmere sweater that was pulled over a yellow, blue and white shirt with a high collar and a pair of Hugo Boss slacks, also in eggshell. Mimi took a moment to appraise the man that stood in front of her before moving her eyes quickly away. "Hi, John."

"Hey, Mimi. So, good to see you."

"Did you get my messages?"

"I sure did, Mimi, and I have every intention of returning them today."

Mimi caught the look that passed between John and Brenda. John sat on one end of Brenda's leather couch, while Mimi sat across after removing her coat and scarf and giving it to Brenda to hang up. It didn't go unnoticed, even on the sly, that John gave her the quick once over, studying her curves like the reading of a lie detector machine.

Brenda returned and sat in the lone chair that made up the leather ensemble. Mimi's eyes darted between Brenda and John, trying to read something into the two's sudden coziness.

"So, John, I didn't know you and Brenda were so close."

Brenda seized the moment to interrupt Mimi, derailing any further questions she may have had. "Mimi, Trevor was beat up."

Mimi's hand went to her mouth. "Oh, my goodness. I'm so sorry, Brenda. Is...is Trevor okay?"

"Yes, he's okay, but he was beaten up pretty bad." Brenda sighed. "I called John to ask his advice. I'm afraid for my son."

Mimi went to Brenda and kneaded her shoulders. "I've been there…with…with Afrika." Mimi hesitated. "But I'm here for whatever you need."

"Thanks, Mimi. I'm blessed to have you and John in my corner. I don't know what I'd do without the both of you."

Mimi kissed Brenda on the cheek. "We've got you. Right, John?"

"That she does," John replied. "If you want me to go with you to see the attorney next week, I'll be happy to do so."

Brenda sighed as she wiped a lone tear from her face. "I may have to call on you, John."

"I can go with, you," Mimi interjected. "That way, John won't have to take time off from work. Since I'm free, I'd be more than happy to accompany you."

John scratched his head. "Well, that's up to Brenda. If she needs me, I'll make myself available."

"I want to see Trevor," Brenda blurted out. "I need to see my son. I need to see for myself that he's all right."

"It's too late today, but I'd be more than happy to go with you tomorrow," Mimi offered.

"Okay," Brenda said without hesitation. "I want to go in the morning. If you could be here by nine-thirty, I'll be ready."

"It's a done deal," Mimi said.

"Look, I better go," John said standing up.

"Please don't leave on my account," Mimi said. "Forgive me; I didn't mean to interrupt your strategy session."

"It's okay, Mimi. Since you're here, why don't we go ahead and work on the tea party. I'll walk John out."

"Okay," Mimi said as she observed John. He seemed antsy for some reason...like he was suddenly uncomfortable with her being there. On the surface, it appeared that John was only there to help Brenda with Trevor's defense; however, she had a nagging suspicion that wasn't all that was going on. John crossed the room and hugged Mimi and followed Brenda out of the room. Mimi couldn't see them from her vantage point, but the thought that something else was going on wouldn't leave her.

CHAPTER FIFTEEN

The house was still when Jamal entered the condo. He pricked his ears for signs of life—that Sheila was still in the land of the living. He took off his coat and laid it on the back of the overstuffed chair in the living room and proceeded to the bedroom to check on Sheila.

He sighed before entering the room. This had become more of a burden than he could've ever imagined. An HIV-positive report gave him every excuse to leave Sheila in the mess he'd found her, but he'd fallen hard for that girl, and it wasn't in his nature...his DNA to abandon something he held dear.

Memories of his mother struggling to take care of three small children when their drunken father had deserted them came rushing back. Jamal wasn't upset by his father's leaving because in his drunken stupor, Jamal's father had abused his mother physically and mentally one-hundred times over. And his absence was the best thing for his mother's survival—for his and his siblings' survival. However, Jamal's mother struggled to make ends meet and keep food on the table, while bouncing from one part-time job to another. Jamal vowed that he'd never let his family suffer.

He moved toward the bed where Sheila lay. She was sleeping soundly, and for that he was grateful. Jamal knew that Sheila was suffering, but he had no idea that the disease would take control of her so quickly. All he could think of was how Magic Johnson had overcome. After ten or more years with HIV, he was still a picture of health, had a family, and owned real estate all over the country.

The one thing Jamal was most ashamed of was that he hadn't consummated his marriage with Sheila. Although he'd ask for her hand in marriage and had whisked her away to Vegas, the thought of penile penetration with or without protection didn't protect him in his mind. It was common knowledge that rubber shields hadn't lived up to their expectations on occasions and rendered a female pregnant, but the thought of getting the HIV virus was bigger than a sperm fertilizing an egg.

As he turned to leave the room, Sheila shifted and called out to Jamal. She must've felt him, heard his thoughts as he stood over her.

"Hey, baby, you're back." Sheila struggled to sit up and leaned against the pillow that hugged the headboard. Jamal sat on the edge of the bed after wrapping Sheila's arms with the comforter.

"Yeah, I had a long day today, and tomorrow I've got to get some work done." He patted the indention that Sheila's foot made. "Are you hungry?"

Sheila's voice was scratchy and hoarse. "A little bit. Guess who stopped by this afternoon?"

"Your mother?"

"Noooo."

"Uhmm, Phyllis?"

"The hell with her. She's no friend of mine. I haven't seen that bitch since Victor's funeral."

"No need to talk like that and get yourself all riled up."

"It just makes me so mad, Jamal. I thought she was my friend, and like so many others, she tossed me to the side. Not one of my co-workers has been by to see me."

"Okay, sweetie. Let's not talk about them. Who came by this afternoon?"

"Brenda Christianson."

Jamal stood up. Anger was now in his voice. "What in the hell did she want? I'm sick of that bitch rolling her ass up over here with her demands."

"Now who's getting all upset?" Sheila paused and caught her breath. "Calm down and let me tell you what happened." Sheila gave Jamal the low down, while he rocked from one foot to the other. "She really had remorse and said we could stay here as long as we like. I mean for real, Jamal, this is her property and we weren't paying a cent. I can't blame her for going off."

"That's well and good, Sheila, but her scum of a husband..."

"Who is no longer alive..."

"Whatever, but he's the cause of your illness. And somebody must pay. You have mounting medical bills that you didn't count on, and you're out of work. I've put my consulting business on hold the last couple of months to see after you."

Sheila threw up her hands. "I understand that this is a lot for you to take on, and you can leave at any time, Jamal. I don't want you to feel as if you're trapped and must stay with me. You've given me the one thing I've always wanted, and that was to have a man who loved me for who I was and care about me unconditionally. But I don't want you to feel like you must stay, Jamal. I won't be angry."

"Be quiet, Sheila. I married you for better or worse. I knew what I was getting into when I married you. True, I hadn't been prepared for the HIV to become full-blown…at least not as fast as it did. I thought you would beat this and that the medicines would keep you going until a cure was found. I wanted to believe," Jamal shouted and grabbed his face so Sheila wouldn't see the tears.

Sheila struggled to get out of bed. She held onto Jamal. "Baby, I'm so sorry. I wish things were different. I really messed up my life. Fooling around with a married man never pays."

There was silence as they held each other. Silent tears streamed down both of their faces. They rocked until Jamal loosened his grip and helped Sheila lay down in the bed. She looked up at Jamal. "At least we don't have to worry about the rent."

"I'm suing her. I saw an attorney today about how to best go about it."

"You did what?"

"We've got some major obstacles and we're going to need help. Brenda Christianson has money, and the sins of her husband are going to help us pay for it."

"Jamal, what are you talking about? Didn't you hear me say that she's letting us stay here for free?"

"Maybe she's anticipating that you won't be with us long."

"That was a mean thing to say, Jamal."

"I'm sorry, baby; I'm calling it as I see it. Brenda

Christianson is no dummy, and I've got to be a step ahead."

"Please rethink this, Jamal. I don't want to have a war with this woman. I'd like peace in my last days."

Jamal looked at Sheila and felt sorry for her. There were times when he wondered what prompted him to marry her when he knew good and well that she was HIV positive—his ticket out of the relationship. "It's in our best interest, Sheila. Now don't you worry your pretty little head off."

"Brenda Christianson isn't going to get off that easy," Jamal said under his breath as he left the room. "Her ass is going to pay. She should've thought about how she talked to Sheila before her sudden change of heart."

CHAPTER SIXTEEN

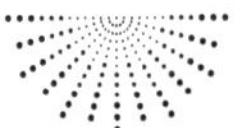

Sleep deprived, Brenda woke up early the next morning with only thoughts of Trevor on her mind. She was a mixed bag of nuts—her brain scrambled in every which way. She was unable to get her thoughts and mind going in the same direction so that she'd be clear about how she wanted to pursue Trevor's defense. Well, that's what the lawyers were for, but it seemed that the mother in her wouldn't let that be.

Pulling the comforter away from her body, Brenda rose from the bed. She briefly stopped to glance at the clock that sat on the nightstand. It was seven-thirty, which gave her two hours before Mimi would be at her doorstep.

Mimi. Brenda smiled and relished in the awkwardness she found herself last evening. Even more, she wished she could've tapped into Mimi's mind to get a glimpse of what she was thinking. Brenda saw Mimi squirm, especially because she'd been trying all afternoon to get in touch with John and on a humbug, he was at her house issuing some much-needed TLC. Brenda smiled again.

She and John played it off, but Brenda knew that Mimi didn't buy the scenario they'd laid out for her.

Brenda moved swiftly through the shower. She didn't have as much time to pamper herself as she'd like, but it was enough for her to begin feeling better about seeing her son. Trevor was her heart, and she needed to see him in person, assess for herself that he hadn't been harmed in such a way that he would require medical attention. But Brenda worried about his state of being. It might be a good idea to step up her appointment to see Reynaldo.

Feeling fresh and rejuvenated, Brenda pranced in front of the mirror. She wore a simple egg-shell-colored turtleneck top and a pair of black slacks. A pair of pearl stud earrings graced her earlobes. Since she was going to the jailhouse, Brenda kept her make-up simple—foundation, a light-colored lipstick and a hint of mascara. With a half hour to spare, Brenda exhaled and proceeded down the stairs with Beyoncé close on her heels. She waited for Mimi's arrival.

Before Brenda hit the landing, her cell phone rang. She pulled it out of her bag but paused and stared when she recognized the caller. Brenda closed her eyes and thanked God.

"Hi, baby," Brenda said, not wanting to waste another second.

"Hey, Mom, how are you doing?"

"It's good to hear your voice, Asia. I've been so worried about you."

"You know where I am; you could've called."

Gritting her teeth, Brenda refrained from saying something about Asia's smart mouth. Asia was still grieving her father, and Brenda knew it was going to take time. "How are you doing? Classes going okay?"

"Yes, to both questions. Look, Mom, I'm not mad at you. I... I can't come home right now. Too many memories of Daddy and Trevor are there, and the best way for me to cope now is to stay away. Believe me I've tried. I guess when Afrika talked to me this morning about family and asked if I had spoken to you, I felt a little guilty."

"I understand, baby. Believe me I do. It's been hard on me, too, but I haven't had any choice but to deal with it. While I have you on the line, I'm planning a small, intimate get together for you and me, Afrika and Mimi. I plan to have it on the veranda, and since you like white, I thought we'd make it a "white" party."

"I don't know, Mom. I don't feel like drudging up the past. You know it will happen when we get together. We won't be able to avoid it."

"What if I promise you we won't? This party is to celebrate moving on with our lives. I think we all are moving toward a better place, and I want to celebrate—kick the funk off. I'm trying to forge ahead, and this is one way to do it. The food will be catered, and I talked to Mimi about singing a few songs. She's interested in starting a singing career."

"Good for her. Are you and Mimi okay with each other?"

"Asia, Mimi will always be my best friend. Things happened, but they are in the past. Remember...celebration."

"Okay, Mom. I'll come. Do I need to tell Afrika?"

"I believe her mother was going to tell her. You can share the information with her if you like. I'm so happy at this moment. I love you."

"I love you, too, Mom. Well, I've got to go study—getting ready for finals. So, what are you doing today?"

Brenda hesitated, not sure that she wanted to divulge that information. However, in order to move on, she had to embrace reality, and Trevor being locked up behind bars was a reality. It was part of the future and there was no way to ignore it. "I'm getting ready to go and see Trevor."

Silence. "Tell Trevor I love him." And the line was dead.

CHAPTER SEVENTEEN

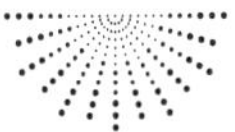

Brenda and Mimi headed toward the building where they had to in-process to see Trevor. A stream of people accompanied them to the first phase of visitation.

"I hate coming here," Brenda sighed. "People look at you as if you're the criminal...that you're a bad seed like the person you came to see."

"Ah, come on, Brenda. Nobody is paying us any attention. They would have to think the same thing about themselves if your statement was true. I understand, though. You hate it here and rightfully so. But you've got to do what you have to do to save your son."

Brenda swung her neck in Mimi's direction but decided to let her comment roll off her back. After all, she was telling the truth, but she didn't need anyone else telling her."

"So, what did John advise you to do as far as Trevor's defense?"

Now Brenda was agitated. She hadn't anticipated that question, especially since her focus was on Trevor. Why in the hell did Mimi want to know? It wasn't her son. The only reason Mimi asked was that she suspected something else...that there might be something going on that she wasn't privy to. Well, Brenda was going to let her sweat.

The wheels in Brenda's head turned fast and at the appropriate moment, an answer came down from heaven. "John advised me to let the attorney I'm paying all that money to handle things. I guess I was so up in arms about Trevor getting beat up, the only thing I could think of was how to solve the immediate need."

"Spoken like a true mother. John is wise and has a lot of sense. I understand why you called him."

"I hope you don't mind, Mimi. I couldn't think of anyone else to call, and he told me to call him if I needed him. Panic...that's what it was."

"Girl, you don't owe me any explanation. I don't have any claims on John. As I keep saying, I'm a happily married woman and plan on staying that way. John is my past; not my future. We all need someone to call on from time to time, and now is your time."

Brenda smirked under her breath. She knew that Miss Thang was outdone and was more than a little jealous at seeing John at her house last night. Brenda loved Mimi, and her blossoming relationship with John was going to stay her secret...at least for now. She looked at Mimi and figured she owed her a response. "I'm glad you're not tripping; we're just friends."

THE LADIES FILED INSIDE, but Mimi was unable to see Trevor as her name wasn't on the visitor's list. Brenda apologized to Mimi but was grateful for the time alone with her son. When Trevor came into the room partitioned by bullet-proof glass, Brenda's heart dropped to the bottom of her stomach.

Trevor looked frail and disheveled. Brenda's heart ached and she longed to hold him, hug him, and make everything all right. When he caught sight of her, Trevor's eyes were pleading, begging to be taken from Satan's den. Brenda's heart sank further down to the utmost pit of her despair.

Trevor put one hand on the glass that separated them and picked up the phone with the other. Brenda placed her hand tight over his, almost as if some type of suction device drew it there. She picked up the phone.

"Baby, Trevor, how are you?"

"I hate it here. You've got to get me out, Mom. I'm not going to last up in here. If I get convicted, it will be my death."

"What's going on? Aren't there guards all around watching everything?"

"The guards are a joke. Yeah, they have weapons and everything, but half of them are afraid of these criminals. These dudes think they own the joint and everybody in it. I'm being threatened by this ugly dude who calls himself Hammer, and he says he's going to make me bow down."

"Bow down to what for heaven's sake?"

"Listen, Mom. This place is no joke. Things might have been different if I hadn't pleaded guilty to murder. And what's worse, I dream about Daddy almost every other night. He keeps pointing his finger at me and says he's going to get me. Damn, I'm glad it's a dream."

"Thank God it's only a dream. Trevor, I'm going to do everything in my power to get you out. But you've said it yourself...in fact admitted out loud to killing your father, and now they're going to make you pay."

"I wasn't in my right mind, Mom. I saw Daddy pointing that gun at Freddie's mom and saying all kinds of crazy, mean, and nasty things. And my brain went into overdrive; I had to do something. If it hadn't been me, Freddie would've killed him. I didn't set out to kill him; you've got to believe me. But I couldn't let him go on; he hurt a lot of people. I'm ashamed to admit it, but I don't feel one way or the other about what I did. He had it coming."

"Okay, Trevor, that's enough. The guards are staring at us. I'm sure someone is listening to our conversation. I told you, I'm going to do everything I can to get this case dismissed. I've got to go."

Tears streamed down Trevor's eyes. His one hand was still plastered to the glass where he had first laid it. Brenda eased the receiver down in its cradle and felt the tears slide down her face. She looked up as Trevor was ushered from his station, his hands and feet bound by shackles, and watched until he was out of sight. Brenda's heart was heavy, and before she knew it, she was running to what she called safety.

Brenda found Mimi standing outside humming a song while enjoying the sixty-degree temperature. Mimi stopped humming when she saw Brenda approach.

"You okay, Brenda?" Mimi asked, putting her arm around her.

Brenda reached into her bag and pulled out a pack of Kleenex and wiped her face. "I'm not good. I've got to get my son out of that place."

BACK IN HIS CELL, Trevor sat on his cot, recalling his visit with his mother. He put one foot up on the cot and circled his bent knee with his arms. He prayed that his mother would be able to get him out of the hell hole he was in. It wasn't until recently that Trevor understood the description his pastor painted of hell and what it meant. Before, it seemed like crazy ramblings from a preacher who tried to scare the teenagers into doing the right thing and follow God's commandments, but now he understood that hell was real with real and absolute consequences. And it was a place that he never wanted to go.

Breathing heavily, Trevor dropped his head, resigned to the fact that neither he nor his mother could push the judicial system any faster. He knew his mother would do all she could to bring his case to trial and hopefully get him off, although, Trevor doubted the likelihood of that happening since he blurted out without thinking that he had killed his father. With nothing better to do, Trevor laid down and went to sleep.

Trevor sat up when he heard the guards approach. It was time for chow. It hadn't occurred to Trevor that he hadn't eaten breakfast, but his stomach was ready for whatever they were serving today in the chow hall. Like the other prisoners, he took his plate of spaghetti, salad, and French bread and found a seat in an empty corner where he didn't have to engage in any conversation.

As he began to twirl his fork around the spaghetti noodles, a shadow invaded his space. "When you finish, meet me around the corner. I need a word with you."

Trevor looked up at Hammer but didn't say a word. He fiddled with his spaghetti, but lost his appetite. With Trevor's silence, Hammer stepped away, watching him all the while. There was no talking back. Fear had taken residence.

A half-hour later, Trevor got up from his seat and placed his tray on the conveyor. He quickly glanced in the direction where Hammer had been seated with his crew, but Hammer wasn't in sight. Trevor's legs began to shake but he pushed forward, anxious to get back to his cell. He had no intention of meeting Hammer.

Trevor pushed on and out of nowhere, he felt an arm encircle his neck. Swiftly he was pulled into a dark hallway and into a steam room, out of sight of the general population. Trevor's eyes were closed, but when he got up enough nerve to open them, Hammer stood before him, while one of his henchmen continued to hold his neck in a hangman's noose.

"Yo, you still defying me, boy," Hammer said. Throwing his hand up in the air and then pointing his thumb down to the floor, Hammer moved closer to Trevor. "I told you I was gonna break yo ass down and it appears that I'm gonna have to show you how that's done."

Trevor said nothing. Out of nowhere, a jagged piece of glass materialized in the hand of the henchman who still had his hand around Trevor's throat. As Trevor examined the piece of glass that was now in front of him, his eyes bulged like helium balloons.

"Now, young playa, yo time is up. There ain't no ifs, ands or buts; you will play by my rules. Tomorrow night is when you show me what you made of. We dealing with a rival gang in here, and they leader has ordered a hit on me, but we gonna hit first. And you gonna do the killing. You have no soul, so playa, this should be easy for you. You don't need to know more than what I'm saying. You been given what you need to do the do. Comprendes?"

Trevor said nothing but kept his eyes on the piece of glass. When there was no response, the henchman, squeezed Trevor's neck and brought the piece of glass up to the side of his face and pricked his skin. Trevor shook.

"I'ma ask you again; do you understand?" For the first time Trevor's head rocked forward in an affirmative response to Hammer's command. "That's more like it," Hammer said, then let out a guttural laugh. "Let him go, Meatball." Hammer turned to Trevor, "You disappoint me, playa, and you'll meet the same fate as yo intended victim." Hammer laughed again.

Meatball pushed Trevor to the floor and then he and Hammer were gone. Trevor wiped the tears from his face and picked himself up from the floor. He pushed air from his mouth and wiped at his face again. His hand produced only a speck of blood, but he would have a scar where he was grazed. Trevor wasn't happy, but for the moment, he was glad that he was still alive to contemplate what he was going to do.

CHAPTER EIGHTEEN

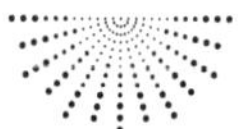

The nightmares wouldn't stop. Trevor dreamed he was in hell and he saw his daddy waiting for him at the next corner with a gun that looked like the one Trevor had used to kill Victor. Trevor tried to rid himself of the dream, but then there was another. Hammer was standing in the shadows watching him execute a Hispanic prisoner who was said to be the "numero uno" commander for a rival gang that had a hit out on Hammer.

Trevor wasn't a killer. While his father, Victor, was an evil man in Trevor's eyesight, he had not intended to kill his father. He was in the wrong place at the wrong time and circumstances at the time of Victor's demise caused Trevor to do the unthinkable. While Trevor refused to say it out loud, he did regret that moment—the moment he killed his daddy, but there was no love lost.

A sudden noise made Trevor jump and turn toward the prison bars. It was still very early in the morning, but he was sure that he caught sight of someone moving fast away from his cell. He sat up and looked around, and with a small fragment of light shining from one of the florescent lights in the corridor, he saw it. What appeared to be a small piece of folded paper sat on the floor just inside of his cell.

Trevor eased up off his cot, not wanting to make any noise and draw any attention to himself. In bare feet, he tiptoed to the where the object lay and quickly picked it up and tiptoed back to his cot. Trevor held it in his hand and shook it, assessing the weight of it. Looking around and seeing no one, Trevor unfolded the paper until a steel object that had a smooth, sharp edge and measured about four inches in length was exposed. Trevor touched the sharp edge and put it to the paper. It sliced the paper without a struggle. Without further hesitation, Trevor rewrapped the piece of steel and concealed it under his mattress. Trevor couldn't determine what the makeshift knife had been in its original form, but he was sure of one thing. The piece of steel that was now in his possession was the weapon he was to use to do the evil deed that evening. So, help him God.

THE STARK QUIET of the morning was interrupted by Beyoncé's constant purring. Brenda sat up in the bed with a start, pulling the eye mask from her eyes that had enabled her to sleep through the night after the awful day she had spent on yesterday. She heard it too and listened with keen ears to the thump, thump on the stairwell.

This was a moment that she wished she had a gun. Before her life was turned upside down, Brenda hadn't been in fear of her life, considering that she lived in a quiet upscale community in Chapel Hill. Beyoncé pounced off the bed—her tail wagging, turning back to look at Brenda to see if she was going to investigate.

"Mom, are you awake?" came a familiar voice.

Her ears perked up. "Asia, is that you?"

"Yes, it's me."

Brenda clutched her arms to her chest and then threw her hands heavenward. God had answered her prayer. Her baby girl had come home. Brenda pulled her feet over the side of the bed just as Asia pushed the door open to her room.

"Hey, Mom."

Brenda looked at Asia as if she was a long-lost sister being reunited after years of separation. She stood up, threw her arms out, and covered the distance that Asia left between them. She wrapped her arms around Asia and hugged the life out of her. "I'm so much better now." Brenda unfolded her arms and dragged Asia to her bed. "Sit, baby, and let me look at you."

"Come on, Mom. It hasn't been that long." Before Asia sat down, she glanced around the room, making mental notes of things.

"Everything is the way it was the last time you saw it. Nothing more; nothing less."

"So, what are your plans for today?"

"Before we talk about my plans, how is Asia doing? It was hard for you to come home, but I'm so glad you did."

"I've been selfish. You suffered as much as the rest of us. I... I couldn't bear to come here, Mom. Too many memories—good and bad."

"How are you and Afrika getting along?"

"We are in a wonderful place. Afrika won't acknowledge Dad as her father. Can't say that I blame her. I was so pissed in the beginning when I found out that she was my sister, although it really was the way I found out, but I'm glad I came to my senses since it wasn't Afrika's fault that Victor Christianson was her dad. And to think Dad tried to kill her...his own flesh and blood."

Brenda sighed. "Let's not spend time rehashing the misdeeds of your father. He wasn't all bad."

Asia began to laugh. "I heard you tell Aunt Mabel that he was rotten to the core."

Brenda looked at Asia and joined her in laughter. "Well, the truth is the truth, but I'm not trying to publicize it."

"I think we have to talk about him to get it out of our system. If we don't, we'll go on for years blaming ourselves for what happened. Look at Afrika's mother. She kept that secret for all of those years, and when no one was looking that secret exploded like an atomic bomb."

Staring at her daughter, Brenda reached out and touched Asia on the nose. "When did you get so wise?"

Asia sat down next to her mother and stared at Brenda. "The apple didn't fall too far from the tree." Asia smiled and Brenda did so in return.

"I'm glad you're here."

"I'm glad I came home. And... I'm looking forward to our "white" party. Afrika is excited about it, too."

"So, you've stopped calling Afrika by her nickname, Nikki?"

"Yeah, we agreed that since our mothers named us after continents that we wanted to be called by our given names. It's one more thing that ties us together."

Brenda stared into space. "Who would've thought that

while we had been worlds away, it was the one thing that bound us together—Asia and Afrika."

"Okay, Mom. You're getting melancholy on me. Back to my first question. What are you doing today? Let's go the spa and do lunch."

"That's a wonderful idea. First, I've got to talk to Trevor's attorney."

"How is Trevor?"

"He's not doing so well."

"He doesn't belong in that hell hole."

"No, he doesn't; it's unfortunate that he was in the wrong place at the wrong time. By the way, have you heard from Zavion?"

Asia was quiet and withdrew for a moment. It was obvious that Zavion's name had provoked the mood that Asia was now in. She sighed then got up from her mother's bed. She twisted and bit her lips, then turned to her mother. "I haven't heard from Zavion since the day he walked out of our house. The news about Daddy was devastating to all of us, but Zavion hated him more than anyone else probably realized. I called him a few times, but after he didn't return my phone calls, I left him alone. To tell you the truth, I haven't even thought about him until you mentioned him."

"Sorry about that. I was thinking about his mother, wondering if she had the disease. Victor's secretary, Sheila, has full-blown Aids."

Covering her mouth with her hand, Asia swung around to meet her mother's gaze. "What?"

"Yes, and I've taken the test. Although I haven't received the results yet, I'm not afraid, Asia."

Asia searched her mother's face for assurance. "How can you be sure?"

"I don't know for sure, but your father and I hadn't been intimate in a long time." Brenda smirked. "It was my saving grace."

"Okay, enough of this kind of talk. Get up, Mom. I'm taking you to breakfast, and then we're going to the spa. You need to focus on yourself. Come, come; I'm starving."

CHAPTER NINETEEN

The disease had progressed at a rapid pace. Evelyn Slater's fate was sealed; she was going to die. There wasn't going to be any fanfare like Victor received at his homegoing. Victor was a vile and malicious person, but he left the earth looking like a king.

Evelyn lay balled up in a fetal position in a dark and cool room. Every other day, Freddie would drop by and check on her, feed her some chicken soup, and offer companionship for the hour or two he visited with her. Evelyn's son, Zavion, was involved in his college basketball career—a shoe-in to be picked up in the first round of the NBA draft. His notable absence was probably more attributed to his grandmother Sadie, Evelyn's mother, who abhorred her street hustling, drug addicted lifestyle. To be a born-again Christian, Sadie didn't seem to have a forgiving bone in her body—at least where it concerned Evelyn. Evelyn had even taken her mother's last name back, but that did nothing to endear Sadie to her daughter.

After Evelyn's husband died, her luck seemed to turn

around. During one of her more sober moments at a local nightclub, she met a good-looking, educated man who looked as if his wardrobe came straight from the House of Versace. Victor Christianson turned heads that night, and people were saying that he was an administrator on the campus of North Carolina Central University. Evelyn was looking good, too, in her four-inch, above-the-knee-red dress that devoured her gorgeous shape and put her on display, and before long and after a couple of Long Island ice teas, the rest of the night was history.

CHAPTER TWENTY

Mother and daughter enjoyed a bountiful breakfast of buttermilk pancakes and omelets, Brenda preferring a western omelet filled with ham and cheese, tomatoes, onions, red and green peppers to a plain ham and cheese omelet for Asia. After their bellies were filled, they picked themselves up and headed to the spa for a day of pampering, something they both needed and were overdue.

They both chose to get massages utilizing the hot stones, finishing up with deep-tissue massages. After their massages, they treated themselves to facials, burying their faces under a cucumber mixture to exfoliate and moisturize. They ended their day with pedicures and manicures and felt like divas who could conquer the world.

"This was fun, Mom," Asia said, giving her mother one of her famous smiles. "It was great sharing this time with you. I feel like a weight has been lifted and that I can go on."

"I know the feeling; it's like shedding old skin. I feel

renewed and I want to get into something...maybe spend some money, buy myself a new dress or a new car."

"You're feeling real good, mother dear. Now if you're feeling real generous, I hope you don't mind buying your wonderful daughter any of those things. I'd be so grateful. In fact, if you want to get yourself a new car, I'd be more than happy to take your Lexus off your hands." Mother and daughter shared a laugh.

"I don't feel that good, Asia." Mother and daughter laughed again. "I'm glad you suggested we come to the spa. How about we head over to Saks and see what new handbags they've got in? I might get into trouble if I step foot at a car dealership."

"You don't have to ask me twice."

Brenda and Asia headed for the car. As Brenda closed the door, her phone began to vibrate. She quickly pulled it from her purse and saw Reynaldo Aziza's name. "I've got to take this. Reynaldo, what's up?" Brenda asked after hitting the green phone icon.

"Look, Brenda, I stopped by the prison today. Your son is not doing well. He claims that one of the inmates is setting him up to kill somebody tonight."

"What are you talking about? I saw Trevor yesterday and he didn't mention anything to me. Maybe he was trying to, but..."

"Listen. I've spoken to the warden and shared what Trevor told me. They told me in no uncertain terms that they were already aware that something was about to go down at the jail tonight. I told him that my client was targeted to make the hit—coerced in fact, and he doesn't feel safe…that his life is on the line if he doesn't comply."

"Jesus, Reynaldo, you've got to do something. Please don't let those thugs hurt my little boy."

Reynaldo was quiet for a moment. "I've asked for Trevor to be removed to county jail, and I'm waiting on the verdict. The action must be swift so that this Hammer guy doesn't get whiff of it. I need your blessing on it."

"Damn, Reynaldo. Of course, you have my blessing. You didn't have to ask me for it. Is there something I need to do?"

"Not now. I'm calling in some favors to see that this happens. When we're successful, and I trust that we will be, I'll call and let you know."

"How long will that be?"

"Calm down, Brenda. I can't be sure; however, we're hoping to execute this matter in the next few hours."

"Let me know right away what happens. Please don't let anything happen to my baby."

"I'm doing all I can. Gotta go." And the line was dead.

Brenda sat in the car stone faced with her phone still in her hand.

"What is it?" Asia asked in a soft voice. "What's going on with Trevor?"

"That was Reynaldo Aziza, Trevor's attorney. Trevor is in trouble. He told me there are inmates who want Trevor to commit a murder tonight. Reynaldo is in the process of trying to get Trevor moved to safety."

"Commit murder? Oh my God," Asia gasped. "I can't take it. I would die if something happened to Trevor."

"We've got to remain positive. Nothing is going to happen to Trevor. I trust Reynaldo, and if he says he's working on it, I believe him. He hopes to give me confirmation in the next few hours. You don't mind if we postpone our shopping trip, do you?"

"No, Mom. What kind of sister would I be, shopping in Saks to buy a new handbag while my brother is fighting for his life? Not a very good one. In fact, I wouldn't feel good at all. Let's go home and wait. I need a drink."

"Asia!"

"I'm kidding, Mom, but I do need something to calm my nerves. This news just killed my spa treatment."

Brenda sighed. "Yeah, but Trevor is going to be all right."

CHAPTER TWENTY-ONE

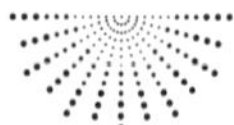

Things were working out faster than Reynaldo had anticipated. It paid not to burn bridges; you never knew when you needed someone to be in your corner. Reynaldo Aziza was well respected within the judicial system, although some thought he was bought with mob money because he was slick, his dress impeccable, and always driving the latest automobile. But that's who Aziza was and he along with his partner, preferred to play by the law, bending the rules when applicable.

He reached into his coat pocket and took out a pack of sugar-free gum, and put a piece in his mouth to quiet his nerves. Young Trevor was no match for the ruthless, hardened killers that were in residence in Raleigh's prison. He was a perfect target and Aziza hoped that he wasn't too late to put something in place to rescue him.

Unable to just sit at his desk, Reynaldo got up and walked down the hall to his partner, Jonathan's office. He had meant to ask him about the client who had stopped by several days earlier, who he had overheard talking about Brenda Christianson. This was as good a time as any to find out what that was all about. With the back of his fingers, Reynaldo rapped on Jonathan's door.

"Hey, partner, what's up?" Jonathan asked as he peered from behind his large, horn-rimmed eyeglasses.

"Man, I'm working that Christianson murder case...you remember the kid that killed his father."

"Yeah, I remember. Kid confessed to the murder. That's gonna be a hard one to prove self-defense or for that matter anything else. That kid had no remorse for his old man."

"You're right, but I think Trevor has had a change of heart. Victor Christianson wasn't a model citizen and Trevor happened to be in the wrong place at the wrong time."

"That may be true, but that doesn't give anyone a license to kill, model citizen or no model citizen."

Reynaldo sighed. "Yeah, you're right. Now, however, he's been targeted by a tough crowd and has been selected to pull a hit tonight. You remember that dude named Hammer that wreaked havoc in Durham."

"Yeah, the gang leader. Killed a whole lot of rival gang members and innocents. So, what are you going to do?"

"I'm working on trying to get him removed from where he is to a safe place."

"Good luck with that man. If you're successful, Hammer is going to be some kind of pissed off."

"Well, he's going to be pissed off because I've called in a few favors and everything looks favorable for this to happen. I'm waiting for the call that everything was successful."

"Good. I hope you can make that happen. I'm sure it'll put his mother's mind at ease."

"Speaking of Brenda Christianson, I happened to overhear you talking to a client about her the other day. What was that about?"

"Now you know, Aziza, that's attorney/client privilege."

"We are working for the same firm, aren't we? I don't remember that we kept secrets from one another."

"You mean to tell me you haven't kept me in the dark about anything?"

"Of course not, Jonathan."

"You're lying, Aziza. Anyway, the gentleman is the husband of the woman who acquired HIV from Victor Christianson, Brenda's husband, and he asked me to represent him. It seems like the lovely Mrs. Christianson can be a little ruthless, borderline heartless."

"How so?"

The client, Mr. Jamal Billops, said that Brenda Christianson went to the condo where he and his wife live and ordered them out by the end of the week, even after Billops explained to Mrs. Christianson that his wife, Sheila, was very ill."

"That doesn't seem like her."

"Well the rest of the story is that the condo belongs to Brenda. Her deceased husband, Victor, bought it so that he and his then secretary-girlfriend, Sheila, could rendezvous and have sex and whatever else there. It was their playground."

"Jonathan, did Jamal Billops tell you that, and if he did, where in the hell was he when his wife was getting her groove on with Victor Christianson?"

"Billops and Sheila weren't married at the time, but I believe he may have been aware of Sheila's involvement with Christianson."

"And the fool married her?"

"We've heard worse stories than this. Anyway, getting back to the story, after Victor was killed, the condo went to his wife. Her name is on the deed."

"That seems very cut and dry to me, Jonathan, and I don't blame Brenda Christianson one bit for kicking her husband's whore out of her house. Was she paying rent?"

"Look, the client came to me to file a suit against Brenda..."

"What in the hell for, Jonathan? I'm sorry the woman has HIV, but she and her husband got some nerve. And when did she and this Billops guy get married?"

"You're too emotional, Aziza. I realize Brenda is your client."

"Come on, Jonathan. I can't believe you even entertained that fool. What kind of money do you think he's going to get? Brenda is the victim and Sheila Billops' time is up. Victor is the person she should've had her beef with, but unfortunately, he's dead. I don't know what you told Billops, but I'm thinking you weren't in your right mind when you agreed to represent him."

"Well, we haven't spoken since that day. I'm not sure how I was going to proceed with this."

"You better give the man his money back. I'm going to shoot you down. Brenda needs her strength for her son, not some foolish mess. Maybe I can talk her into letting them stay there a little while longer."

"Seems like you've got your mind made up. I've got a lot of work to do. You know...other clients."

Aziza laughed. "See you, buddy. I'll let you know what happens with Trevor. In the meantime, you better let Mr. Billops down slowly because if he files any suit, I'm coming down on you and him like a bulldozer from hell. Further, I wouldn't want the firm to get a bad reputation due to your unwise decision. But in truth, it is a conflict of interest."

"The hell with you, Aziza. I'll see if I can get up with this Billops guy. I think he needed someone to talk to."

Reynaldo looked at Jonathan like he was crazy. "The psychiatrists' couches are in the next building."

It was Jonathan's turn to laugh. "You're wrong for that, Aziza. You're wrong for that, but that was pretty damn funny."

"I'm glad you thought it was. I'm out." Reynaldo pulled his iPhone out of his pocket. No word yet.

TREVOR'S BODY stiffened when he heard the rustle in the hall. It was late afternoon, and he knew that in a few hours it would be night. The blade that had been dropped at his cell early that morning was still stuck under his mattress.

He sat up straight against the wall. His ears perked as the sound of soft-soled shoes drudged the concrete. Trevor was afraid to look out beyond his cell, but he couldn't help it as the sound seemed to move closer. Two white men approached and stopped in front of his cell and motioned for him to be quiet.

Unable to move, Trevor sat as one of the men opened his cell with a large key. Fear consumed Trevor. His body felt paralyzed from the top of his head to the soles of his feet. Once the door was unlocked, the two men came in and one put his finger to his mouth. Before Trevor could react, he reached down and felt warm liquid drench his pants. He didn't remember the last time he had peed on himself, if at all.

"Be quiet," the shorter of the two whispered as he cuffed Trevor's hands and feet. "Come with us."

Trevor sat still and the two men nudged him from the bed. "Dude we have to hurry, so we can get you out of here without too much notice."

"Who are you?" Trevor whispered.

"Shhh if you don't want to get killed. We're here to save your ass."

A black hood was placed over Trevor's head, and he felt a hand grip his arms on either side. The men moved at a fast pace, prompting Trevor to move his feet in the same manner. He didn't know who these men were that he had entrusted his life to...shoot, he wasn't sure that they were the enemy, but he did what they said.

For an undetermined amount of time, Trevor remained hooded. He heard a series of doors open and shut. There were whispers as he was moved along until finally he felt the coolness of outside hit him in his face.

A door closed with a thud and he turned in the direction of the noise. Then he felt arms pulling him along and what felt like concrete under his feet. Abruptly they stopped.

"Step up," one of his captors said.

Trevor did as he was told. He realized he was on a bus, as he navigated the three steps that lifted him high off the pavement. He heard the hissing sound of doors being closed, and then there was silence. With the hood still on his head, the bus jerked and then began to move.

The ride lasted all of thirty minutes. Trevor sat stark still unable to grasp what was happening to him. At the end of the ride, he was taken off the bus, still led by two sets of hands on either side of him. Pleasantries were passed back and forth as he entered a building, and Trevor waited. He must've been at a processing station, and then he was led to what he later determined and realized was another cell.

Claustrophobic, Trevor almost lost his equilibrium when he heard the cell door shut. Seconds later, the hood was removed from his head, as well as the shackles on his hands and feet. When he adjusted his eyes, Trevor was surprised to see his attorney, Reynaldo Aziza in his cell.

"Hey, Trevor, you're safe now. You don't have to worry about Hammer. You've been relocated, and we'll be monitoring and checking on your well-being."

Trevor was speechless. He rubbed his wrists where the cuffs had dug in and looked from Aziza to the two gentlemen who'd escorted him from his old cell. "Thanks," was all Trevor could muster at the time. "Thank you."

"No problem. I'll call your mother and let her know you're safe."

CHAPTER TWENTY-TWO

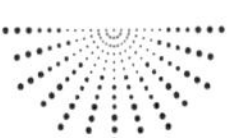

Mimi busied herself listening to the music of Mariah Carey, Whitney Houston and others. Headphones were glued to her ears as she swayed back and forth, popping her fingers, and belting out number after number. She wasn't going to be deprived this time of her dream. One way or another, she was going to get the attention of some record producer and become the next singing phenomenon on her way to collecting her Grammys. Shoot, she might even star in a few films, as it seemed that singers who'd made it in the music world were also crossing over to the silver screen and making a name for themselves. Mimi smiled at her silent thoughts.

After a couple of hours of belting out tunes, Mimi picked up her iPhone from the coffee table and looked at it. She was hungry, and she thought of John. It would be nice to get a bite to eat and chat with an old friend. They hadn't done that in quite a while—the two of them, and it was long overdue.

Mimi pulled up her contact list and found John's number and touched the icon to place a call to him. The phone rang and rang. Mimi hung up and tried and again but received the same results.

Sitting back in her chair, her mind drifted back to the cozy setting she found at Brenda's house. Maybe she was a little jealous seeing John there, but Mimi's instincts said different. There was something going on between Brenda and John.

"Let it go, Mimi," she said out loud to herself. "You're making more of it than need be. You've got a good man."

Before Mimi put her headphones back on, her head turned in the direction of the front door. She stood alert at the sound of the door knob turning and then thrust open with herculean power. The smile on her face said everything, though. Her baby, Afrika, was standing in the door frame—picture perfect. She was a happy woman.

"Hey, Mommy," Afrika said as she put her book bag down in the nearest chair and went and threw her arms around Mimi's neck. She sealed it with a kiss on the cheek. "How's my favorite mother in the whole wide world?"

Mimi kissed her back. "How is the best daughter in the whole wide world?" Mimi gave Afrika a big squeeze and hug. "Love you."

"Love you too, Mommy. What have you been doing? I see your earphones dangling from your arm."

"Baby, if I expect to get a Grammy in the near future, I've got to have some hit records with sales of over a million copies."

"You're going to do it, Mommy. No one has a voice like yours. And you don't need to go to *American Idol*, *The Voice*, or any of those other reality shows to prove what you can do. You're bad without them."

"Thanks for that vote of confidence. I'll be sure to acknowledge my wonderful daughter in my credits."

"Good."

"So, did you get an opportunity to speak to Asia?"

"Yes, I did, and guess what?"

"Please don't keep me in suspense."

"She went home this weekend. Her spirits were high when she left school; so, I hope she and her mother are having a fun time together."

"Oh, I hope so, too. Look we've got to purchase something to wear for the white party. I'm really looking forward to all of us getting together. Hopefully, there won't be any talk of Victor and we can forget about the old and ring in the new."

"I'm kind of looking forward to it, too. Asia and I don't talk about Victor. I wish I never knew he existed, let alone that he was my biological father. But he was and I've forgotten him just like that." Afrika snapped her fingers. "Anyway, my daddy is over in Afghanistan fighting for our country. Have you heard from Dad?"

"Not in a couple of days. I'm sure he's real busy. If I don't hear from him by tomorrow, I'll call him."

"Tell him I love him."

"I will, Baby."

"What do you have to eat in this joint? I'm hungry."

"I don't do much cooking since I'm by myself. However, I'm a little hungry, too. Why don't I treat you to lunch?"

"I'm not going to turn that down. I'm going to use the bathroom and then we can leave."

"Sounds like a plan. I'm thinking we'll go to PF Chang's, since we don't go there often."

"Okay," Afrika said. "It is one of my favorites."

"Well hurry up so we can get the show on the road.

BRENDA PACED THE FLOOR. It had been two hours since Reynaldo had called about the fix Trevor was in and how he was trying to orchestrate a move for him. Waiting patiently wasn't one of Brenda's virtues, at least not lately, and as the clock ticked on, her patience was at a premium.

With Beyoncé at her side, she turned on the flat-screen television in the family room and watched the action on the screen with a blank stare. Beyoncé jumped on the couch next to Brenda and stared at the screen like her feline self knew what was going on. Brenda's nerves were tied up in knots; there was nothing she could readily do to help her son.

Brenda looked up as Asia entered the room with two glasses of wine. "To calm your nerves, Mother dear; Trevor is going to be all right. You said so yourself." With her head hung, Brenda prayed another silent pray.

Brenda jumped at the sound of her phone. She snatched it up and pressed the TALK button when she saw Aziza's name pop up on the screen. "Reynaldo, what happened?" Brenda said out of breath.

"Trevor is safe."

"Oh my God. Thank you, thank you, thank you."

"Tomorrow is Saturday, but I'd like for you to stop by the office around noon. I'll give you all the particulars then. Right now, he's safe and doesn't have to worry about Hammer."

"I'll be there. God has answered my prayers. Thank you again, Reynaldo. I owe you big."

"Don't sweat the small stuff. Save it for when I have to

defend Trevor. Okay, I'll talk to you later. I wanted to give you that piece of good news to put your mind at ease."

"I couldn't have asked for better news. Bye, bye. Talk to you later." The line was dead.

Brenda looked at Asia and smiled. "The day has turned out fine after all. Trevor is safe."

"This calls for a celebration. Bottoms up."

"Bottoms up." After Brenda emptied her glass, she looked up to the heavens. "Dear Lord, thank You for answering my prayers."

CHAPTER TWENTY-THREE

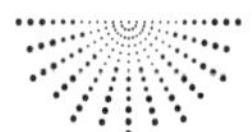

Jamal checked in on Sheila, who was fast asleep. It was early afternoon and he had yet to conduct any viable business. In fact, business was falling off, thanks to his having to take care of Sheila, running her back and forth to the doctor for every little thing.

In the beginning, Jamal believed he and Sheila would sail through her bout with HIV and be another Magic and Cookie Johnson success story. But Sheila refused to take the drugs, and then she lost her job and all the benefits that came with it, including a great health care package. Now they were operating on the little that he had, but something had to change and Brenda Christianson was the answer.

Although the condo was nice but small for his taste, Jamal was thankful that they could stay there rent free—at least for now. He'd given up his modest condo, pre-Sheila, utilizing the opportunity to stay with his girl at no cost.

He went into the other bedroom that served as his office and sat down at his desk and poured over some financial documents. He had built a nice portfolio of clients for which he handled their financial planning. But he hadn't had the get up and go to expand his territory and his business was beginning to suffer.

Jamal thought about Brenda Christianson day and night. Her arrogance the day she came over and ordered them to leave the premises stayed with him. Jamal and Sheila needed money, and Brenda Christianson was going to be the treasure chest to their normalcy. A couple of times, Jamal had entertained leaving Sheila, but it wasn't in his nature to abandon a relationship that he brought to fruition. He was the product of a strong Baptist minister grandmother, who taught about love and long suffering. Jamal shook his head; he did love Sheila, but his love for her was taking a toll on their marriage and their finances. He'd got them into this mess, and he would get them out. Tomorrow, he'd call the attorney and tell him to proceed with the lawsuit against Brenda. And he was going to win by any means necessary.

CHAPTER TWENTY-FOUR

Putting on their warm coats, Mimi and Afrika headed to the car for their shopping venture and dinner. Mimi smiled, happy to have her daughter home, even if it was only for the weekend. They drove to The Streets at Southpoint Mall, found a parking space, and proceeded to the White House, a unique store that sold women's apparel. As if the dresses were waiting for them, mother and daughter found two white, laced-sheath dresses that would be most appropriate for the occasion. While North Carolinians didn't wear white until Easter, Easter was close enough to the date of their "white affair" to be appropriate. Mimi and Afrika didn't stop at the white dresses, they filled their bags with a couple of other cute ensembles that they couldn't pass up. After their purchases, they headed for Nordstrom and did damage in the shoe department.

"Enough," Mimi said, her arms full of purchases. "Your dad gives me a hefty allowance, but I've done enough damage to call it quits. Anyway, I'm ready to eat."

"Mommy, you are so funny when you get buyer's

remorse, although we both know that you aren't going to take not one of those items you purchased tonight back to the store. I vote for returning to the car and getting our eat on."

"I see that you're holding real tight onto those bags of yours. But it was fun, and I'm glad we had this opportunity to share this moment together. We haven't done anything like this in a long time—at least before the shooting."

"Mommy, let's not talk about it...the shooting. All it does is conjure up images of that man who had the nerve to be my father. What kind of father would try and kill his own child?"

"Do you and Asia ever talk about your dad?"

"I've already told you we don't talk about that man. Victor Christianson was never my dad. Yes, he was Asia's dad, but never mine. Please, let's not talk about Victor anymore or I'll have to go back to the dorm."

"Okay, baby. My mouth is sealed until the food comes. I'm glad we don't have far to drive."

"Thanks for today, Mommy. It was fun."

Mimi drove out of the main mall area and crossed the street to restaurant row and another group of stores. Mimi's mouth watered for the oriental cuisine that was served up at P.F. Chang's, specifically the spicy Dynamite Shrimp and the Banana Spring Rolls. They had a twenty-five minute wait.

Once seated, they toured their menus, although they already knew what they wanted. After the waitress took their orders, Mimi and Afrika engaged in small talk. Suddenly, Afrika began to squint.

"What is it, baby?" Mimi asked Afrika, as she began to turn her head in the direction Afrika was looking.

"Don't turn around, Mommy. I see your friend, John, a couple of booths down with a group of people. He's sitting next to this good looking Nubian woman."

"What does she look like, and can I turn around now?"

"No, Mommy. Then they'd know we were talking about them."

"Well, don't look now, but guess who just entered the restaurant? And you can't turn around."

"Well, tell me, Afrika, since I can't turn my head. I have no earthly idea who it could be."

"It's Brenda and Asia. I wonder if they're here to join John."

"Why would you say that? Do they see us?"

"Not as far as I can tell."

"Well, I'm going to go back there and see if they want to sit with us."

Before Mimi could respond, Afrika was out of the booth and headed in the direction where Brenda and Asia were standing. Was this a coincidence? And then they were following Afrika, as if this had been preplanned and scooted in the booth that was comfortable for the four of them. Afrika scooted in next to Mimi so that Asia and Brenda could sit together.

"Fancy meeting you guys here," Brenda said after she was settled in.

"How about that?" Mimi said. "We came to the mall to shop for our outfits for the white party."

"For real?" Asia blurted out. "Mom and I were going shopping today, but we had to change our plans."

"There's nothing wrong, is it?" Mimi asked, looking at Brenda who she realized had just discovered John sitting several booths over. "I know that you were concerned with

Trevor's well-being when we were at the prison the other day."

Brenda brought her attention back to Mimi. "No...no, no. Trevor was moved to a different cell, and we stayed around the house to make sure that the transfer went well."

Mimi was puzzled. "Why did they move him?"

"Trevor wasn't happy with the treatment he was getting from some of the other inmates. I'm praying that his trial will go smooth and that Reynaldo will be able to get him off on some technicality."

"I'll be praying with you," Mimi said.

"I don't mean to change the subject," Brenda continued, "but isn't that John Carroll over there?"

Mimi turned her head already aware that John was sitting in the booth with a group of people. "Yeah, that looks like him. Do you know who those other people are with him?"

"No," Brenda was slow to say. "They look as if they're having a lot of fun. That must be his girlfriend. She's very attractive."

Mimi smiled. "I tried calling him earlier today, but his call went to voicemail. I guess he's a busy man." Mimi laughed but noticed how uncomfortable Brenda seemed to be.

"I guess so," Brenda responded. She picked up her menu and concentrated on making a selection. Brenda occasionally peeked from behind her menu to glance at John.

"I hope John finds someone he can share his life with. He's a nice guy. If I wasn't married to Raphael, I wouldn't mind talking to him."

"Mommy, please," Afrika retorted. "You better not let

Daddy hear you talking like that. Asia and Ms. Brenda, I must apologize for my mother. Sometimes she says the dumbest things."

Brenda looked at Mimi, then back to Afrika. "Mimi is just running her mouth. I hope John finds someone special, also. It would be good for him."

Mimi didn't say another word and seemed satisfied that John wasn't exclusive to Brenda.

CHAPTER TWENTY-FIVE

"Where are you going?" Brenda asked Asia, who was dressed in a spiffy, chocolate velour, Baby Phat jogging suit with pink piping running down the side seam of each pant leg and sleeves of the jacket.

"I'm meeting Afrika at the mall. I hope I'm lucky in finding something to wear for our white party."

"I thought we'd do that together since our outing on yesterday was postponed."

"We'll, do something later, Mom. Afrika and I plan to go to the movies afterwards. We're... we're meeting some friends."

"Friends like whom?"

"It's been a long time since Zavion and I broke up, and now I've found someone special. In fact, I believe I'm in love."

Bucking her eyes, Brenda stared at Asia with renewed interest. "In love? Wow, I'm flabbergasted that you would be into someone else after all that's happened. Love is…"

"It hasn't gotten that serious yet."

"My point exactly. If someone is in love, it is serious, and I'm not sure..."

"Look, Mom. Afrika and I are going shopping and then to the movies. We plan to have a good time."

"Does Afrika have a boyfriend as well?"

"Yes, she's rekindled her friendship with Keith. They're good for each other. Now, I've got to go. See you later. And you aren't ready to go anywhere with that colorful caftan on." And Asia was out of the door.

Brenda hugged the door and watched as Asia got in her car and drove off. Her baby was growing up or to hear her say it, she was already grown up, and there was little Brenda could do to dictate what Asia did or didn't do. She was still her mother and would offer advice as needed, but it was her new reality; she had to let Asia decide her own future.

BEYONCÉ PURRED and brushed up against Brenda's feet. Brenda picked her up, went into the family room, sat on the couch, and placed Beyoncé on her lap, brushing her fur. In the quiet of the room, she allowed herself to think about last evening when she saw John sitting next to the beautiful woman at the restaurant.

Even after John stopped by their table and explained that it was an office birthday party and they were celebrating the young lady's birthday, Brenda couldn't help but notice how attentive John was to her. The young lady must've been in her late twenties. Her make-up was flawless and looked like the handy work of a professional make-up artist. And her jet-back hair, probably a well put-together weave, fell below her shoulders. Brenda thought that the young lady flirted a little too much with John, to the point that it had made Brenda a tad bit jealous.

Brenda put Beyoncé on the couch and proceeded to the front door to get her mail. As she was about to reach into her mailbox after stepping out onto the porch, Brenda was startled at the sound of the gray, Ford Explorer that eased its way up her circular driveway. *What was he doing here*, she wondered? Maybe he was there to offer an explanation because he felt guilty about being seen with the young lady who seemed to have eyes for only him.

Unable to move, Brenda waited until John stopped the car and got out. He looked so handsome with his bald head sticking out beyond his white shirt, partially hidden by brown-tweed jacket and brown slacks. He reminded Brenda of a baked Alaska that she wanted to devour on site.

"Hey there; pretty dress."

"Thank you. It's called a caftan."

"It's still pretty. Well, I guess my surprise is spoiled since you've spotted me already."

"I ventured out to get the mail. However, I'm still surprised to see you. Last night you seemed to be preoccupied."

"Come on, Brenda. Natalie is only a co-worker. I try to be nice to everyone, and while I wasn't trying to sit next to her, my other co-workers set me up so that I ended up sitting next to her. Anyway, Natalie has a boyfriend, and I think they may be engaged. But all of that has nothing to do with us. So why don't you get your mail and invite me inside."

Brenda looked at John, as if he had some nerve. How in the world did he flip the script that quick and made her the bad guy? Regardless of what it seemed, she was enthralled with John's take charge attitude. Before she knew it, a smile splashed onto her face. She retrieved her mail from the mailbox and went into the house followed by John who'd taken the liberty of putting his arm around her waist. She liked.

Beyoncé leaped from the couch when Brenda returned with John. Beyoncé wasn't interested in their conversation. She found her little bed, rolled up in it, and lied down.

"Your cat really loves you. What kind is it?"

"Persian, and her name is Beyoncé."

"Beyoncé? Get out of here. Now I've heard it all. Why in the world...Beyoncé?"

"Because she dances to Beyoncé's music. You should see her when Beyoncé is singing *Single Ladies.* She rocks."

"Well, I see that you have mad love for her, but that's not why I'm here."

"Why are you here, John?"

"Come on, Brenda." He sat close to her on the couch and reached for her arm that extended beyond the sleeve of the orange and blue caftan. "Again, last night was exactly what I told you it was—a birthday party."

"I haven't heard from you in a few days, so..."

"So, you thought what? That I had moved on to the next conquest? Please, give me some credit." John shook his head.

A sour look crossed Brenda's face. The smile that had briefly come out had all but evaporated. "Please don't insult my intelligence, John. I appreciate you coming by, but let's be clear; I'm not that shallow of a person."

"I never thought you were, but give me some credit. I've long since been a player. Let's put Natalie's birthday party/dinner aside and talk about us. First, how did your visit with Trevor go?"

Brenda relaxed her face. John seemed to know what it took to mellow her out. She shared with John her visit to see Trevor and his being moved to a more secure location due to the intimidation he received from the other inmates. "Damn, I missed my meeting with Aziza."

"Who's Aziza?"

"The attorney who's representing Trevor. I was supposed to meet with him so that he could give me all the particulars about Trevor being moved and how he was going to proceed with the case. Damn."

"Why don't you call him? I'm sure he'll understand. After all that's why we have phones. Plus, you can tell him you had an unexpected visitor, and that's not a lie."

Brenda wanted to say something smart but she thought better of it. Instead she smiled. Brenda felt so comfortable being able to share this personal information with John. He pulled her to him. They hugged. She called Reynaldo who understood and made an appointment for Monday.

"Have you heard anything else from the Health Department?" John asked when Brenda got off the phone.

Brenda sat up straight and sighed. "No, not a word. I haven't looked at today's mail yet."

Brenda went and picked up the mail from the coffee table where she had set it upon entering the house. There were several large postcards advertising store sales and two business type envelopes. "Time Warner Cable is going to kill me," Brenda said as she opened the envelope. "Their rates keep going up and up."

"If I could do with only basic cable, I would reduce some of the services I have on my cable."

"Oh...," Brenda said, interrupting John's train of thought.

"What is it?"

Her hand began to shake uncontrollably, as Brenda scrutinized the envelope. "It's a letter from the Health Department. I'm scared, John. I am scared."

"Brenda, you have nothing to worry about. Everything is going to be all right. You told me yourself that you hadn't been intimate with Victor in long while. Let's hope that translates on paper."

"I can't open it, John. Please open it for me." Brenda grabbed her chest and jumped up from her seat and began to hyperventilate.

John got up from his seat, went to where she was standing and held her. "Come on, Brenda. In this envelope is the verdict you've been waiting on. Have faith, baby. I can't open it; it's personal. You should be the one to open it. I'll be right by your side when you do."

Tears traveled down Brenda's face. "John, what if I have the HIV virus? What am I going to do?"

"You're going to fight like hell. There are medicines available that have allowed many to live well beyond their life expectancy with HIV. Magic Johnson is a prime example."

"But I don't want to have HIV."

"I know, baby. Why don't you open up the envelope?"

The tears continued to fall, and Brenda sat back down on the couch followed by John. He held her tight, encouraging her to be of good cheer and to have faith, but refusing to look directly at her.

Brenda used her finger to slice open the envelope. Slowly, she retrieved the one-page letter from inside the envelope. She closed her eyes and said a prayer, asking

God to let the report be a good one. With shaking hands, she took the letter that was folded in thirds and opened it. Brenda's nerves were getting the best of her, but she finally dropped her eyes and carefully scanned the document.

John jumped. Brenda's screams were surely heard all over the subdivision. She jumped from her seat and raised her hands and began chanting, "Thank You Lord, thank You Lord, thank You Lord." She jumped around and hugged herself, her tears stinging her face. When John felt it safe to do so, he jumped into the fray and hugged Brenda and rejoiced along with her.

"John, I'm HIV negative. God is good." Brenda continued to pump her fists in the air. "I'm sorry, but I've got to cry these tears of joy. God has blessed me with a new beginning. Oh God, oh God, I'm so thankful. The letter says that I have to take another test in six months to ensure that I'm indeed free of the virus." With that Brenda dropped to her knees. She prayed in silence and got back up.

She amazed John. "I'm so happy for you. This is a day of restoration."

"Yes, it is, John. And I'm going to celebrate."

"Why don't we celebrate together?"

At that moment, Brenda sat still and wiped the tears from her eyes. She looked at John with sincere eyes, knowing what he meant—at least what she thought he meant. While she'd just won a victory, there was no way in hell she was going to throw her newly found freedom by the wayside.

"You mean celebrate, as in us—you and I—having sex together?"

"No, Brenda. I don't want to have sex with you."

Brenda was embarrassed and somewhat puzzled. She stared at John not understanding.

Sensing her awkwardness, John held her and kissed her gently on the lips. "I want to make love to you, Brenda. I believe we both want it. I wouldn't even suggest a hit it and quit it for the home team. You mean more to me than that. This is a monumental day for you, as it means life devoid of HIV."

"Wow," Brenda said, still embarrassed. "John, I'm on such a high, I can't tell you how good it feels. All I want to do is thank God for my life. It means that I can see my daughter graduate from undergrad and possibly get married. It means that if I'm to be a grandmother, I'll be able to hold my grandchildren and give them love. While you are special to me, John, I can't compromise my life by making love to you right now...not when God has spared my life. While I want to be with you, you'll have to take an AIDS test and pass it before I can give myself to you whenever that might be. Remember, Victor was my husband, someone I trusted, the reason I had to get the test in the first place. Give me that, John. I'm not willing to compromise myself for a momentary thrill."

John seemed dejected. "You make a lot of sense, Brenda. There's something extra special about you that has me acting a fool. I appreciate you being candid with me, and I'll always respect you and your feelings. I hope that doesn't mean I can't kiss you."

Brenda smiled and leaned into John. "No, it doesn't mean you can't kiss me."

His lips were moist like sponge cake at the very touch of them. John caressed her mouth with his lips until he parted them with his tongue. It was sensual, downright erotic, and Brenda wanted to lose herself to him. John continued to explore her mouth with his tongue, probing into the depths until she could no longer withhold her joy as she generously kissed him back.

There was no mistaking how she felt and that she would most graciously give herself to John at that moment, but lust wasn't about to win over the gift God gave her—her freedom. He would have to submit to an Aids test before she'd allow him to camp in her campground with all the rights, privileges, and benefits that two lovers most often shared. Or do the correct thing, which was wait at such time they were man and wife, if that were to be.

But Brenda wasn't ready for John to discontinue his sensual lovemaking with her mouth. It felt so good. Against her body's wishes, she pulled back and watched John lick his lips in L.L. Cool J fashion. She wanted to melt.

"I'm falling in love with you, Brenda, and I'm going to the clinic first thing on Monday and get an Aids test."

Brenda couldn't contain her excitement. Without a word, she cupped John's face in her hands and kissed him passionately. "I've fallen for you, too, John. It could easily be love, but I'm not willing to express that sentiment this moment. However, I'm sure it's why I felt that twinge of jealousy last night when I saw you sitting next to that attractive female. But all is forgiven. Today, I'm the happiest person alive, and I can honestly say I'm ready to move on."

"I love you, and that's the truth of the matter, and I'm sure you'll admit in time that you feel the same about me. Now come here and let me hold you since everything else is off limits. But as soon as my negative report comes back from the clinic, I'm going to sweep you up and take you on a romantic getaway."

"Not so fast, buddy. I do love the coast. Maybe we can go to one of the beaches so we can watch the sun rise and set on the ocean."

"I'd like that a lot."

CHAPTER TWENTY-SIX

Early Monday morning, Jamal was up putting in a couple of hours in his office. He finished a few phone calls and scrounged on his desk for Jonathan Locke's business card. "Where is that card?" Jonathan demanded as he pushed back papers, looking under some while discarding others that were scattered on the floor in an effort to locate the misplaced card.

"What are you looking for?" his wife's voice whispered at his back.

Jamal turned around and seemed stunned to see Sheila standing in the middle of the room. It was as if a miracle had been wrought. Her face seemed full and the colorful wrap she usually wore around her head was nowhere to be seen. Her braids flopped to the sides like a Douglas fir tree. Still in a gown and wearing a beautiful smile on her face, Sheila appeared to have come back from the dead.

"Sheila, baby, are you, all right? I mean...you look like you haven't been sick a day in your life."

"I feel pretty good today, Jamal. When I woke up, my

body felt like the hands of God were wrapped around me and had squeezed the sickness out of me."

Jamal got up from his seat, went to his wife, and hugged her. She was still frail, but to see that smile was more than he could ask for now. He took her beautiful face in his hands and stared. "Baby, you look wonderful. You look happy."

"What were you doing?"

"Ahh, I was going over some accounts and setting up some appointments to meet with some new prospects."

"That sounds good, Jamal. I don't want you to worry about me. My illness has taken you away from your business, but I'm glad to see you back in the grind."

"Come and sit down in the chair, Sheila." Jamal wasn't sure he wanted to share with her what he was about to do, but he didn't want to keep it away from her either. "Look, I'm going to call Attorney Locke today to see if I can meet with him to discuss moving forward with the lawsuit against Brenda Christianson." Jamal saw the smile evaporate from Sheila's face.

"Why do you want to do that, Jamal? She said we could stay here for as long as we like. She has every right to kick us out."

Jamal took a long hard look at Sheila. "We are behind in our finances. Your medical expenses are over the rainbow. When I married you, I didn't have sufficient medical coverage to cover your current illness, although I thought you'd still be working. Somehow, we've got to come up with the funds to take care of our debt, and Brenda Christianson is the answer."

"I thought you owned property before I met you? Staying here, we've been mortgage free, other than utilities. I don't understand why we could be in so much debt."

Jamal didn't say a word. He watched his fragile wife sit down in the chair and wait for a response. His temperature was at a boil, but he attempted to quiet it as he continued to look at Sheila. "I married you knowing that you had contracted HIV, something you brought on yourself."

"Don't go there, Jamal. I didn't beg you, not once, to marry me. In fact, it was settled in my mind that I would bear this burden alone, but no, you insisted that we get married. My problems were my problems." Tears began to flow from Sheila's eyes. She abruptly stood up from her seat and began to walk. After one step, her knees buckled and she fell to the floor.

Jamal ran to her and kneeled. "Sheila, I'm sorry. You're right, baby; I was aware of what I was getting into. I only want to make it right for us."

Jamal scooped Sheila off the floor and carried her to the bedroom and placed her in the bed. She turned away from Jamal and wept.

After Sheila's crying had subsided, Jamal grabbed his coat and headed out the door. His mind was made up. He was going to proceed with the lawsuit regardless how Sheila felt. Brenda Christianson owed them, and she was going to pay.

JAMAL PULLED into the parking lot of Aziza and Locke Attorneys at Law. He sat a moment, recalling the morning with Sheila. Guilt at what he said to Sheila made him rethink his mission to see Jonathan Locke, but as the minutes ticked, he resolved within himself that he was doing the right thing.

Luck was the word for the day. While Jamal had every intention of seeing Jonathan Locke, he couldn't believe his good fortunate that the busy attorney had a few moments for him, even without an appointment. Jamal walked down the hall to Locke's office with a purpose, and presented himself as if he was somebody of great stature when he entered the room.

With his glasses perched on his nose, Jonathan Locke peered over them when Jamal entered the room. Jamal nodded his head and Jonathan pointed to a chair. "I only have fifteen minutes that I can afford you, Mr. Billops," Jamal took a seat. "What can I do for you?"

"When I was in here the other day," Jamal began, "I indicated that I wished to pursue a lawsuit against Brenda Christianson for medical and other financial hardships placed on my wife due to Mrs. Christianson's deceased husband having infected my wife with Aids. I realize it is a delicate situation, but as part of Victor Christianson's estate, I believe my wife is due some type of retribution."

Jonathan sat back in his chair and listened to Jamal before finally taking off his glasses. "Mr. Billops, I've thought a lot about your request, and I've concluded that you're going to have a heck of a time winning this case. First, Victor Christianson, per your knowledge which isn't proof, infected your wife with the virus, and he's dead. It is not known that he had the Aids virus. Mrs. Christianson is his beneficiary, and in view of all the documents relevant to her estate, she doesn't owe you anything. I understand from my partner, who represents Mrs. Christianson, that she's made you a generous offer by allowing you to stay in the condo you and your wife now reside free of charge. Again, I say that's most generous and done in good faith."

"You weren't there before she had her change of heart, Mr. Locke, when she talked to me as if I was scum with no regards to our situation. She was ready to throw us out on the street that very moment, and even though she had a change of heart, it's too late."

"What do you do for a living, Mr. Billops? Why aren't you providing a haven for your wife? You have been living in the condo that belongs to Mrs. Christianson free of charge for almost a year, and many would call that theft. And if Mrs. Christianson should decide to press charges, she'd be well within her rights."

Jamal jumped up from his seat. He moved forward and stood directly in front of Jonathan's desk and pounded on it. "I came to you for help, but instead I'm hearing you spout out what you think that mean-ass bitch deserves. I came here for justice." Jamal hit the desk again. "And I'm going to get it come hell or high water."

Jonathan rose from his seat. "It's time for you to get the hell out of my office. I, in all my good conscience can't represent you. I'd be taking money that you don't have without the results you want. Besides, it is a conflict of interest since my partner is representing the would-be defendant. And if you ever darken my door again, you best learn how to conduct yourself in a civil manner. I don't take kindly to loud-mouth assholes, who think they can come in here and bully me into representing them. Now get out of my office."

Jamal scowled at Jonathan, turned around, walked out

the door, and slammed it, rattling the interior windows within the building. Jamal opened and closed his fists, but decided to walk out of the building before he did any more damage. He was furious, but he resolved in his heart that Brenda Christianson was going to pay.

CHAPTER TWENTY-SEVEN

Monday traffic seemed heavier than usual, but it may have seemed that way as Jamal's mind was clouded. Wandering all over town ceased to soothe his nerves. The audacity of Jonathan Locke to deny him representation and to say in another breath that there was no way possible he would win a lawsuit against Brenda Christianson. The last thing Jamal wanted to do was go home to Sheila after he had disrespected and made her feel terrible.

Thoughts of driving to Brenda Christianson's home entered his mind, but Jamal gathered his senses in a hurry. He wanted to hurt somebody, make someone pay for the woes he had suffered, but there was no one that immediately came to mind, other than Brenda, that he could unleash his wrath on or talk to.

After expending a half tank of gas, Jamal headed toward home. Before he reached the condo he decided to stop by the ice cream shop at The Streets at Southpoint and buy Sheila a pint of her favorite ice cream as a peace offering.

For a moment, the ice cream seemed to pacify all the drama Jamal had endured that morning. Sure, it was a quick fix, but if it would melt Sheila's heart and guarantee a smile on her face. He'd made the right choice.

Happy with his ice cream purchase, Jamal jumped in his car and headed toward home which was less than a mile. When he pulled into the entryway to his home, he was taken aback at the sight of an ambulance lurking near his condo.

Without locking the car, Jamal grabbed the pint of ice cream and moved toward the crowd. He looked up and saw Ms. Pomeroy shaking her head as if in disgust, pointing her finger. Jamal pushed his way through the crowd, then dropped the pint of ice cream when he saw Sheila lying on the gurney that the paramedics shoved into the back of the ambulance.

"Hey, that's my wife," Jamal shouted all out of breath as he neared the ambulance.

One of the attending paramedics turned around. "We're on our way to Duke, if you want to follow."

"What's wrong with her? She was all right when I left a couple of hours ago."

"Mr...."

"Billops, Jamal Billops."

"We're responding to a nine-one-one call. We had to break-in when we arrived. Your wife is in a coma. We need to move now."

"Jesus!" Jamal shouted as he raised his fist in the air. "Hang in there, Sheila. I'm on my way."

The crowd disbursed as the ambulance drove away. "Where were you when she needed you?" Ms. Pomeroy shouted down from her balcony.

"Mind your business, old lady. She's my wife and my

concern. Don't you worry about us." Jamal turned away and walked toward his car.

"All you mens are alike," Ms. Pomeroy said to no one in particular. "You get a woman, take advantage of her, and throw 'em out like the pit of a ripe peach you done sucked to death."

CHAPTER TWENTY-EIGHT

Several weeks passed and it was beginning to look a lot like spring. Brenda and John chatted daily —late into the night. Theirs was the beginning of a blossoming friendship whose petals were ripe for opening. Only a small piece of paper with the operative word "negative" typed on it stood between them unleashing the passion they felt between them—Brenda didn't want to spoil her blessing.

In the meantime, Brenda and Mimi finalized plans for their tea party or white party as they had come to call it, which was to take place the following weekend. Everything was simple down to the catered meal and the number of guests who'd be attending—four in all. Her surprise came when Mimi shared the song she was going to sing. *Do you want to hear my song?* Mimi asked when they met. *It's an original; I wrote it specifically for our gathering. It's entitled Free to Love. I love the title*, Brenda told her. Mimi performed the song for Brenda, which was met with approval.

After meeting with Reynaldo Aziza, Brenda felt more

comfortable about Trevor's pre-trial well-being. She delved back into work. Now finished with her last client for the day by phone, the doorbell rang. Puzzled, Brenda looked at the clock on her desk and noted it was one-thirty in the afternoon.

The doorbell rang again, and Brenda raced through the house to answer the door. She peeked through the peephole, and her lips turned up into a great big smile. Upon opening the door, she was welcomed with a great big kiss.

"Well come in, stranger. Why didn't you call to say you were coming over? What if I hadn't been home?"

"Hold up, baby. I took a chance by coming here unannounced, but I had to."

"So, what is it that you're so excited about that you couldn't have called first?"

"You don't have anyone else here hiding in one of your closets, do you?"

"I'll never tell. Now please satisfy my curiosity."

"I'm going to satisfy more than that." With that said, John whipped out an envelope from his inside jacket pocket.

"What is this?" Brenda asked, taking the envelope from him. When she turned it over, she saw the return address as being the Health Department. Brenda looked from the envelope to John. "Does this mean...?"

"Brenda, this means that I'm a very healthy boy with no major defects. The blood is flowing clear and free through my veins. I promised that I'd take you away when I received the good news, and I'm here to do just that."

"Oh my God!" Brenda exclaimed. "You are...you are HIV negative."

"Yes, I am. I received my clean bill of health in the

mail today. I call it my Good Housekeeping seal of approval, and I ain't ashamed to let everybody know."

"This is wonderful, John, but I can't go today. I've started back counseling full-time, and I have patients to see. I can take a half day off on Friday, and we can go to the beach. Is that okay? I don't mean to spoil your enthusiasm about what this day means."

"Well, I'm a little disappointed, but that doesn't mean we can't have a celebratory get together right here, right now."

Brenda put her hands on her hips. "You naughty boy; I believe you ran all the way over here with hopes of making love to me."

"Jeez, Brenda, don't make it sound dirty or that I'm lusting after you. Yes, I want to have an intimate sojourn with you. Most importantly, I wanted to share my good news."

"What will we tell Mimi about us?"

"Brenda, why are we talking about Mimi? She has a husband. I'm in love with you, not her. She's going to always be my girl but not *my* girl. You do understand."

Laughter filled the house. Brenda held her sides for fear that she'd bust out of her skin. "You're so comical, John." She pulled him toward her and he wrapped his arms around her waist.

IT WAS A NEW EXPERIENCE. Brenda's stomach was tied up in knots. For the last twenty years, she'd been a lover and a wife to only Victor. Tied to her marriage vows, not even the thought of being with another man had penetrated her senses until now.

As she and John moved up the staircase to her bedroom—the one she once shared with her late husband — the rumbles and anxiety grew. Brenda knew that John was checking out her hips; she felt them move up and down as she climbed the stairs. It was somewhat intimidating as this man followed her, especially since she wasn't accustomed to giving herself to anyone else. Even with all the kissing and teasing that went on between them, disrobing in front of John and exposing her sacred jewels was a mission that for a brief moment Brenda thought about aborting.

Brenda's lovable Persian cat, Beyoncé, followed behind the couple as if she was part of the package, but at the door, Beyoncé was denied access. Once inside, John drew Brenda to him and kissed her passionately on the lips. He alternated between her lips and ear lobes before finally allowing his tongue to slow drag down to her neck. It was intoxicating.

"We'll take it slow," John murmured in short breaths as he unbuttoned Brenda's olive-green, silk blouse that sat atop of her cappuccino-colored skin and olive-colored, lacy bra. He removed it from around her shoulders and gently slid it down her arms. Brenda shivered.

Brenda's breathing was erratic, and she began to pull back a little. "Baby, there's nothing to be afraid of," John coached. "I'm going to be so gentle that you'll believe that an angel has you floating on his wings."

"You flatter me, John. I...I... don't...I haven't been with a man in a long time. Not even with Victor."

"Experiencing true love with someone that you haven't been with will always be a new adventure. Having a sexual encounter is like riding a bicycle. You never forget the strokes. You may add some new ones, but true and sensual lovemaking comes from the heart."

"So, you're an expert."

"I don't claim to be, but I'm damn near close."

Brenda smiled. "I'm going to entrust myself to you."

"You're safe in my arms. And so that you know, you're getting ready to embark on a journey that's going to take you far away from here. How does high above the clouds sound?"

"You sound awfully sure of yourself. And, if you don't deliver, I want a full refund."

"It won't be necessary. Now stop talking."

John took off his clothes and Brenda took off her pants until she only had on her bra and panties. Brenda avoided looking at John. And then she felt his arms, after he had pulled back the satin comforter on the bed, picked her up, and laid her on the blue-satin sheets.

John passionately stroked Brenda's lips, took them into his mouth, and sucked on them. Finally, he parted her lips and explored her mouth as if he had discovered the fountain of youth.

JOHN RAN his hands the length of her arms. Brenda was vulnerable, and he wanted to take it slow so that she could experience the essence of what it felt like to be made love to. While he had her in a lip lock, he eased the straps of her bra down her shoulders, eventually unsnapping the band that kept her twin mounds of pleasure intact. Brenda's constant moaning gave him the courage to continue. He stroked her body tenderly, as he allowed his hands to cup and squeeze her breasts until she moaned for more. He pulled down on them until his forefinger and thumb were wrapped around her nipples. Brenda moaned some more and he planted his lips around them and sucked each one gently. Sparks flew like the fourth of July.

As if a magic button had been pushed, Brenda's body trembled as he continued to suck and caress her breasts. Her hands began to look for a place to belong, and she grabbed John's shoulders and began to massage them before moving them down the length of his arm.

John continued his assault with his tongue moving down toward her sensitive terrain, marking the spot at her belly button until he found the top of her lacy bottoms. Brenda gently touched John's hand as he tried to slide her panties over her hips.

Brenda sat up abruptly, pushing John out of the way, killing the good mood. "I don't know if I'm ready for this," Brenda said, her body shaking. "I thought I was ready, but I don't think I am. And John, I can't go all the way without you wearing a condom. I'm sorry, but I can't do this."

"Oh, you don't have to worry about protection. There was no thought of pleasuring you without my protective shield."

Brenda gasped. "How presumptuous of you to think I was going to submit to your desires just like that."

"Look, Brenda, I ran over here with my good news, and we agreed that when I received a clean bill of health, we would let caution fly to the wind and enjoy each other."

"I don't remember it quite like that, John."

"Maybe those weren't the exact words, but they're

close enough. I'm positive that you know that to be true because you were there." John pulled Brenda close. "You're afraid, especially in light of the disease Victor inflicted on others. You were one of the lucky ones, and maybe I am pushing you too fast."

"John, I am in love with you." Brenda closed her eyes and reopened them. "There's nothing more that I want than to be with you. Ever since you paid me a little attention and your intentions were made known, I've been like a giddy school girl. Somewhere in the back of mind, I've had this crush on you. I'm sorry about today. I...I..."

"It's okay, baby. Don't worry about it. Another opportunity will come and when it does, we'll let love dictate. It may mean that we don't consummate our growing love for each other by being together intimately—at least for now. It's going to be hard for this brother to resist a good-looking sister like yourself, especially one he's in love with and happens to be sitting in front of him in her birthday finery."

Brenda blushed and picked up a corner of the comforter and pulled it partially over her. She lowered her head. After a minute's pause, she lifted her head and held John's face in her hands and placed a long, hard kiss on his lips. "Since we've been sitting here, I've been thinking. We've talked about getting away. Why don't we go away to the beach this weekend, since the following weekend is my tea party with Mimi and the girls? It'll give me time to think about making that ultimate step with you."

"This weekend isn't good, but I do like what you said about making that final step."

"Don't get too happy. I said I would think about it. After all, I don't want you to think that I'm a loose woman who's willing to drop her panties at your beckoned call. And I hope that what is happening between us isn't only about sex."

"No, Brenda, it's not only about having a sexual relationship. I'm in love with you. I apologize if I in any way made you feel…insinuated that I was pursing you to have sex. Quite the contrary; you're a beautiful, intelligent woman who I admire and have totally fallen in love with."

Brenda smiled. "Okay, I was only checking to see if you're the real deal." Brenda began to laugh.

John's smile broke into laughter. "Girl, you scared me." He pulled the comforter away from her and kissed her left breast. Her nipple became erect at his touch and he found his mouth around it once again. He sucked, manipulated, and caressed it until moans of pleasure emitted from Brenda's mouth. He moved to the other breast and suckled it and before he knew it, his hand found her secret garden and he tendered it well. Without another word from Brenda, he whisked her panties from her body and took a private moment to look at her. John shook his head; he was pleased.

Not hearing any complaints, John reached for the condom that he had slipped under the pillow. He eased it out of the wrapper, and placed it firmly on his erect member. Brenda's body longed for him with each touch of his mouth on her, and within moments John introduced her to ecstasy.

Brenda's body convulsed and shuddered as John gave her the ride of her life. There was no turning back, as Brenda begged him not to stop at the top of her lungs. John felt Brenda moving to his rhythm, enjoying the ride with unselfish abandon. He felt her tongue glide down his chest, circling his nipples. And then the beast rose simultaneously as the two lovers sought to be the first to surrender. And when the climax had reached its peak, there were no immediate words as to what this pleasure had wrought. For sure, there were no regrets.

CHAPTER TWENTY-NINE

Mimi was ecstatic. She'd finally gotten her first real singing gig. Out of the blue, she received a call from an old friend she knew from Hampton University who went by the name of Minx, whose brother was looking for a jazz singer for his band. After meeting with the band member, her new life was moving at a fast pace, so much so she hadn't even had time to call and tell Brenda of her good fortune. There were rehearsals that lasted sometimes six or seven hours, but tonight she was going to perform at a cocktail social for one of the big Whigs in town who had organized the event as a fundraiser for a political candidate.

Now that she had a chance to breathe, Mimi decided to call Brenda and tell her the good news. She felt bad that she hadn't spent any time with her best friend, except for a call here and there to finalize their tea party for the following weekend. And even then, the telephone calls were short and sweet. The last time Mimi saw Brenda was at the restaurant when they both ran into John.

Come to think of it, Mimi hadn't spoken with John

either. It was apparent, he was trying to distance himself from her. Raphael had given John a run for his money and let John know in no uncertain terms that his wife was off-limits. So why was she trying so hard to get up with him? Mimi resolved in her mind to let John stay in his environment, and she wouldn't bring him up again. Anyway, she didn't have time for him. She was on her way to becoming a recording artist. Surely after people recognized her for her vocal talent, producers would come running out of the wood work. She was patient.

Mimi picked her iPhone up from the table. She placed a call to Brenda, but the phone continued to ring. Mimi hung up and called again but with the same result. Mimi would call Brenda tomorrow. There would be plenty to tell her.

"Do you want to get that?" John asked. "The caller seems awfully insistent."

"It's Mimi," Brenda said in a soft tone. "I'm not in the mood for any conversation other than what's going on here."

John smiled. "Can't get enough, can you?"

Brenda smiled back. "You figured that once you had me in your clutches that I'd only want more. If the condoms last, baby, I'm ready. I haven't felt this way in a long time. You've created a monster—a monster with a big appetite for you. But I will say, that if this is what love feels like, I don't want to come down from the clouds. I don't have any idea what it feels like to be strung out on drugs, but from the pictures I've seen, I'm strung out on something."

"Baby, this is the first day of many days." John was thoughtful. "I'm hoping that this will be the beginning of forever."

Brenda squinted her eyes. "What does that mean, John?"

"Don't worry your little self about it now. It'll become crystal clear soon enough. Are you ready for fourths?"

"I'm past ready."

CHAPTER THIRTY

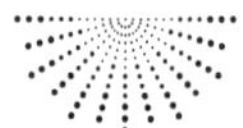

Mimi wore a black-and-white-print cashmere shell and cardigan that enhanced her high-waist Italian Viscose crepe, black pants. She set it off with a four-inch, Italian leather shoe that shined like it had a touch of patent leather.

Painting her lips with a magenta-colored lipstick, Mimi smiled as she took one last look at herself in the mirror. Her beautician had smoothed her hair back, and placed a twelve-inch ponytail on top. Without a doubt, Mimi looked fabulous and she basked in this new-found freedom—not having to look over her shoulders to protect herself from a crazy Victor Christianson. All that was missing was her loving husband, who she missed dearly.

Slipping into a fur-trimmed cashmere poncho, Mimi picked up her purse and headed to the venue. Excitement dripped all over her, and she couldn't wait to entertain the high-profile guests who were the who's who of the Raleigh-Durham community.

Off in her Mercedes, Mimi sang a medley of tunes, each vibrating throughout the car. She felt poised, on point, and ready for the show to begin, and she prayed that if not tonight, that somewhere in her immediate future, a record producer would materialize and jumpstart her career.

The venue was at an upscale club on the edge of Raleigh and Durham. Pulling into the parking lot, Mimi noticed that a few cars had begun to trickle in. She was asked to arrive at least an hour early, and she wanted to be on time for her first event, although she had gone through sound check earlier that afternoon. The band was comprised of an eclectic group of men whose ages ranged somewhere between forty and sixty. Their sound was great, but Mimi had no desire to sing behind them forever.

Valet parking was at her disposal, and she hopped out of the car as soon as her door was opened. She sashayed into the clubhouse and gave a grand smile when she saw some of the band members stop and turn in her direction when she entered the room.

"Hey, guys," Mimi said, waving the tips of her fingers as if it were an effort. She dropped her cape off at the hat check-in, brushed her clothes down and joined the band in elegant splendor.

"You sure look good tonight, Mimi," one of the band members said.

"Thank you, Charles," Mimi returned. "I'm really looking forward to this evening."

"If you sing like you did at rehearsals, it's going to be a fabulous night," the band director, Clifton Sayers added.

"Thanks, Clifton. I appreciate the opportunity to join your band and throw down for this town."

"Well, knock them dead, diva," Clifton said. "And I mean diva in a good way."

Mimi smiled and began to warm her vocal chords

along with the band as guests began to arrive. It was a star-studded event. There was a certain sparkle, elegance, grace, a little Hollywood when black folks dressed up for an affair. They put on their best party dresses, high-heel shoes, and tuxes.

Heavy hors d` oeuvres were being served. Jumbo shrimp, watercress sandwiches, beef and chicken sticks, and a large assortment of other creatively decorated finger foods were brought around on trays for the guests' palate. Mimi learned that a sit-down dinner followed an assortment of speeches, per a copy of the printed program she snuck into her purse. After cocktails, the band would have ample time to rest and after dinner would perform again for either the guests' listening pleasure or their dancing feet.

The low chatter cooled down when Mimi began to belt out her numbers. She sounded so much like Anita Baker but with an edgier sound that could've been Jill Scott. The applause was uplifting, and Mimi could tell that the guests were mesmerized. Clifton Sayers, the band director, was pleased and while the guests had moved to another room for dinner, Clifton took the opportunity to text his brother about Mimi's performance.

Mimi looked out into the sea of patrons and scanned the room. She half expected to see Brenda. Brenda and Victor were part of this crowd. Since Victor's death and Trevor's incarceration, Brenda hadn't ventured far from home. That was one reason why she was excited that Brenda wanted to have the tea for her and the girls. It was a sign of moving on.

An hour and a half passed. Speeches and testimonials were given, and by the response of the audience, the night seemed to be a success. Guests began to trickle out of the main ballroom. Some gathered their wraps and continued outside, presumably for home, while others waited for the band to play. After all, it was a weeknight, and many had early starts the next morning.

Mimi captured the hearts and souls of the guests who remained, and there was a crowd. After a few songs and the band moved toward ending their final set, the crowd went berserk, shouting for an encore. Mimi was pleased. Whistling echoed throughout the room and the band sang a few more numbers before the host stepped in and announced that it was the final song.

"Mimi, you've got some pipes on you," Clifton said, congratulating her on a good night. "I sure hope you'll be with us a long time. My god, girl, you're a jewel."

Mimi grinned, delighted at the wonderful compliment. "Thank you, Clifton. It was easy with this band. They say behind every good singer is a good band, and the Clifton Sayer Band is the best."

Clifton smiled. "I've already sent Minx a text about your performance. Said he was going to fly down from New York for our next one, which will be at DPAC."

"DPAC?"

"I forgot you haven't been in Durham that long. DPAC stands for the Durham Performing Arts Center. It's one of the more upscale places to go for concerts and plays in Durham. It draws a more sophisticated crowd."

"Wow. That sounds great. When will it take place?"

"You should've received a schedule of our events. It's next Sunday."

"Whew," Mimi said.

"Is that a problem?"

"No. I have a very important engagement with my daughter and a dear friend and her daughter next Saturday; I'm glad that I don't have to make any schedule changes. Well, I look forward to performing again."

"We don't have many engagements, although, after tonight, we might be filled up for the summer months."

"Well, Clifton, tonight was wonderful, and I'll see you at rehearsal on Friday."

"Same here, Mimi. May I walk you to your car?"

"Thank you, but I valet parked. I don't have far to walk."

"Let me walk you to the curb anyway," Clifton said, checking Mimi out on a sly. "I've gotta make sure that the star of my band is properly escorted to her car."

Mimi batted her eyes, although not intentionally. "Okay. First, I must stop by the coat check and pick up my wrap. I'm sure it's a little chilly outside."

"I'm right with you. Lead the way. And if I didn't tell you already, you're a beautiful addition to our band."

"Thanks." Mimi was anxious to move on. Surely Clifton saw the big rock that sat on her married left hand. She was flattered, but the only one who mattered was her Colonel, Raphael Bailey, her man. She would be most happy when he returned from Afghanistan.

CHAPTER THIRTY-ONE

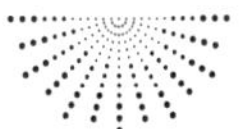

It was a new morning and a new day. Dark still covered the earth, however, if not for the alarm on the clock that broke the deathly silence in the house at five-thirty, she'd still be asleep. Brenda tried to roll over until she realized there was an obstruction. She grabbed her chest, then enjoyed a private grin. For the first time in years, she entertained an overnight guest—an overnight guest in her home and in her bed.

Looking toward the ceiling, Brenda began to reminisce about the wonderful, insatiable, erotic, and fun-filled day and night she had with one John Carroll. He was a tender lover and ironed out all the kinks that had settled in her body. It was like heaven, and she wanted to be the recipient of his good loving on a regular basis.

The irritating sound of the alarm clock pierced the room again. This time John shifted under the satin sheets before finally jumping up. "Damn, I've got to get up and go home so I can get ready for work."

"I saw how comfortable you were under those sheets,"

Brenda said, before blowing a kiss in his ear as she lay on her side.

John rubbed his bald head and eased up from under the covers. "That and the fact that you made some mad, passionate love to this boy last night. Brenda, you are a wonderful lover. You took your time and enjoyed it."

"We enjoyed it." Brenda pressed her lips together. She looked John square in the eyes. "I can get used to this on the regular. I'm not sure what you did to me; it could've been a date rape drug. But baby..." Brenda said, unable to finish her sentence all the while shaking her head, "I don't know if Diana Ross really knew what she was singing about when she sang about a love hangover. I can attest to the fact that I have one and it's about to drive me crazy."

"Why don't I come back tonight so we can enjoy the experience again? Right now, I've got to get my tail out of this bed and get ready for work. On a serious note, I enjoyed making love to you, Brenda, and I'm glad that you enjoyed it, too." John reached and kissed Brenda on the cheek. "After I brush my teeth, I'll give you a taste of the real thing."

"Okay."

Brenda watched as John scrambled out of bed. He ran through the shower, put on the clothes he'd come to her house in, before slapping her with one of his hearty, wet kisses. She was stung. Now he was gone, and she couldn't wait for his return.

Lying in bed, Brenda reached back into her history with Victor. She was head over heels for Victor when they first met as young freshmen college students, and she thought he made her blood boil. But as she lay in the darkness, she couldn't recall a moment when making love to Victor was this intoxicating, exciting, erotic, all-consuming, or whatever other adjective described fabulous. That memory wasn't forthcoming. John had strung her out and left an undeniable mark on her. She was smitten and in love with him. Yes, there had been lust but she truly was falling head-over-heels in love with this man.

Up and in a wonderful mood, Brenda met with two of her clients, although she wasn't as attentive as she should've been. She wrote a few notes on her legal pad, but John Carroll was all that she could think about. After her last client departed, she tapped her fingers on her desk and thought about calling John. Before she could pull up his number, her phone rang. It was Mimi. This was her best friend, but now she'd acquired a new best friend. Brenda smiled and quickly answered the call before Mimi hung up.

"Hey, girl," Brenda said, her face flushed thinking about John.

"Wow, you're in a good mood. Who floated your boat?"

"Girl, why do you always think that someone else has to be the reason for my good mood?"

"My bad," Mimi said. "I didn't mean to imply anything. I was just checking on my best friend."

"Sorry about that, Mimi. My last two clients left, and I think I was happy to have the rest of the afternoon free."

"Good. Why don't we meet for lunch? I've got something to tell you."

Brenda was all ears now. She never knew from what field Mimi would be coming from. "What is it? In fact, why don't I fix us some sandwiches and you can come by here?"

"Oh, okay. That'll be fine. How about in thirty minutes?"

"That'll give me time to run to Chick-fil-A and grab something."

"That doesn't sound homemade."

"It would've been until you said thirty minutes. Come on. I want to hear your good news."

"I'll pick up the food; I'm on the way."

CHAPTER THIRTY-TWO

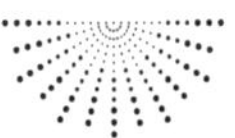

Mimi rolled up into Brenda's driveway in thirty minutes flat. She flounced out of the car dressed in a cocoa, cashmere leather-trimmed pocket wrap, layering a burnt-orange, ribbed turtleneck top and brown stretch jeans. It was obvious that Mimi was riding on a high and she couldn't wait to tell Brenda her good news, as if she was the only one who had any. She carried a bag that contained two Chick-Fil-A salads and sandwiches.

As soon as Mimi tapped the doorbell, the door opened and Brenda stood to the side with a welcoming smile.

"I like that," Brenda said, eying Mimi's get up, moving her finger up and down for effect. "You dropped some money on that outfit, and you're wearing it, girlfriend."

"Thanks, Brenda. You look fabulous yourself. I'll put the food in the kitchen."

"Girl, these old pair of jeans and shirt don't stand a chance next to your outfit. Some days, I don't feel like getting all dolled up, but when I do, watch out. Next

Saturday, I'm going to be wearing my white and without a doubt will be camera ready in my fabulousness."

Mimi laughed. "I'm looking so forward to it, Brenda."

"Me, too. Let's eat on the patio; I'm anxious to hear your good news."

After getting settled and taking a few bites of her chicken salad sandwich, Mimi ran down her performance last evening before giving her the low down on how she got the gig and the sometimes torturous and grueling rehearsals she'd been through. She ended by telling Brenda that her good friend Minx, who was the brother of the band director and was friends with several record producers in New York, was coming to see her at the band's next performance.

"Well, certainly I've got to be there," Brenda said. "I don't want to miss my best friend's coming of age. You're finally on your way, Mimi, even if it did take almost a lifetime."

Mimi dropped her head momentarily, but brought it back up and smiled at Brenda. "A short setback, but it's all good. It's all about God's timing, and I guess this is my time."

"You're right."

"So, anything new your way, Brenda? You should've received your tests results by now. I trust and hope everything will be all right."

"I believe everything is going to be all right." Brenda wasn't sure why she hadn't shared her good news with Brenda. Maybe it was that she had a new best friend by the name of John with whom she shared it with first—taking liberties with the good news. She dismissed her thoughts and came back to the present. "I'm not sweating the small stuff. Victor and I hadn't been husband and wife for a long time. I've already claimed the victory."

"Good for you," Mimi said. "I want to see you happy. You seemed to be a little distracted this afternoon, and it's probably because I talked so much about myself."

They both laughed. "Yeah, you did seem a little stuck on yourself."

"Really? I hope I wasn't being an ass. I only wanted to share my good news with my best friend. I don't talk to anyone else. John certainly seems to be ignoring me, but I've let it go. I've been too busy with my new career. Anyway, John filled a temporary void with Raphael being so far away—just friends, nothing else. John will always be a dear friend, and one day, maybe we can pin him down and do lunch."

Brenda was solemn, nodding her head as Mimi spoke. No, John didn't have time for Mimi; she was monopolizing all of it. And she wanted to keep it that way. She closed her eyes for a minute and reminisced on their lovemaking last evening. "Uhm," Brenda said, catching herself.

"Are you all right, girl?" Mimi asked, a line forming across her forehead. "Maybe you should see a therapist."

"No, I'm fine...I'm good," Brenda said, looking away from Mimi. "I was thinking about Trevor; that's all," she lied.

"Well, I can see that I'm not good company."

"Don't say that, Mimi. I always love our time together, it's just that I have so much on my mind right now. I'll be all right. Now let's finish our lunch; I want to hear all about the band and the songs you sang last night."

Mimi watched Brenda. Something wasn't right, but it was up to Brenda to get help if she needed it.

CHAPTER THIRTY-THREE

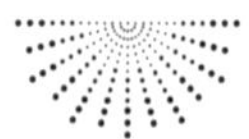

Brenda and John spent a lot of time together the next seven days, but today was the *White Party* and all of Brenda's attention was going to shift to Asia, Mimi, and Afrika. She looked forward to this day, as much as the rest had claimed they did, but she had to force the last seven days of unspeakable, mind-blowing, erotic, captivating sex and lovemaking to the bottom of her list... well not totally at the bottom. She was riding a wave of romantic bliss, and she didn't want to let go.

The decorators had come and gone, and the caterer had put the finishing touches on the hors d` oeuvres. Brenda relieved Mimi of her duties for fear she would run into John since she couldn't get him to leave her bed until early that morning. What a relief. And Asia and Afrika were coming together. Now that everything was in place, she was poised and ready to receive her guests.

They looked like angels who had gathered for a heavenly tea party—the mothers, Brenda and Mimi, and their daughters, Asia and Afrika. Asia and Afrika were the vision of twins, one light the other slightly darker, with their hair both slicked back into ponytails. Little did they know when they met as college freshmen a year ago that they shared DNA—their father, the great Victor Christianson, who had been characterized as a ladies' man, a man whore and a rapist. Their mothers who were best friends, Brenda and Mimi, found each other after an eighteen-year absence, only for Brenda to discover that her husband of nineteen years had raped her best friend; and she kept it a secret. This was a time for healing...for moving forward.

"Mimosas for everyone," Brenda said, pulling a glass off the tray that the caterer passed around. Raising her hand up high with the Mimosa in hand, Brenda gave a short toast. "To us!"

"To us," the others said in unison before taking sips of their Mimosas.

"Divas all," Brenda said, taking another sip of her Mimosa. "This was supposed to be a tea party, but once Mimi and I started planning, it has become something else. Look at us. We're four drop-dead, beautiful chicks. We've got to get a picture of us together to commemorate this day."

"Yes, we are," Asia responded, enjoying herself.

"Everything looks wonderful, Brenda," Mimi began, as they all gathered their things and moved to the area where they were to spend the afternoon. Mimi scanned the terrace, the beautiful decorations and place settings. "I can't wait to sink my teeth into the shrimp cocktail." Brenda laughed. "We couldn't have asked for a more gorgeous spring day," Mimi added.

Brenda smiled. "That it is, and today, we're going to celebrate us."

"You're in an awfully good mood, Mom," Asia said,

pointing her finger at Brenda. "I can't put my finger on it, but you seem different."

"Me?" Brenda looked around the room. "I don't know what Asia is talking about. Can't a girl have a little bubbly and some fun?" Everyone laughed.

"I'm glad you're in a good mood," Mimi added. "It's a far cry from how you seemed the other day."

"I've thought a lot about what you said, Mimi, and I realized that I must leave the past in the past."

"That's right, girl." Mimi took another sip of her Mimosa, as she watched Brenda carefully.

"How are you doing, Afrika?" Brenda asked. "You've barely uttered two words."

"You and my mom have taken over the floor as usual."

Asia slapped Afrika's wrist. "Girl, you've got that right, but I'm glad we've gotten together like this."

"Yeah," Afrika replied. "It's long overdue. And to answer your question, I'm fine. In a couple of days, we'll have completed one year of college."

"And I'm moving to Brier Creek," Asia put in. "Afrika is spending the summer with me."

"Ohh," Brenda said, giving Asia a once over. She hadn't any knowledge of this. "Wow, Mimi, a lot has happened in a year. Takes me back twenty years."

Mimi smiled halfheartedly. "It does."

"Thanks, Mrs. Christianson for suggesting we have this party," Afrika continued. "I'm sure it means a lot to my mom." Afrika went to Mimi, kissed her on the forehead and gave her a big hug. Before anyone could say anything else, Asia got up and hugged Brenda—the first step on the road to healing.

"Okay," Brenda interjected, unfolding her arms from around Asia. "I've catered a simple but scrumptious meal for us, after which my best friend is going to render us a song. I've already heard it, and I'm sure you'll understand its meaning and know it's coming from Mimi's heart." Mimi nodded her head in approval and smiled.

Afrika and Asia looked in Mimi's direction, but Mimi offered no other hint. She smiled and passed the baton back to Brenda.

"So, what's on the menu?" Asia asked, rushing to move beyond the melancholy mood.

Gathering her composure, Brenda rattled off what sounded like an appetizing meal. "Since each of us loves the fruit of the sea, we're having grilled shrimp on a bed of saffron rice along with the largest lobster tails the caterer could find. I'm sure you'll find the crab cakes delectable since I had them flown in straight from Maryland."

"You don't have to say any more," Mimi screamed. "Let the eats begin."

"Well, you know how much my baby, Asia, loves crabmeat. So, I have a pasta that's laden with Alfredo sauce full of crabmeat to die for."

"Okay, Mom, stop teasing. Bring it on."

"I didn't get to mention the salads or dessert."

"You don't have to," Mimi cut in. "Let's say grace so I can plop one of those scrumptious shrimps into my mouth. Look at it; it's begging me to rescue it from that crystal glass."

Everyone laughed. Brenda asked Mimi to bless the table, after which she summoned the caterers. The ladies feasted and shared small talk. Asia and Afrika talked about school and the new semester, while Brenda and Mimi talked about life as it was now. Mimi shared her good news about the singing gig and how her career seemed to be ripe for taking off. Everyone clapped and gave high-fives.

"I need more butter," Mimi said, licking her fingers. "And the crab cakes are divine." Everyone laughed.

A high-pitched sound met the diners' ears when Brenda clinked her glass softly with her knife. "I have some news," Brenda said, after the laughter had died down.

"What is it," Asia asked as she pushed back her chair, giving Brenda her undivided attention.

"I've got some good news." A smile sprung across Brenda's face. She pulled out an envelope that she had kept underneath her place setting. Mimi's eyes bulged and watched Brenda with restrained interest. Brenda pulled a one-page letter out of the envelope. Then she looked at the trio who stared with utter distress on their faces. "This letter represents my freedom." She held it high in the air.

"Oh my God! Oh my God!" Mimi shouted, jumping up from her chair. "For real, Brenda?"

Brenda put her finger to her mouth to summon Mimi to be quiet. "This letter is from the Health Department and it states that I... am... HIV negative."

Not another second passed before the whole group was up and out of their chairs. They erupted into a chorus of cheers and chants of *yes* and *all right* for Brenda, each one in turn giving Brenda a huge serving of hugs. It was so infectious, that everyone one hugged each other, crying tears of joy. It looked like an angelic choir—all dressed in white.

After several minutes of rejoicing, Brenda pulled away and wiped her eyes.

"Thank you. This piece of paper means the whole world, although I didn't doubt that I'd receive this answer.

The Lord already told me when I prayed what His answer was going to be and that I had to believe. Of course, I will have to go back for six month check-ups for a period." Brenda grabbed her chest. "God is good, and now I'm free. I'm free to love."

Asia went to her mother and hugged her again. Brenda picked up her linen napkin and dabbed her eyes again. "Guys, I think this is the most appropriate time for Mimi to sing her song. I said we weren't going to dwell on the past, but there's a reason why we're here today. That's because we've all been victims of the past, but by our testimonies we are free. And while I had no idea what I was going to say today, Mimi's song is befitting for all of us. Come on Mimi before I shed more tears."

Mimi wiped her face, taking her time to come and stand in front. She looked at her daughter, Afrika, and smiled. Then she looked at Asia and Brenda and smiled and let her head drop slowly before lifting it back up.

"You all won't believe this but my song, which I wrote only a week ago, is entitled "Free to Love." Wow, I can't believe how Brenda moved us into this moment. She's heard the song, and I hope you'll embrace it, too; I'm also free to love. It's not that I didn't have a wonderful life with my husband and daughter. There were things...secrets that held me back from being free...things that kept me from experiencing life without always looking over my shoulder...things that kept me from realizing my full potential. I feel Brenda's love." Mimi exhaled. "Here's "Free to Love.""

I've watched my life float by like a tumbleweed in
the wind

Mirrors reflecting how my life wasn't supposed to
be...and then again
Secrets had me bound
But there was no one around...that I could tell, I
could tell.

I never thought the hurt and the pain of that day
would ever go away
I hadn't realized how many people I had betrayed
along the way
Because I refused to share
the dark secret that would've set me free, set
me free
Free to love my man
Free to love my best friend
Free to love the best of myself
Free to put the shame to rest
But when I did, I was free to love

And now I'm free to love; I'm free to love; Yes, I
am free to love, I'm free to love
Free to love my man
Free to love my best friend
Free to love myself
Free to put the shame to rest
Yes, I'm free; I'm free to love

There wasn't a dry eye. And the hugging began; the healing began. No one moved until the crying subsided.

CHAPTER THIRTY-FOUR

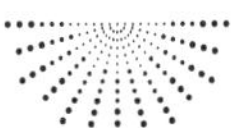

The tea party wasn't a tea party, it was an intimate day with best friends—Brenda and Mimi, Asia and Afrika. They continued to swap feel good stories, allowing the afternoon to drift away. Brenda smiled. She was at peace and the group was at peace along with her, knowing that she was no longer in danger—out of harm's way. And oh, didn't Mimi sing that song—"Free to Love." How appropriate was it at a time like that? Karma, nothing but pure karma.

The ladies lounged and sipped on cups of hot tea, their minimum drink limit of Mimosas fulfilled. Mimi looked at her watch, gawked and yawned having realized that the beautiful spring day was soon coming to a close.

"I guess it's time for me to be getting home," Mimi said, yawning yet again. "Sleep is trying to invade my body."

"Mommy, where do you have to go in the morning?" Afrika asked in a playful, sarcastic tone.

"Church, that's where I'm going. I've finally joined a church not far from the house."

"For real, Mommy? Hallelujah!"

"Well, Miss Afrika, if you'd call and talk with your mommy more often, maybe you'd learn a little something about your mother's activities. In fact, I want you all to come to my next singing event that will be held at the DPAC."

"For real, Mommy?"

"Yes, indeed," Mimi answered with a smile.

"We should all go and support Mimi," Brenda said, taking another sip of her tea. "Today was only the beginning of getting together—mothers, daughters, and best friends." She winked at Mimi.

"I like that," Asia said. "But don't try to monopolize our time; we have other social obligations to meet."

"Like what, Asia?" Brenda asked, as if she didn't already know.

"Now, Mom, I don't think I need to spell it out for you."

"Okay, I won't pry at this moment, but we've got to talk some more." Asia and Afrika winked at each other.

Mimi stood up. "I really need to get a move on. I believe it's all those Mimosas I drank."

"I'll drive you home, Mommy. I was planning to spend the night anyway."

"Great. Brenda, this was a lovely party. I had the best time. I'm so happy about your good news."

"Me too, Mimi. And look at our daughters. They're mirrors of us."

"So, true," Mimi said. "Okay, Afrika, let's go."

They all stopped what they were doing when the doorbell suddenly rang. Fear jumped on Brenda's face, as if she'd suddenly been stricken with a stroke. John knew that she was entertaining Mimi and their daughters, and surely, he wouldn't show up on her porch, especially with all the cars in the driveway. Without a doubt, she longed to be in his arms, but not now.

The doorbell rang again. Asia got up and went to the door with the others following close behind. When Asia opened the door, she stepped back with a startled look on her face.

IT HAD BEEN months since Asia laid eyes on Zavion. In fact, the last time she recalled seeing him, it was at her house...at that very spot when he ran from her home without a word. The moment was still vivid, like a Kodak picture that had been captured and placed in a scrapbook. Asia remembered what he had on and the look on his face when he learned that her father was Victor Christianson, his half-brother's illegitimate, deadbeat dad who had abused his mother.

Four pairs of eyes stared back as Zavion crossed the threshold followed by his brother, Freddie. They looked haggard and worn and their clothes were wrinkled, almost as if they'd slept in them. Zavion's jeans fell midway across his behind, which shocked Asia who remembered him as being clean cut.

Asia inched back, unsure of what this surprise visit was all about. There were no smiles on either brothers' face, and since they hadn't been in touch the whole time Trevor had been incarcerated, Asia assumed it had nothing to do with him.

Brenda moved forward and stepped in front of Asia.

"Hello, Zavion...Freddie. Ahh, we're surprised to see you. Is everything all right?"

Asia watched as Zavion stared at her then turned to look at her mother. "No, Mrs. Christianson, everything isn't all right."

"What's wrong? How can I help you? We haven't seen you boys in months."

Zavion rolled his eyes. "Our mother is dead."

The blood drained from Brenda's face. She stood there gawking at Zavion and Freddie. "I'm so sorry about your mother. I... I didn't know she was sick."

"No disrespect, Mrs. Christianson, but how can you say you didn't know? Her life played out in the newspapers. That bastard, Victor Christianson destroyed our family."

"Hold on, young man. There's no need to talk like that. I can understand your feelings," Brenda said, her body shaking.

"Do you? Hell, you don't have any idea. Victor Christianson knew and he didn't give a damn about my mother —left her sick and penniless. She died alone, Mrs. Christianson. Nobody in this world cared about my mother and what would happen to her."

Brenda looked at Zavion with eyes of compassion. "Again, I'm sorry for your loss. Why don't you boys come in for a minute so we can talk about this more calmly?"

"You don't get it, do you?"

"I don't get what?"

"Your husband, my brother's father was responsible for my mother having Aids."

"Well, I heard reports that she was the one who transmitted the Aids virus to my husband. Son, this is not our conversation."

"Somebody's got to pay. You've got money. In fact, my mother should've had some of what that sorry bastard left you."

Asia stepped forward. "You have no right to speak to my mother that way, Zavion. Honestly, you've got some nerve coming here. Eight or nine months have gone by since my father's death, and not once have either you or Freddie inquired about Trevor. After all, it was my brother, Trevor, who saved your mother's ass."

"Okay, Asia. We aren't going to solve anything like this."

"Come on, Mom. I can't believe his nerve."

Freddie moved from the shadow of his brother and spoke for the first time. "If it wasn't for a sorry, lowdown excuse of a man who didn't care about his children, we wouldn't be having this conversation."

Asia pushed the palm of her hand toward the brothers' faces. "He was my father, too. I'm sorry your experience wasn't great, but we can't pay for the sins our father committed. Where is your grandmother?"

Zavion sneered at Asia. "Leave my grandmother out of this. She has nothing to do with it."

"I believe she does," Asia countered. "If I recall from some of our conversations, your grandmother wasn't too pleased with your mother's lifestyle either. And if my memory serves me right, your mother was a drug addict."

"That's enough," Brenda shouted. "Everybody in the family room."

Zavion maintained his unpleasant and callous demeanor, while Freddie wore a softer countenance. Reluctantly, they followed Brenda into the family room. Asia, Mimi, and Afrika brought up the rear. There was so much tension in the room, it was stifling—like someone had cut off the air supply. Freddie and Zavion sat on the couch while the rest of the group sat in one of the two free chairs and on the sectional. Brenda remained standing.

Several minutes went by without anyone saying a word. When it appeared that everyone was comfortable at best, Brenda stepped in front of the boys with her hands cupped together.

"Where is your mother now?"

Both Zavion and Freddie looked up at Brenda. A scowl so mean was still present on Zavion's face. Blue veins pushed up the skin across his forehead, giving it the appearance of a roadmap on a GPS navigation system. His stare was cold and hard. "She's in the morgue," Zavion said.

Brenda bent down so that she was eye level with the boys. She picked up Freddie's hand, since he was the calmer of the two. Without penetrating their eyes, she looked between the two of them. "Have your grandmother contact me. I'll give you my number to give to her. I will help with some of the funeral arrangements."

Asia jumped up from her seat, but Brenda waved her back down and mouthed something that only Asia could comprehend. Brenda patted Freddie's hand, and before she could move from her squat to a standing position, Freddie began to cry; he lost it. Brenda bent down again and held his hand.

Zavion looked at Freddie and seemed to be contemplating something. Slowly he reached over and put his arm around Freddie's shoulders. Brenda dared to look, and she saw tears rolling down Zavion's face, although he refused to make a sound.

Mimi got up from her seat and went behind the boys and placed a hand on each shoulder and offered a prayer.

It was what the boys needed. It was obvious to everyone in the room that their souls were hurting.

Both Asia and Afrika got up and stood next to Brenda and waited for Mimi to finish her prayer. When all was quiet, Zavion gave Freddie a little push."

"We've got to go," Zavion said. His face was dull but it had lost some of its bitterness. "May I have your number for my grandmother...please?"

"Yes. Sure. Let me get a piece of paper and a pen," Brenda said.

When Brenda moved to the kitchen, Zavion chose that time to look up at Asia. "It's been a long time." He shook his head. "Sorry about all this, but I'm an emotional wreck right now. I don't care what my mother did or who she was, she's my mother."

Asia stayed her distance and eyed Zavion carefully. "Look, I apologize for some of the things I said. I've gone through a lot as well, and because my circumstance isn't your circumstance doesn't mean that I don't hurt or feel betrayed. Victor Christianson was my father."

Zavion ingested Asia's words and was about to respond when Brenda reentered the room with a piece of paper with her telephone number written on it. "Again, let your grandmother know that I'm willing to help with the funeral."

"Thanks," Zavion said in a soft, muffled voice. "I'm sorry for my rudeness. I'm sure my grandmother wouldn't have been proud of how I conducted myself. Thank you."

Brenda hugged each of the boys followed by Mimi. Asia refused to say anything else to Zavion. Brenda escorted the boys to the door, and as they were about to leave Freddie turned around and looked at Brenda.

"How is Trevor?" he asked.

"He's fighting for his life."

CHAPTER THIRTY-FIVE

Brenda, Mimi, Asia, and Afrika sat in the comfort of Brenda's family room, rehashing the last half hour's turn of events. It was exhausting at best, but having Zavion and Freddie Slater show up at the front door was mind boggling.

The reason behind their visit made Brenda shudder. It had only been a few days ago that she received the good news that she was HIV negative. Now, right in the middle of her good news and a very electric day, her late-husband's sins had come to destroy the peacefulness she'd just acquired, having to be reminded of his dirty deeds. She hadn't seen this coming, but it made her think about Sheila.

Brenda looked at the somber group. "I'm going to help Sheila."

"You're going to do what?" Mimi asked. "For God's sake, Brenda, wasn't she Victor's mistress? She disrespected the sanctity of your marriage, knowing full well that Victor was a married man."

"Yeah, Mom, I don't understand you. Sheila is getting what she deserved."

"No one deserves that dreaded disease. It could've been that I had received a positive HIV report, but I didn't. God spared my life so that I could watch my children grow up and become productive citizens. Even though Trevor's reality is what it is, God is going to work that out, too."

"I hear you, Mom, but you're going overboard, as if you should feel guilty about Zavion's mother's death. She was a drug addict and a whore who didn't care about her children. That's why Zavion and Freddie had to live with their grandmother."

Brenda sighed. "Yeah, maybe you're right. Maybe I'm going overboard. Maybe I shouldn't feel sorry for Sheila, Zavion, or Freddie. But I saw Sheila with my own eyes. She was suffering some kind of awful from that dreaded disease. I was mean and evil to her, when all she asked was that she be able to stay in the condo for a little while because she was so sick."

"But what makes that your responsibility, Brenda?" Mimi pounced. "Sheila got married to a man who had a job, and they continued to live in your condo without paying one red cent. If she was any kind of person, one of them should've come to you and offered to pay rent."

"That's how I felt in the beginning, Mimi; that's exactly how I felt the day I went over there to throw them out. Some would call me crazy for what I'm about to do. I'm sure if they were in my shoes, they'd spend all of Victor's money on themselves and to everyone else be damned. But there's a scripture in Matthew in the Holy Bible that says we're to love those who despitefully use us.

"I'm a psychologist. It doesn't mean that I pity

everyone who has a hard luck story or that I try and fix every broken vessel I encounter. Somewhere deep within me, I have a conscience, and every time I have a memory flash of me reading that piece of paper that gave me life, I feel the hand of God. It's almost as if he has his hand on my shoulder guiding me toward something. And since that letter came in the mail, I've felt this obligation to do something positive for someone. So, whether you agree or not, and I really don't give a damn, I'm going to help Sheila."

Everyone was quiet. It seemed as if each soul present searched their heart for a truth. Suddenly, the quiet was broken as Mimi began to sing her song, "Free to Love."

Asia and Afrika fought back tears. Mimi sang on. Brenda shut her eyes and moved her head from side to side.

Free to love my man
Free to love my best friend
Free to love myself
Free to put the shame to rest
And when I did, I was free to love.

CHAPTER THIRTY-SIX

Evelyn Slater's funeral was held in the chapel of a local funeral home—the old, Greystone building a pillar of the community that dated back to the late 60's. Only a handful of family and friends gathered for the services. Zavion and Freddie wore dark shades and black suits, each one taking turns to console their grandmother.

The service was short, although the minister's arousing sermon stirred up some hardened hearts. One of the ladies from Zavion's grandmother's church read the brief obituary, while another sang "The Lord's Prayer." There was only one floral spray that stood next to the coffin and it was from Brenda, while Mimi opted to send a nice peace lily, so that grandma could take it home.

In less than an hour, the service was over, and the family processioned out of the chapel. Grandmother Slater stopped in front of Brenda when Zavion pointed her out.

"Thank you, ma'am, for your act of kindness...for what you've done for my daughter and grandbabies. I appreciate it." Then she turned and moved on until her silhouette disappeared beyond the chapel doors. The remainder of the viewers singled filed out of the building. Now, the chapel was empty.

Mimi rubbed Brenda's back. They watched as the family filed into the limo and followed the hearse out of the parking lot. Other mourners followed the procession, but Brenda and Mimi stayed behind.

"I'm sure it felt good to help those boys and their grandmother regardless of what their mother had done and who she was," Mimi said at last.

Brenda bowed her head and exhaled. "It did, Mimi. It did. It wasn't only for them, it was for me, also. I'm not sure what God is trying to show me and what his true calling is on my life, but this was something I needed to do."

"Sometimes we have to walk in the valley alone," Mimi said.

"You're thinking about having kept your secret all those years."

"How did you guess?"

"Remember, I've known you practically all of my life. As soon as the words left your mouth, it popped into my head. You know, Mimi, at first, I was pissing mad that you had waited all that time to tell me Victor raped you. I didn't want to believe it, although in my heart of hearts I believed it to be true. We were best friends, and we shared everything and never lied to each other. I guess that's why it hurt so much when you finally told me after you'd vanished without a trace."

"It was a hard burden to bear alone, but I kept the secret because I loved you. But when I finally put the shame to rest, I was free to love."

Brenda laughed. "You're getting your mileage out of that song. I can't wait to hear you sing at the DPAC."

"Girl, I'm so excited. In fact, I have practice in a couple of hours. I can't believe I've finally gotten the opportunity to share my gift."

"You're working on that Grammy, aren't you?" Brenda said with a chuckle.

"And American Music Award."

"Sounds awfully greedy to me."

"I dream big and in living color. I think I'll invite John to come. I may have to leave the message on his voicemail since I don't seem to have much luck contacting him these days. What do you think?"

"That's a nice idea. I hope you have luck getting a hold of him."

"Me, too. Well, let me take you home so I can get to rehearsal on time."

"Thanks for coming with me for support, Mimi. As much as I didn't want to come today, it was important that I be here. I'm glad I did."

"Glad I was able to support a friend.

The two friends hopped in Mimi's car and headed away from the funeral home. Brenda pulled out her cell phone to check her messages. She had a half dozen text messages from John and they all said the same thing, *I luv you & can't wait 2cu in a few. I've taken the rest of the day off.*

Brenda cringed. She hit reply and began to type, *Luv u2. I'm on my way home and Mimi is dropping me off. Stay away from the house until I text u. Should be there in 20 min.* Brenda pressed the SEND button.

Mimi startled Brenda. "Girl, I see you've got the text thing down."

"Yeah, one of my clients was requesting an appointment."

"On your personal phone?"

"There are some who need access to me for special reasons. I call them my VIP clients. The list is very small, but they have access day and night should they need me."

"Ahh, they should feel extra special to be put on Brenda Christianson's VIP list. Handle your business, girl."

Brenda smiled. She was going to do just that when her VIP showed up for his appointment, which was in forty-five minutes. She couldn't wait.

CHAPTER THIRTY-SEVEN

Brenda couldn't wait to get inside. With cell phone in hand, she threw her purse down on the small settee at the far end of the foyer and began to type a text to John. She couldn't believe how great her need, but she was ready to see her man. And she didn't have long to wait. He said he'd be there in ten minutes.

Brenda flew up the stairs and refreshed herself, first taking a long, overdue tinkle. Next, she brushed her teeth, pulled off her street clothes, gave herself a five-minute sponge bath, dusted herself with powder, splashed on her favorite perfume, before finally slipping into something more comfortable. The yellow-and-white linen caftan was sexy, with a long, devious split that ran from the hem to the middle of her thigh. The loose, V-neck collar showcased her girls nicely with the help of a new push-up bra she'd recently purchased from Victoria's Secret. Before she could take another breath, the doorbell rang.

Fanning herself to quiet the flames of desire that had already risen inside, she took a deep breath and descended the steps. She glided across the marble floor as regal as a queen. Holding back the smile that threatened to erupt on her face at any moment, she opened the door. There John stood with a beautiful bouquet of red roses, and he handsome as ever.

Loss for words, Brenda took a breath and waved John in. She closed the door behind him and stood with her back up against it. John took her in with his eyes and ambushed her, almost forgetting about the roses.

He held her hostage as he kissed her passionately, the two of them coming up for air ever so often. And then he pulled her away from the door, the roses still in his hand, and threw his arms around her shoulders. He moved backwards while Brenda steered them toward the family room, their mouths still glued together. Five more minutes passed, and then Brenda pushed back.

"Well, hello," she said out of breath.

"Hello, baby. You are so beautiful and utterly delicious." He untangled his arm and pushed the flowers toward her. "Oh, these roses are for you."

Brenda blushed and took the roses from John. He kissed her again. "Let me put these in some water," Brenda said all smiles, as she lightly stroked John's chest before proceeding out of the room. She knew John was looking and she threw her hips into overdrive, as she sashayed out of the room.

John hadn't moved from the spot Brenda left him. She returned with the flowers positioned in a Waterford crystal vase that she placed on the intricate pewter sofa table that leaned up against the back of the sofa.

"They look beautiful there," John said as he watched Brenda place the flowers on the table and then tap into her every move. "I can't think about anything else but you. I've never been this whipped. My work is suffering since I always seem to be in this daydream...with your image in front of me, sapping up my peripheral vision."

"I'm flattered, unless your comment is motivated by something else."

John bucked his eyes. "Oh, so you're in my head and know what I'm thinking? You couldn't be. If you did, you'd know that I speak nothing but the truth."

Brenda came and stood in front of John. "If truth were to speak, it would say that you were in my daydreams, my night dreams...that you were all up in my system. John, it's worse than I imagined...this desire, this want, this need I have for you." Brenda scratched her neck absentmindedly. "I don't know what I'm going do."

"Why don't you shut up and kiss me again?"

Brenda's smile was infectious. John's smile was even broader than Brenda's. He pulled her to him, and they kissed again. And they came up for air once more.

"Ummm, we we're in the moment, Brenda. Hate it when you cut it short. Right now, I need a glass of wine, and then...I want to make love to you. Sweet love—that sensual, sexy, sugary kind of love…the kind of love that makes you weak in the knees."

"I'm game for that," Brenda said sweetly. "I'll get the wine. Oh, but before I do, I forgot to tell you that Mimi is going to call you."

"Brenda, surely you didn't stop in the middle of my raging desire to make love to you to talk about Mimi."

"I'm sorry, baby, but I may forget to tell you later. You're getting ready to make me lose my mind and I won't remember."

John laughed so hard that he almost choked on his saliva. "You got that right, girl. So, if you need to tell me something about Mimi, spit it out now so we can get back to us."

"Mimi is singing now." John clapped and Brenda frowned at him. "Be nice. This weekend, she will be singing with this band at the DPAC."

"Oh, good for her," John said with surprise in his voice, ready to get back to where he left off.

"She finally got her chance to sing to an audience."

"I believe it's been her life's dream. I really couldn't have competed with that."

"Yeah, although I know that her dream extends far beyond her present gig. Anyway, she's invited the girls and me to hear her. She told me that she was going to call and invite you. All I'm saying is do me a favor and return her call."

"And say what?"

"That you're going. We can meet at the venue, and if everything goes the way I hope it will, maybe you and I can leave together."

"The picture is becoming much clearer to me." John laughed. "Brenda, you're a sly fox, but I love how you work it."

"Just looking out for a friend."

"You know I love Mimi. It's not that I'm avoiding her, but then again, I guess I am. She and I have history, and when I saw her for the first time in nineteen years, I'll admit it aroused a curiosity in me that I had no business giving in to, especially when I found out my girl was a married woman."

"Oh, really?" Brenda said, a little too quickly.

"You have nothing to worry about; John Carroll has eyes for only one woman, and her name is Brenda Christianson. My love for you is not a pretense. My heart is sold out to you, and...and I'm hoping that what we have will go well beyond what we have today. I'm in it…to win it...to win your heart and soul forever."

"Oh my God. John, what are you trying to say?"

"I'm saying that I'm in love with you, Brenda Christianson, and that I hope our love will endure. I hate to sound like an old cliché, but I want to be with you always...to love, to cherish, and...and to death us do part."

Brenda began to shake where she stood. Her sweet, brown eyes became round as saucers. John went to her and held her tight. "Don't be afraid, Brenda, I've got you."

Brenda buried her face in John's chest. Moments later she pulled back and looked into his eyes. "I love you, too, John, and I want to be with you forever."

John smiled and patted Brenda on the butt. "Girl, you've made me a happy man today. Now go and get that wine so I can wine and dine you correctly." He winked. "Oh, and I'll make sure to let Mimi know that I'll support her on Saturday."

Brenda winked back and set off to get the wine. Her life was moving in a different direction, and she felt good about it. For a second, she thought about Mimi and the song she'd penned for her and the girls. Yes, she was now free to love.

CHAPTER THIRTY-EIGHT

It was a beautiful spring evening in downtown Durham. The sea of concert goers, decked in their after-five attire, looked as if they belonged on the red carpet. Black and white was the color combination for the season, although it was late spring, and the men and women wore it as if they were going on stage to accept their personal Soul Train or BET Award.

Brenda, Asia, and Afrika stepped high in their four and five-inch heels, drop-diamond earrings, and strutted in a low-cut, just-at-the knee crepe dress for Brenda; a one-shoulder dress with a large rhinestone brooch on the collarbone for Asia; and a sleeveless, scoop-neck sheath that was three-inches above the knee for Afrika. There was no mistake that they were a stunning trio as they strode up to the second floor to await entry into the theatre with almost every male in the house doing double and triple takes when they passed by. The ladies smiled with confidence and enjoyed the courtesy looks of their admirers.

Every now and then, Brenda took liberties to glance

around the room. It wouldn't have been so obvious if she didn't look as if she was in search of a long, lost friend.

"Mom, what's up?" Asia asked, curiosity written on her face.

Brenda locked her face in place and stared at Asia. "What do you mean, what's up?"

"We are the finest women at this event and everyone is checking us out, but you're acting like you've never seen people before."

"It's your imagination, Asia. Don't try and analyze me."

"Hey," John Carroll said from behind, causing Brenda to jump as she swung around to get a look at the intruder. Her face remained blank as she forced herself not to act surprised.

Brenda bucked her eyes. "Hi, John, what are you doing here?"

Asia twisted her lips and whispered something to Afrika. Both girls began to bounce their eyes between Brenda and John. "You ain't foolin' me, mu dear," Asia whispered in Brenda's ear. Brenda ignored Asia.

"You ladies are absolutely beautiful," John said as he scanned each lady individually. "Anyway, Mimi invited me to hear her sing. I should've figured that you all would be here, especially you, Afrika."

Afrika rolled her eyes. "Of course, I wouldn't miss Mommy's performance for the world. This is practically her debut into the songstress club. I'm sure it won't be long before she lands that record deal she's been after all of her life."

John looked at Afrika thoughtfully. "You sound so much like your mother, except that you're more confident." Afrika let down her guard and smiled.

"They're opening the doors for us to go in," Brenda said, interrupting the current conversation. Mimi was certainly the reason why they were there, but Brenda didn't want John to stroll down memory lane and reconnect with her. Brenda knew it was jealousy sneaking around in her brain, but she couldn't help it.

"I hope you all don't mind if I sit with you," John said. "It's much nicer to sit with people I know...who know Mimi."

"It's no problem," Afrika spoke up. "It is reserved seating, though. If we miss you, I'll make sure to tell Mommy that you came."

John pretended to look at his ticket and then at Brenda's. He purchased the tickets and was aware they were all seated together. "It appears I'm in the same row."

Asia glanced at her mother, as if she was getting the picture.

Afrika led the way into the auditorium followed by Asia and Brenda with John bringing up the rear. He took little sneak peeks at Brenda, brushing up against her a time or two to let her know that he was hers. When the girls weren't looking and the room was dark, Brenda took the liberty to pat John's arm. It was almost like an aphrodisiac—foreplay on the sly.

The announcer came out and introduced a local jazz singer by the name of Gabrielle Rider, who came out and belted a few songs. She was excellent and received several standing ovations. The red, punked hair distinguished her, and her voice was golden. Both John and Brenda jumped up from their seats and clapped when her brief set was over.

A hushed silence came over the auditorium. The moment everyone had paid their good money for had arrived. The curtain was pulled back and exposed a colorful group of middle-aged men that consisted of a drummer, a pianist—both regular and electronic, two sax players, an acoustic electric guitarist and a plain electric guitar player, and xylophonists. They played a contemporary jazz number that everyone in the audience swayed to.

Afrika reached over and whispered to Asia. "I wonder when Mommy is coming out." It was hard to hear above the crowd, who had already been consumed by the music.

"Girl, she's probably the main attraction."

"Yeah." Afrika leaned back, clapped her hands, and smiled.

Three minutes passed, and the man playing the baby grand piano got up out of his seat. He went to center stage and pulled the microphone out of its stand. "How are you all doing tonight, Durham?"

"Great!" the audience yelled in response.

"My name is Clifton Sayer and this is the Clifton Sayer Band." Clifton waved his hand at the band, and the crowd was with him, clapping hard in appreciation. "Tonight, we have a special treat for you. A gifted, talented singer has joined our band, and I'll tell you now, she has a set of pipes on her. If you thought Ms. Rider could sing, wait until you hear this woman. She has electrified the crowds since she started singing with us, and I don't want to hold out any longer from you getting a taste of what this sultry singer has in store for you. My fear is that some amazing record company exec will find their way here and steal her away from us." The audience laughed.

"Let her sing," someone belted out.

"I'm going to do that right now. I'd like to introduce to you someone who is also from the area and once attended North Carolina Central University..." Eagle shouts went out through the crowd. "I present to you Ms. Mimi Bailey, singing along with the Clifton Sayer Band. Hit it band."

The band hiked up the volume and Mimi strolled in like the legendary acoustic queen she was destined to become. She held a mike in her hand like she had been on stage for years. She wore a long, black, sheer number that sat over a short, black miniskirt and camisole. She wore a pair of round, large platinum-gold, diamond encrusted earrings that looked like sand dollars and her feet were adorned with a pair of black leather, jazzy ankle boots with a sterling-silver broach that sat at the nape of the shoe. Her make-up was flawless—her eyes outlined in dark eyeliner and eyelids dusted in slate gray. Her round lips glistened with a hot red lipstick, but when Mimi began to sing, no one cared how she looked or what she was wearing. They were lost in her melody.

Brenda sat back in awe. She remembered Mimi singing in her formative years and only a week ago heard her sing the song she had penned for her and the girls. But she wasn't ready for Mimi's performance tonight. It was totally mesmerizing, and Brenda could tell that John was in awe also. Even Asia and Afrika sat on the edge of their seats, totally blown away by the power and strength of Mimi's voice and the beautiful melody that floated from her lips so effortlessly.

"She's good," John said, not taking his eyes off Mimi. "She's got that Anita Baker and Jill Scott thing going on. But it's so smooth."

"I noticed that, too. She's damn good," Brenda allowed herself to say.

Mimi was in the middle of the song and held the note so long, people jumped to their feet and were shouting *yes* and *you go, girl*, without ever sitting back down. Afrika and Asia gave each other high-fives before standing to their feet and shaking their heads to the rhythm of the beat. Tears rolled down Afrika's face.

"I think our girl may be on her way to stardom, if the right person hears her," John said to Brenda.

"Yeah, and to think she hid her extraordinary talent from the world all these years because of Victor."

"There's something about God's timing. It wasn't Mimi's time until now."

"I guess you're right."

Mimi sang eight songs with the band and the crowd continued to be mesmerized through the rest of her performance. No one wanted to leave. The audience continuously clapped and called out her name. The audience demanded an encore, and Mimi rose to the occasion and gave them what they wanted. While Mimi wouldn't know it right away, her life was about to change, and the City of Durham was going to take credit for making her a star.

CHAPTER THIRTY-NINE

The girls were excited. Afrika couldn't wait to hug her mother and tell her how good she sounded. "I'm going to call my dad tonight and tell him how my mother broke Durham down and how she was truly a diva in her own right."

"Well, you know your mother is like my second mother," Asia interjected. "I knew her before she was famous and now I'm one of her groupies. Girl, this means we're going on the road and jet set with her, especially when she goes to the big cities."

Afrika laughed. "You are so crazy, Asia. But you're right. Tonight, has opened a whole new world for her. I realize she doesn't have a record deal, but I'm optimistic and with Facebook, Twitter, and YouTube, she's on her way."

"You're right. I saw a lot of people with cameras and cell phones recording our mother's performance."

"Listen to you; you've already claimed my mother as yours."

"Like I said, Afrika, I'm getting on her ship. We hang

with your mom, we're going to meet the men who can sport a real Rolex and got bank up the yang-yang."

"Asia, you're talking foolish. Ahh, ahh, ahh..."

"Ahh, what?"

"Don't look now, but Zavion is at our three o'clock position." Asia turned her head right into Zavion's stare. "Fool, I told you not to look."

Zavion was suited up in a black-and-white tweed jacket, white shirt, black slacks and a black-and-white, geometrical-design tie with gray hues. His close-cropped hair was edged to perfection. His fingers were intertwined with a five-foot-eleven, pure-milk chocolate-colored sister, whose black and white stretch dress snatched every corner of her high-fashion model body. Her feet were slung in a pair of Jimmy Cho's that she rocked without trying, and her lips were painted bright red.

"Who's that?" the woman said, as Asia read her lips. He raised his hands to quiet her, although his eyes never left Asia's face. And then he advanced with the size-three sister hanging on, although it was obvious she wanted no part of this face-to-face.

"Hello, Asia... Afrika," Zavion said.

"Hi," the sisters said in unison.

"I'm sorry I wasn't able to say anything to your mother at the funeral," Zavion went on, biting his bottom lip. "I had a lot on my mind and was trying to get through the day the best I could for me and Freddie."

"I'm sure she understood," Asia said, demurely. "It's good seeing you again."

"Yeah," Zavion said, not able to take his eyes away from Asia's. As if finding a way to tear away, Zavion looked at Afrika. "Wasn't that your mother singing?"

Zavion's friend perked up. "That was your mother? She was killing it. Damn she was good."

"Thank you," Afrika said, with indifference. "I'm proud of her."

"Whenever she has her release party, be sure to invite Zavion and me. That would be absolutely fabulous."

Afrika didn't say anything. She parted a fake smile and grabbed Asia's hand.

"Well, I'll let you all go," Zavion said, sneaking another peak at Asia. "Maybe I'll see you all around sometime. I'm leaving school early to enter the NBA draft."

Asia seemed stunned. "You aren't staying for your senior year? You're not graduating?"

"With all that has happened with my mother, it's the best thing for me to do."

"Oh," was all Asia could come up with. "I wish you luck with the draft."

"Thanks." Reluctantly, Zavion did an about face, and Asia watched as they walked away.

"Make sure you let us know about the record deal," Zavion's date shouted back.

"Do you believe that crap?" Asia asked.

"Naw, but I'm sure you noticed how Zavion was giving you the once over."

"I don't care what he was giving. He ran away from my house without a word, and then he shows up out of the blue ten months later demanding money like it was his right. I hadn't done a damn thing to that guy. It appears he's had a quick recovery since his mama died."

"Don't be so critical, Asia. That boy is in a lot of pain. I believe he still has feelings for you, though."

"Afrika, don't go there. You didn't experience the rejection. And I'll be damned that just because I ran into him at this affair with his brainless twit of a girlfriend, who probably paid for his ticket to the event, that I'm not going to forget all about his ugly ways. Besides, I can't help that I'm looking drop-dead gorgeous…"

"Okay, I was only saying..." Afrika threw up her hands and then began to laugh.

"Please. Now let's find my mother so we can get out of here."

"It looks like she's hanging on to John's every word."

"You noticed that, too?"

"You would have to be Stevie Wonder blind to not notice."

"Let me handle my mother." The girls walked over to where John and Brenda stood giggling at each other. "Ready to go, Mom? Maybe we can catch up with Mrs. Bailey and wish her well."

"I'll get with Mimi later. John has offered to take me home. This way you won't have to drive all the way back to Chapel Hill."

"It's no bother. You've forgotten already that I moved into my apartment at Brier Creek this week. Chapel Hill is in between."

"Asia, I'm fine."

"Well, Mr. Carroll, you take good care of my mother."

"I'm going to escort her home, and I'm sure she'll call you as soon as she arrives to let you know that I dropped her off safely," John said with a straight face.

"All right, I'll be waiting on your call, Mom," Asia said with a hint of laughter in her voice. Both she and Afrika watched them walk away. "My mother isn't fooling anybody. Something is going on with the two of them."

"It's obvious to me, too," Afrika lamented. "Let's find my mother."

CHAPTER FORTY

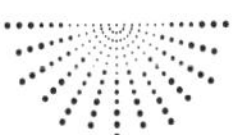

Mimi was in her element. Every member of the band complimented her on how she sizzled and set the theatre ablaze. She was overwhelmed and wished that Raphael could've been there to witness her singing debut. She knew he would've been proud.

"Mimi," Clifton called to her. "We've been summoned. There's someone who'd like to speak with you."

Mimi blushed, patting and fanning her face at the same time, as she looked for her purse. "Who is it?"

"It's a surprise. What are you looking for?"

"My purse so I can dab a little lipstick on these lips. They've been singing all night, and since I'm going to meet someone that you call a surprise, I have to look my best."

Clifton laughed. "I hear you, girl. You were on it tonight, Mimi. You sang your heart out."

"Thanks, Clifton. I owe this opportunity to you. Oh, here's my purse."

"Okay, dab on your lipstick and let's go. I don't want to keep your surprise waiting."

Mimi took out her compact and patted down her face. Next, she took out a tube of lipstick and put enough on to color her lips nicely. She winked at herself in the tiny mirror and closed it. Now she was ready for what lay ahead. "Ready, Clifton."

Clifton took his prize singer by the arm and escorted her to another dressing room. With a swift knock on the door, Clifton pushed the door open before anyone answered and walked in with Mimi. Three well-dressed business types stood around talking but hushed when Clifton and Mimi walked in. They looked and smelled like money. The tallest of the three wore dreads that were tied back in a band and hung down the length of his back. His smile produced a gold tooth that was common back in the day. Mimi surveyed the gentlemen more carefully and then recognition set in.

"Minx," she said, as she zeroed in on the guy with the dreads. It had been years since Mimi last saw him.

"Mimi the Diva," Minx said, moving away from the group to give her a platonic kiss on the lips. "Girl, how long has it been? I can't even recall the last time I saw you, but I will say this, you're still as fine as you were then."

Mimi blushed. "Flattery works with me...sometimes." The gentlemen broke out in laughter.

"Well, one thing that these gentlemen will agree on," Minx began again, "is that the woman who belted out those songs tonight has a voice—a golden voice. Girl, you sang from your heart and soul, and I'm wondering why you waited so long to showcase yourself."

Mimi couldn't contain her smile. "I had opportunities, Minx, but there were things that got in the way, which I can't talk about, that hindered me from pursuing my dreams early on. But that's water under the bridge now, and I'm comfortable with the future."

"It was your husband that kept you back," Minx started in. "Jealous men tear women's dreams apart all the time."

"No, Raphael would've been fine if I chose a singing career."

"Is he here tonight?"

"He's overseas...in Afghanistan."

"That's right; I remember he was in ROTC at Hampton."

"Well, he's now a full-bird colonel, and his tour of duty is about over. But he wants me to live my dream; he knows I want this bad."

One of the other gentlemen dressed in a lightweight, charcoal-gray gabardine two-piece suit moved forward and offered his hand to Mimi. "Mimi, my name is Howard Austin, and I'm the executive producer for AZILET Records. "I was amazed tonight at the power and strength of your voice and how you took the songs and made them yours—so musically eloquent that chills ran down my spine. The fact that you held that one note for almost a minute..."

"You were counting?" Minx asked.

"You're damn straight I was, buddy. But as I was saying, you have the gift. I can't think of any other way that you could've showcased your talent...you know, with you being older than the norm for those trying to currently break into the business. There's a lot more to you, Ms. Mimi..."

"Mimi Bailey. Thank you, Mr. Austin, for your kind words."

"It was on account of what you did tonight that I can say what I said. But not to prolong this reunion and get together, I'm prepared to offer you a record deal tonight. You've already auditioned, and need I say more. Let me introduce you to my partner, Yohan Giles."

The third gentleman moved forward to shake Mimi's hands. His hand was smooth like a baby's behind and probably hadn't done one ounce of manual labor a day in his life. Mimi noticed how manicured his hands were, adorned with expensive diamond rings on three of his fingers that enhanced the manicurist's work. He wore a hat on his head, but tipped it when he shook Mimi's hand. He was bald, and for a moment he reminded her of John. She wondered if he made it to the performance.

"Yohan is our creative director, and if should you except our offer, he will guide all aspects of your career—from the material you'll sing, public relations, tour, and you name it."

Mimi already felt boxed in and she hadn't signed her name on the dotted line. She had visions of singing her own songs and performing them in the way she saw fit, however, if this was going to get her in the door, she couldn't let this opportunity pass; there might not be another.

"Wow," Mimi said on exhale. "This is happening so fast."

"And to think," Yohan said, speaking for the first time, "many don't get this opportunity their first go-round."

"Please don't interpret my hesitation as being ungrateful. Believe me; I want this. However, I'd like to discuss all the terms of the contract as well as have my attorney review it."

"We'd really like to get you signed tonight," Howard Austin said.

"Hold on a minute," Minx interrupted. "Mimi is good for this, and if she wants to take a moment to have her attorney review the contract, I think she should be afforded that opportunity. I can tell she's a shrewd businesswoman, especially being married to a full-bird colonel." Minx winked at Mimi. "Am I right, Mimi?"

"I couldn't have said it better, Minx." She turned in the direction of the other gentlemen. "I do want this opportunity Mr. Austin and Mr. Giles."

"It's Howard and Yohan," Howard Austin said. "Let's talk money and let me know what you think. You can sleep on it, take it to your attorney, but I'd like to have an answer no later than Wednesday morning eastern-standard time."

Mimi smiled. "I'm ready to hear the terms of the contract."

"You won't be sorry, Mimi," Minx said. "Big brother has got your back."

"Okay then."

"So, Mimi," Clifton said after being silent for the last twenty minutes, "does that mean you've already quit the band?"

Mimi looked between Howard and Yohan, who were shaking their heads. "I guess the answer is yes. But I will fulfill my commitment for the remaining dates since there are only three left. I owe you that much."

"I appreciate that, Mimi," Clifton said. "I miss you already."

"Here are the terms of the contract," Howard began. "We're going to offer you..."

CHAPTER FORTY-ONE

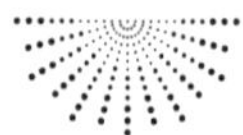

"Afrika, are you awake?" Asia shouted loud enough for Afrika to hear in the next room.

"Yeah," Afrika said groggily. "What's up?"

Asia got up, went into Afrika's room, and sat on the edge of the bed. "Let's get up and grab a bite to eat in Chapel Hill."

Afrika hit her pillow. "Girl, it's Sunday morning. What's up with you? I need my beauty rest."

"I can't sleep and I've been doing some thinking."

Afrika lifted her head off the pillow. "Been thinking about Zavion, haven't you?"

"Why do you keep on insisting that I have Zavion on the brain? Please."

"Tell me I'm lying. And if you say that I am, I won't bring it up again." There was an extended period of silence. "Uhm hmm."

"I don't have feelings for him, Afrika, but for some reason, I can't keep my mind off him."

"Especially after seeing the new girl hanging all over him. So, what are we going to achieve by going to Chapel

Hill? You plan to go to his grandmother's house? Do you even know where his grandmother lives?"

Asia sighed. "Okay, you've figured me out. No, I don't know where his grandmother lives, but I know Zavion spent a lot of time on a particular basketball court. There's a possibility that..."

"Okay, okay, okay, I'm getting up so that I can help you satisfy this gnawing urge to find peace with Zavion...so you say."

"Shut up, Afrika. You don't understand. I need closure. I need answers. I had fallen for him once, and in one instant, he tore my heart out when he ran out and evaporated into thin air. He and I aren't brother and sister like you and I are sisters. I understand how he must've felt finding out that Daddy was the man who'd made his mother's life miserable and was Freddie's daddy, but that wasn't my fault."

"On second thought, maybe you should stay your ass here and let me make breakfast for you. You've got the makings of one of those people who has the capacity to ruin somebody's day and turn a sane person into a schizophrenic. Please don't ruin my weekend."

"I'm serious, Afrika. I've got to find Zavion, and you're going to help me."

Afrika sat up in bed and watched as Asia took off like lightening. It was going to be a long summer. She had no plans to become involved in Asia's mess, especially when she was trying to establish a relationship of her own. Afrika got up and sloshed her feet into her slippers. "Oh hell; here we go."

Brenda's eyes popped open as if they were an alarm clock. She lay still listening as the silence of the morning captured birds chirping and other audible sounds of life. Not moving, her ears became instant radar and flushed out the sound of human breathing—short staccato breaths emitted by another life form in close proximity.

Catching her breath, Brenda's body became taunt—straight as a board, remembering suddenly that she wasn't alone. In fact, her memory served her better than it wanted to, and the sins of the night came rushing back like a mighty wind.

She pinched her lips together to seal in the laughter that threatened to come out, as she recalled so vividly the crazy lovemaking she and John had participated in the previous evening. It was surreal, as they threw caution to the wind and let their souls lead the way. Some would call them freaky—sweaty bodies in a love frenzy—but truth be told, they were downright nasty, testing their love for each other to the limit. That's what Brenda's freaky side of her brain tried to tell her, but the other side declared that it was love in bloom and that passion and romance was the order of the day. They lusted and they drank from the fountain until their wells ran dry...until they were satisfied. And Brenda obeyed her conscience and never allowed John to enter her unprotected.

Brenda felt moved and dared to look in the direction where John lay. Her mouth opened into a circle. She was busted; John was staring at her like a private eye, who was spying on her private thoughts.

John giggled. "You were far away, but I could easily tell that you were still on a high from last night."

Brenda offered a half-laugh. "What makes you think I was thinking about us or what we did last night?"

"Your nipples were raised at attention and your chest was moving in and out like you were reliving a moment that brought you the utmost pleasure."

Laughter got the best of her. Brenda looked at John and then smiled. "You think you know me."

"It doesn't take ESP to figure out what's going through your mind. Your body language did the talking, and if I must say so, it was a beautiful night, girl. You rocked my world. Our lovemaking was so complete, so sensual, so sexy..."

"Even though I made you wear a condom?"

"Yes; your love flowed freely. Brenda, I'm going to be honest with you. I've been married twice before, but I don't think I've ever experienced the passion that we had...that came so natural for us." He pulled Brenda to him and kissed her passionately on the lips until Brenda pulled away.

"Morning breath," Brenda said, a little nervous.

"I love your morning breath. In fact, I love everything about you. I want you in my life, Brenda." John sighed. He looked away for a moment then turned around and grabbed Brenda's wrist. "I love you, and... I want you by my side for the rest of my life."

Brenda was temporarily immobilized. She wasn't sure how to feel. This was all too soon, but she felt that same something for John, too. It wasn't a school girl's crush. It was as if he was part of her whole and she needed him in her life to exist. One thing she knew for sure was that no man would ever control her again. John was different; she believed that with her whole heart.

John gazed into her eyes. "So, how do you feel about what I said?"

"I'll admit that my heart is registering things it hasn't

in years and I love being with you. I was with Victor for over twenty years, John, and I've been so used to him. He was controlling, dictating..."

"A two-timing, no good, cheating asshole, who used you to get to where he was in his sorry-ass life." A frown formed on Brenda's face. "Don't make excuses for him. Victor had no respect for you, in fact he had total disregard for your feelings. For God's sake, he could've given you the HIV virus.

"I'm not that kind of man. I will always treat you with love and respect. I'll always adore you for who you are—your mind, soul, and definitely body." Brenda smiled. "You mean the world to me, Brenda, and though it may be too soon, too fast, I've felt something for you for a while now. And don't worry about Mimi. I love her as a friend, just as you love her. She already has a man who adores her, and after getting to know Raphael, he's an officer and a gentleman."

"I love you, too," Brenda said without regrets. She couldn't believe how easily it came out of her mouth. "I guess I'm afraid...I'm afraid to love." She shrugged her shoulders. It was my life with Victor that's made me afraid."

"You don't have to be afraid anymore, Brenda. You are free to love."

"Oh my God."

"What? What did I say?"

Brenda clutched her chest. "You won't believe this, John. Mimi wrote this song for me and the girls. The title of the song is "Free to Love." Wow, even when she was singing it, I had no idea how this song...its lyrics would become a central part of my theme. Tears sprouted from her eyes. "I want to pursue this relationship with you." Brenda threw her hands up. "God, I love you."

John reached over and pulled Brenda to his chest and held her. Brenda held him as tight. She had been blessed with a real man who was going to treat her like the good woman she was. Maybe she had to experience life with Victor to realize her true worth and to finally come into her own. Brenda wasn't sure that her thought was accurate, but for sure she was free to love.

She reached up and kissed John on the lips. "I do love you, man, and I want to be with you forever."

John kissed the top of her head. "Will you marry me?"

"Yes," was Brenda's answer.

Suddenly there was noise on the stairway. "Mom, are you up?" came Asia's voice. "I need to talk to you." Before John and Brenda could regain their composure, the door to Brenda's bedroom flew open. "Mom..."

CHAPTER FORTY-TWO

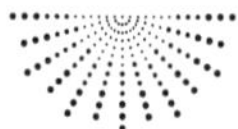

Brenda raised the covers high, but Asia was around the corner of the bed. She stared at John and then back at her mother. To make matters worse, Afrika was standing in the doorway. To Brenda, it seemed that Asia was rather enjoying the embarrassing situation...the untimely predicament she walked into.

"I'll wait downstairs," Afrika said. Her footsteps were heavy on the stairs, an indication she was in a hurry to be far away from the situation she encountered.

"So, Mom," Asia began as she looked at John and tried to keep from laughing. "I guess this isn't a suitable time for us to talk. I should've made an appointment."

Brenda wasn't smiling. "Asia, I already have an appointment and you need to remove your little narrow-ass behind from my office."

"Okay, Mom." Asia raised her hands in surrender. "I'm sorry for the intrusion. I wasn't quite sure what to do."

"I'm paying good money for you to go to college, Asia. You aren't that dumb."

"Ohhh, my mother is a little testy, John." John

remained silent. "Okay, I'm going downstairs; I'll wait for you."

"Why don't you and Afrika go home?"

"Mom, did I do something wrong?" Asia tried to hold in her laughter that was bursting at the seams. She seemed to enjoy her mother's discomfort.

"You invaded my privacy."

"When you called last night to let me know that you had arrived safe and sound, you could've told me you also had company. It certainly would've saved us this embarrassment."

"If you don't get your ass out of my room, I'm going to get up and knock some sense into you. And from now on, knock before you come in. That's what a closed door means."

Asia waved goodbye and shut the door behind her. Brenda and John heard Asia's laughter even after she'd descended the stairs. She didn't even try and contain it. Brenda and John looked at each other and had a laugh of their own.

AFRIKA'S SMIRK said a thousand words.

"Don't say a word, Afrika," Asia said as they made their way to Asia's car. "I told you something was going on between the two of them."

"And if you remember, I told you it was quite obvious. The only difference is that you're…we are eyewitnesses to the truth."

"Damn. That was an awkward mess. Ich. To see my mother in bed with another man besides my daddy was awful."

"But it sure seemed like she was happy."

"Too happy for my liking. I want my mom to move on with her life and everything, but getting it on with John? Ugh. The more I think about it, Mom and John were probably already seeing each other. That piece of paper that said she was HIV negative was the only thing standing in the way. What if the next test shows that she's positive?"

"Why in the hell would you say a thing like that, Asia? Damn, girl. Be happy about the results she received and pray that they'll always be negative. You must be a little more encouraging. Your mother is a grown woman—a single, grown woman. She doesn't need you or anyone else telling her what she can and cannot do."

"You're right, and I don't need you to tell me so. It's just that my father was the only man she's been with for all those years, and even though he's gone, she looks normal being by herself."

"You're being selfish, Asia. Your father, my sperm donor, didn't treat your mother well, and now she has a chance to experience love all over again. And hopefully, it will make her happy."

Asia shook her head. "I can't help but think about the song your mother wrote, "Free to Love." It's like she had a premonition and wrote the song so we could move on with our lives."

"That means you too, Asia. Zavion lost all credibility with me, but I will agree that for you to find closure so that you can be free to love, you need to find him and share how you feel."

Asia smiled. "That's my sis. Let's go find Zavion. I'm not sure what will happen when we talk, but I need you to have my back."

"I've got your back, sis. Now let's go find this man so I can help you kick him to the curb."

"I'm going to leave you here if that's what you call having my back, Afrika."

"Just kidding, sis."

CHAPTER FORTY-THREE

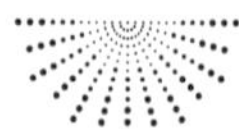

Asia drove around Chapel Hill until she found the basketball court. She suspected it wasn't too far from where Zavion's grandmother lived, which wasn't too far from the University of North Carolina at Chapel Hill. It was in the poorer section of town, but due to its proximity to one of the largest and well-renowned colleges in the nation, it held its own.

Stopping the car and turning off the ignition, Asia and Afrika sat and watched a moment at a group of guys who'd gathered for a session of hoops on a Sunday afternoon.

"I see him," Afrika barked into the silence in the car.

"Yeah, I see him, too."

"So, what are you going to do? I mean, he's with a bunch of dudes, and I don't want to be in the middle of any mess. And you know as well as I, Zavion isn't going to like you busting up to his spot to talk about what happened to y'all eight or nine months ago."

"Don't you think I know that? Why don't you stay in the car, Afrika? It might be best if I handle this alone."

"Oh no, you aren't going over there by yourself, especially after you got me up out of my slumber to help. Ain't no way, Jose, that I'm going to sit in the car."

Asia popped her fingers twice. "Listen up. You can go, but don't say anything. I don't want your tainted attitude interrupting what I need to do. Are you with me?"

Afrika exhaled. "Yeah. Let's go."

The girls got out of the car and proceeded to the basketball court where Zavion and three other guys were shooting the basketball. As they neared the foursome, each guy turned around and stared at the beauties. A couple of the guys gawked with their mouths open, and Zavion watched with apprehension, not knowing if this was a showdown or a simple drive-by to say hello.

Zavion stepped forward and bounced the ball a couple of times. "Hey," he said to both Asia and Afrika. "What are you two doing in my neck of the woods?"

Afrika stepped back and let Asia do all the talking. "Ah um, after seeing you last night, I've been doing a lot of thinking."

Zavion searched Asia's face. "Oh really?" He bounced the ball.

"Yes," Asia said, needing to get it said before she chickened out. It was a little difficult to do with Afrika and Zavion's friends standing around getting an earful.

"What do you want to talk about?"

"Throw the ball, man, if you're going to talk to your girl," one of Zavion's friends said.

"I thought Sherika was his girlfriend," another said.

Zavion threw the ball at the guys. "I'm a holler at y'all later." Zavion's friends waved and commenced to shooting the basketball.

Asia, Afrika, and Zavion moved away from the basketball court and stopped short of Asia's car. "I want to talk about us," Asia said.

"Us?" There was a puzzled look on Zavion's face. "If we're going to talk about us are we going to do this in front of Afrika?"

Asia looked at Afrika and gave her an, *I'm sorry look.* "You're right. I'll drop Afrika off at one of the shops on Franklin Street, and then we can talk."

"That'll work."

The trio got into the car, but Afrika wasn't happy at all. Asia drove the few minutes to Franklin Street and dropped Afrika off close to her favorite smoothie shop. "Sorry to have to kick you to the curb," Asia said. Afrika gave her the evil eye. "Give me a half-hour. If I'm going to be longer, I'll text you."

"Yeah," was all Afrika said as she got out and slammed the door.

Asia could tell that Zavion was checking her out. She didn't mean to wear her shortest shorts and the tightest tank top, but it was a halfway decent day and the sun was out.

"So, what did you want to discuss?" Zavion asked. "I'm in a relationship."

"Yeah, I'm aware of that," Asia said a little miffed, sensing that the conversation was not moving in the direction she intended. She had to get it back on tract—Zavion's girlfriend wasn't up for discussion. "I want to address what happened when you walked out of my house those many months ago without an explanation or a return phone call."

Dead silence. Asia drove six more blocks before Zavion opened his mouth.

"I don't want to discuss that evening."

"Don't you think you owe me an explanation?" Asia asked, taking her eyes off the road momentarily.

"What is there to say? I've hated Victor Christianson all my life, even though I didn't know him. He treated my mother like trash and infected her with Aids. My brother was born, but Victor Christianson never did anything for him. My brother, Freddie, was his illegitimate child that he never intended to claim, but it was my mother's fault for not practicing safe sex."

"Don't you think your mother had some responsibility in how your brother got here? You told me yourself that she was a drug addict and that your grandmother didn't want to have anything to do with her. But I shouldn't be judged by the sins of my father."

"You don't listen. I said my mother was at fault for not practicing safe sex. But oh, it's all so easy for you to say; you had everything growing up. You lived in a nice house and probably wore all designer clothes."

"Some of that's true, but again it isn't my fault that Victor Christianson planted the seed in my mother that sprouted me. For your information, my mother suffered a lot behind the misdeeds of my father. Everything wasn't always great in my household either."

"I'll let you get away with that. But to answer your question, I couldn't bear the thought that you were Victor's daughter. Dating you would only be a reminder of the evil man who hurt and destroyed my family. You were too close to my anger."

Asia sighed. "Well, why couldn't you have been man enough to say that to me, if not at that moment, later? My father didn't deserve the father of the year award, but his doings had nothing to do with me. In fact, the nature and magnitude of what my father did stunned my whole family. My brother, Trevor, went to jail protecting your mother from my father. Not once have either you or Freddie acknowledged that…let alone gone to see him."

Zavion was silent. Asia drove into the parking lot of a fast-food restaurant and turned off the ignition. "You owe me an apology," Asia said, folding her arms across her chest.

Turning his head slightly, Zavion glanced at Asia and then looked straight ahead. "You're right. It was wrong of me to run out like I did, but I'd just received the shock of my life. I apologize. I was scared, shocked, and angry. I couldn't deal with it at that moment, but I do owe you an apology, which I hope you'll accept."

"That was weak, Zavion, but I'll take it. Seeing you last night conjured up a lot of memories."

"Well, seeing you brought back some memories for me as well. You looked beautiful and even today in your shorty-shorts, you look awfully good. I won't stare too hard because I've got a..."

"I understand; you have a girlfriend. Is she the one?"

Zavion stared at Asia longingly. "I'm not sure she's the one for life, but she's fun and complements the person I am." Zavion scratched his forehead. "I'm getting ready to enter the NBA draft and have no idea as to where I'm going and what's truly in my future other than basketball." Zavion reached for Asia's hand. "You will always have a special place in my heart. I hope you'll always remember."

Asia touched the top of Zavion's hand, rubbed it, and withdrew. She sighed. "You will always have a special place in my heart, too. I wish you well with your basketball career. Maybe I'll get to see you play one day."

"That would be great." Zavion stopped and felt in his pocket. He pulled out his cell phone and looked at it. He looked up at Asia, who turned and looked out the window. "It's Sherika." He hit the TALK button. "Hey, Baby. I'll be there in a few minutes." And he hung up.

Without saying another word, Asia started up the car and drove out of the parking lot. Fifteen minutes passed before she reached the basketball court where she'd picked Zavion up. She stopped the car and looked straight ahead. He turned to look at Asia, but she didn't turn around. Zavion reached over and squeezed her arm.

"You'll always have a special place in my heart." Zavion opened the car door, got out, closed the door, and was gone. Tears sprouted from Asia's eyes. She got an answer from Zavion today, but perhaps it wasn't the one she was looking for.

CHAPTER FORTY-FOUR

Fayetteville Street crawled with new freshmen who had come with their parents to get a look at the college they would attend in the fall. Summer school had commenced and students were settling in, hoping to get a couple more classes under their belt so they could graduate on time.

Afrika tossed her leg up and down in annoyance at being dumped off. She dipped her spoon into her Mountain Blackberry Yogurt and scooped out enough to sit on the end of her tongue. She did this in rhythm, with each new dip of the spoon showing her displeasure at having to sit around and wait until Asia and Zavion finished their deep discussion. Asia said a half-hour, but Afrika knew that a half-hour could easily become an hour or two.

Going in for another spoonful, Afrika jumped when she felt her phone vibrate. She pulled it out of her pocket and answered it. "Hey, Mommy, you were the bomb last night."

"Afrika, I feel on top of the world. Guess what?"

Afrika was all ears and let the spoon drop into her yogurt cup. "Tell me. I don't want to guess."

"I signed a contract."

"A contract for what, Mommy?" Afrika teased.

"You know what kind of contract it was..."

"You did it, Mommy? You got a record deal?"

"Yes, baby. Your mommy has fulfilled another item on her bucket list. This was the big one. I was looking for you to come backstage last night."

"We were, but Asia and I ran into Zavion, and we got sidetracked."

"Oh, so do you think they're going to rekindle the old fires?"

"I don't know, Mommy. He was with a girl last night, and she was hanging pretty close. I'm in Chapel Hill now because Asia had this need to see him...to talk to him about the night he ran out."

"So, what are you doing? Being a third wheel?"

"Asia begged me to come with her, and after she found Zavion, they dumped me off on Fayetteville Street. I'm sitting in my favorite yogurt place feeding my face. But I'm not happy about it."

"Well, maybe they needed space to talk."

"Speaking of running into folks, guess who I saw last night?"

"Who, baby?"

"Your friend, John Carroll."

"Oh, he came. I'm so happy. I invited him, but I wasn't sure that he was going to come."

"Well, he saw us and we all sat together."

"That's wonderful. Did you all clap for me?"

"We did. Your voice is awesome. I mean this; you were off the chain."

"Did Brenda seem to enjoy my singing?" Mimi asked.

"She did, but that wasn't all she enjoyed."

"What are you talking about?"

"This morning, Asia and I stopped at her mother's house before going on our hunt for Zavion. Like a fool, I followed Asia up the stairs to her mother's room. Before I had my foot on the top step, Asia had burst into the room."

"I hope she had her clothes on," Mimi said, then laughed.

"Not only did she not have her clothes on, she had a man in bed with her."

Mimi was silent as if she was in think mode. "A man...in bed with her? Who was it?"

"Come on, Mommy. Didn't you get the hints?"

"Brenda is a grown woman who is a widow. She's entitled."

"How about John Carroll? Umm hmmm. Asia busted all up in the room, and it was the most embarrassing thing I've ever witnessed." Afrika began to laugh.

Mimi said nothing. A minute went by without a response.

"Mommy, are you still there?"

"Yes," Mimi said sharply.

"Mommy, you aren't jealous, are you? I wouldn't want to have to report you to Daddy."

"Of course, I'm not jealous. Brenda has a right to see anyone she wants to. I have a husband that I'm deeply in love with, and John Carroll couldn't compete with Raphael if he tried."

"You are too funny. Look, I've got to go. Asia decided to show up; she's honking her horn."

"Okay, baby, love you. Enjoy the rest of your day."

"I'm so proud of you, Mommy."

"Thank you, baby."

Afrika picked up her yogurt and went to meet Asia.

MIMI HUNG up the phone and let the tidbit that Afrika dropped on her germinate. It wasn't the fact that Brenda and John were together, it was the hiding and pretending that nothing was going on between them that infuriated her. Mimi was furious, now that she understood why John was ignoring her calls. Yes, she was happily married, but Brenda knew that she and John had a special friendship. The more she thought about it, the more pissed off she became.

Mimi looked at the clock. She wanted to run over to Brenda's right away and confront her but came quickly to her senses. She'd wait until later in the evening—go over for a friendly chat about the concert on last evening. And she wasn't even going to call. She would surprise Brenda's ass and maybe John's, too.

"I hate liars and deceivers," Mimi said. She flew up to her bedroom in a huff and looked for something to wear.

CHAPTER FORTY-FIVE

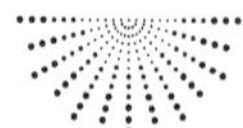

Mimi backed out of her driveway and headed out of her subdivision, as if she was piloting a jet. She hung a left then a right and sped down the main road that would give her quick access to Interstate 40. She sulked and didn't even belt out a tune, which had been customary for her to do when she got in the car. Exercising her lungs was a twenty-four seven job, but singing was the farthest thing from her mind.

After entering the interstate, she drove the several miles that would get her to the exit she needed to take. When she arrived at it, she swerved at the last minute after not being able to move over in time to exit. She took the curve on the ramp ten miles over the speed limit. Mimi caught her breath. She was pissed, but it wasn't that serious.

Her mind settled for the moment, Mimi drove on in continued silence until she approached the street where Brenda lived. She drove through the subdivision at ten miles-per-hour, and sped up a little upon arriving at her destination.

Mimi parked on the street not wanting to alarm anyone in advance of her arrival. She glanced around but saw no evidence of John's car in the immediate vicinity.

She exited the car and strolled up the circular driveway wearing a pair of navy blue, skinny jeans, a hot-pink ruffled, knit blouse that she pulled off the shoulder, and a pair of navy ankle boots. Mimi's hair was pulled back in a ponytail, and she swung it with each movement of her hips. With her confidence in check, she now stood on the porch at Brenda's door and pushed the doorbell.

Surprise was written on Brenda's face when she opened the door. A smile immediately replaced the surprise as Brenda ushered her friend into her home.

"What a surprise!" Brenda said with enthusiasm. She went into the family room with Mimi at her heels. They exchanged hugs before sitting down.

"Still excited about last night's event. I was going to call, but I had to see you face-to-face since I'm still riding on this cloud. There's nothing like a good girlfriend to chew the fat with and get an honest opinion about my work."

Brenda waved her hand at Mimi. "Girl, you were fabulous, and I don't think you needed me to tell you that. Didn't you hear that crowd? They were on their feet, cheering, and screaming your name. Encore, encore they kept saying over and over. We were all proud of you."

That was Mimi's moment to bring up John, but she wanted to wait...not pounce as soon as she got in the door. The moment would present itself again. If it didn't, she'd make sure it did.

"Well," Mimi said, patting her chest. "Guess what other news your friend has for you?"

"Please put me out of my misery. I have no earthly idea."

"Yours truly...drum roll...will soon be a recording artist."

"Ohhhhhhhhhhh my God!" Brenda screamed. She got up from her seat and met Mimi who had gotten out of hers and embraced. Tears formed in Brenda's eyes. "Girl, I knew that one day you'd be in the spotlight. I'm so happy for you."

"Thanks, Brenda. It is a dream that has finally come true."

"This calls for a toast. I've got your favorite Moscato on chill. Hold on, I'll be right back."

"Okay." Mimi looked around the room as Brenda left for the kitchen. She scanned the room like a secret-service agent, looking for any tale-tale signs that a man, specifically, John Carroll, had been on the premises. Everything was in place as Mimi would've expected. No identifying element in sight that would conclude that John had been at the scene of the crime.

Brenda returned as quickly as she left, and Mimi had to suspend her surveillance. Mimi took the glass of wine Brenda offered.

"I want to make a toast," Brenda said. "To Mimi, the woman with the golden voice who's finally made it over the rainbow. To you, my friend."

"Thank you, Brenda. Your words mean a lot." They sipped their drink and then there was a moment of silence.

"Afrika told me that John was there and sat with you all." Mimi saw Brenda flinch at the mention of John's name. She seemed to gather her thoughts, and in Mimi's estimation was trying to act like it wasn't a big deal.

"Yeah, he came out. He said he didn't want to miss your performance for the world."

"So, he enjoyed it."

"Said he did," Brenda said nonchalantly. She got up from her seat and fanned herself. "Are you warm? Maybe it's the wine."

"I'm fine," Mimi said, watching Brenda's movements. It was obvious that she was uncomfortable talking about John and wanted to change the subject. Mimi had no intention of giving up her probe."

"I'm going to turn on the fan for a minute." Brenda turned on the fan and returned to her seat.

Mimi took another sip of her Moscato and peered over the top of her glass. Brenda was definitely agitated. "So, I hear you have a new man in your life."

Brenda turned and stared at Mimi. "So, is this what your visit is all about? You didn't come over here to talk about your recording contract or how well you sang last night, did you? You heard that John was in my bed. Yes, I said it. John was in my bed and you couldn't deal with it. And you had to run over here to see if it was true...maybe to see if he was still here."

Mimi sat up in her seat. "My, my, my, you're certainly on the defensive. My intentions for coming over here were pure. I really did come to share my good news. Only thing is, I heard you had some good news of your own that you apparently wanted to keep to yourself."

"You're a jealous bitch, Mimi."

"Okay, Brenda, there's no need to resort to name calling."

"Maybe not, but I'm getting a little tired of you acting as if John is one of your possessions. You are a married woman with a good husband, and you need to act like it."

"I have no claims on John. As I've said to you time and time again, he's a good friend. You can't get over the fact that he still felt something for me after all the years that had passed, while you were still obliging that sorry-ass husband of yours."

"Shut the hell up, Mimi. Why is it that you always want what I have? You probably came on to Victor and called it rape when you couldn't handle his advances."

Mimi threw her drink in Brenda's face.

"Get the hell out of here, bitch. I don't want to ever see your ass again. And so that you don't have to wonder, John loves me and I love him. And we're talking about forever."

Mimi grabbed her purse and almost ran out of the house.

"You're nothing but a jealous bitch," Brenda screamed after her. "And you can kiss my black ass."

Mimi stood outside the door and let the tears fall. She asked for it, and now she would be estranged for a second time from her best friend. Why did she go and do that? Was she jealous as Brenda said? "Damn, I made a fool of myself. I've lost my best friend...again."

CHAPTER FORTY-SIX

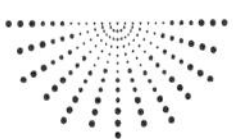

Brenda was livid. How could a good moment with a friend sour in less than an hour? It had a face, and its name was jealousy. Pure, unadulterated jealousy was what it was. She couldn't fathom how Mimi had waltzed her way over to her house on the pretext that they were going to reminisce about her evening, and then turn it into an all-out assault on her character. It was her damn business what went on at her house, and since Mimi had her nose all in it, she got what she deserved.

Huffing, Brenda went upstairs and retrieved her iPhone. While she didn't want to seem petty, the only thing she could think to do now was to call John. Maybe she shouldn't. She didn't want to seem like a crying ass woman every time something went wrong. But John was part of the discussion, and Brenda felt he had a right to know how Mimi violated their friendship.

She hit the speed-dial button for John and waited. Brenda and John had experienced another night of blissfulness until Asia suddenly materialized. Brenda would have to start locking her door since some people had little regard for her privacy.

"Hey, beautiful," John said when he finally answered.

"Hey," was Brenda's reply.

"What's up? I hear it in your voice."

"I really didn't want to come to you with this, John, but I need to let you know what happened this afternoon."

"I've got all the time in the world. Let me have it."

"Mimi found out that we were together last night...this morning. I'm sure Afrika told her."

"Oh, I see where this is going."

"She was going to find out sooner or later, but it was how she handled the whole thing."

"Please don't tell me she acted ugly."

"Worse than ugly. That bitch is jealous of our relationship and you're forbidden fruit. She came over here on the pretense of talking about her performance last night, and when she found the right moment, she pounced like a cheetah. Her accusations had already been rehearsed, but it was the look she gave me...like I didn't deserve to be with you."

"Hold it, baby. Hold it right there. I can't believe Mimi would do this to you. Mimi is a married woman and she has no claim ticket on me. I need to talk with her and put her in check. I love our girl, but this is the last straw."

"It was bad, John. I ordered her out of my house and told her I didn't want to see her ever again."

"You didn't mean that."

"At the time I did, but I feel some remorse for having said it. But she was so conniving and mean about it, and friends don't treat friends that way. All I've ever wanted was for us to be best buds, and after eighteen years when she reentered my life, I was the happiest because my friend had returned home. Today, I didn't recognize that person. I swear she acts as if the world revolves around her. I'm happy for her success, but I deserve some too."

"You're damn right about that, baby. Let me handle Mimi. Don't give this afternoon another thought. This weekend, I'm going to take you away from here. We're going to the beach."

"Thank you, John. You are a loyal friend. I appreciate you for all that you've been to me. I feel much better now."

"Good. Now get your bags packed."

JOHN ENDED his call with Brenda. His nostrils flared as he thought about how Mimi treated the woman he'd come to love. He was going to wait a minute and give Mrs. Mimi Bailey a call. She was going to know this very night that she couldn't have him and Raphael too. In fact, he wasn't on the market. His heart belonged to Brenda.

Thirty minutes had passed since John spoke with Brenda. He picked up his cell phone, pulled up Mimi's number, and hit the dial icon. It seemed an eternity, although it was a mere couple of seconds when he heard Mimi's surprised voice at the other end.

"John," she said. "I hadn't expected to hear from you, although I wondered whether you were able to come to my concert."

"Mimi, you already know that I was there from what I've heard."

"So, what did you hear if I may ask?"

"Look, Mimi, you are a dear friend and I cherish our friendship."

"Somehow I feel a 'but' coming on."

"There are no buts, however, let me say this and cut to the chase. I'm in love. I'm in love with a friend of yours. She means a lot to me, and the truth of the matter is, I'm going to ask her to marry me."

There was deathly silence. John had to strain to hear if Mimi was breathing. He expected that she would react in such a way, but by now Mimi would have said something smart back at him. John held the phone without a word for a few more seconds before he heard the dial tone. He pulled the phone away from his ears and looked at it. A smirk flew across his face followed by a half-hearted smile.

"I guess Mimi got the message," John said out loud. He went to the fridge and pulled out a cold one and nursed it. "Brenda, I hope you say yes."

CHAPTER FORTY-SEVEN

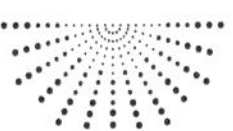

Several days passed and Mimi regretted her beef with Brenda. Was she jealous of Brenda's relationship with John?

She went to the refrigerator and took out a bottle of orange juice and poured some into a glass that she had pulled from the cabinet earlier. She sat down at the kitchen table and swirled the liquid drink around in the glass, while letting her thoughts roam, going back into her memory bank as she pulled up the file marked Brenda.

Her face twitched as she replayed a month's worth of history. She had indeed played the jealous friend when she didn't even have the right to do so. She was a married woman who was in love with her husband with no room for another. Maybe Brenda was right, although it wasn't altogether true about Mimi wanting what Brenda had.

The fact that John reentered her life, only as a friend, when she desperately needed someone to talk to, made their friendship special, and it seemed that Brenda, in Mimi's estimation, was the one who was jealous. True, Victor had stolen half of Brenda's life, but whose fault was that? During college, Mimi had warned Brenda many times over that Victor was a dog, but she married him anyway.

Mimi gulped down the rest of her juice, got up, rinsed out the glass, and put it in the sink. She sighed. Dismissing her recent battle with her friend, Mimi got up and went to her office and turned on her laptop. She needed a break from Durham. A trip to New York would put her in a better mood. Minx had called her on Monday to say that it would be an excellent idea for her to fly to New York and start working with Yohan Giles on her vocals and music. The more she thought about it, the better the idea sounded.

She wasn't ready to leave so soon after the show; she needed time to digest everything and plan a schedule. Sometimes you had to forget all about the perfect schedule and move when called. That was show business and Mimi was ready. The taste was in her mouth, and she bought a ticket on the first thing smoking to New York City. She wasn't even going to tell Afrika.

BRENDA WAS STILL upset with how Mimi had misrepresented herself. Why wouldn't she want to see her happy? John Carroll was single and free. Not once did Brenda put herself out there as bait. John Carroll had cozied up to her, and her arms were wide open. Forget Mimi.

The phone rang and Brenda started not to answer it until she saw Reynaldo Aziza's name in the caller-ID. She pushed the TALK button in a hurry and waited for Reynaldo's voice.

"Hey, Brenda, I hope I didn't catch you at an inconvenient time."

"No time is an inconvenient time for you, as it concerns my son."

"I'm glad to hear that. Look, we've got a court date and it's coming up soon. This case is going to trial, and you'll have to brace yourself for all the ugly to resurface."

"Whatever I have to endure, if it will help free Trevor, won't be as hard as what my baby is facing in that prison. I pray for him daily."

"I visited him today."

"You did?"

"Yes, and Trevor is doing much better in his new venue. You may want to visit him within the next few days to give him some encouragement. He believes everyone has given up on him and doesn't care if he rots in prison."

"That's not true, Reynaldo. I was there not even a couple of weeks ago. It's hard for me to go there, but I'll do whatever I have to do to save my son."

"He's going to need you, Brenda. He's going to not only need your love but your strength and compassion. He's a torn kid. Somewhere in that head of his he has some regrets about what he did, although he's indicated that there was no love lost between him and his father. He was trying to keep his father from killing his friend's mother."

"Yes, his friend, Freddie. You know his mother passed away. She died of Aids."

"I heard. I'm going to subpoena Freddie. He's Trevor's get-out-of-jail free card. His mother would've been my main witness, but with her demise, I've got to go with Freddie."

"I hope Freddie will cooperate."

"Your friend...what's her name?"

"I'm not sure who you're talking about."

"Victor kidnapped her husband. "

"Oh, you mean Mimi."

"Yes, that's right. Mimi."

"What about her?"

"Her husband was being pursued by Victor just before he was fatally shot. He could testify to what transpired before Trevor shot Victor as well as to Victor's state of mind."

"Raphael is in combat in Afghanistan."

"Damn. That's not good for us or for him."

"Maybe Freddie's testimony will be all we need."

"I hope so. It must be compelling. Well, I'll let you go. Everything is full steam ahead. I forgot to tell you that we go to court the middle of August—two-and-a-half months."

Brenda breathed deeply. "Whatever you can do to save my baby, Reynaldo, I'd appreciate."

"I'm going to do everything within my power to see that Trevor gets the minimal amount of time, if any."

"Thank you. That's all I can hope for right now." Brenda clicked the OFF button and rested her head in her hand.

CHAPTER FORTY-EIGHT

Today was one of Sheila's good days. It seemed that a spark of life had entered her body like a plug when inserted into a socket of an electrical appliance. She seemed energized and felt like getting up and fixing herself a slice of toast and a cup of coffee.

Sheila peeled herself off the bed, put on her robe and slippers, and went in pursuit of Jamal. The house was too silent for the mood she now found herself. Maybe he was in his office, although lately, he seemed distracted and distant—not really into his business.

Jamal's back was to Sheila when she entered his office. He didn't hear her come in as he was bent over, shredding documents. She gazed around the room where papers were scattered everywhere. Off in one corner, she noticed three leather suitcases stacked together that appeared to be waiting for someone to pick them up and cart them off to places unknown.

Sheila stood there transfixed, not sure what to make of the suitcases. Maybe they had been there for some time and this was the first time she'd noticed them. Sensing someone in the room, Jamal finally turned around, surprised to see Sheila in the doorway.

"Hey, what are you doing up? Don't you need to sit down or something?"

"Actually, I feel pretty good. I thought I'd fix myself a piece of toast."

"Oh, okay. Uhm…"

"What are you doing?"

Jamal hesitated, looked around the room, and then back at Sheila. "I was going through some of my files. They needed purging pretty bad."

"Are you going somewhere?" Sheila asked, catching Jamal off guard.

Jamal cocked his head, his eyes squinting as if trying to see where Sheila was coming from. "Why do you ask?"

Sheila moved to the middle of the room and stood next to Jamal. She pointed at the wall where the suitcases stood hostage. "Your luggage…I don't remember it sitting over there before." Sheila watched as Jamal's eyes travelled to where she pointed.

"Oh, I was moving some things around in the closet and I sat them over there…out of the way until I was finished with what I was doing."

Sheila took another glance around the room. There were two piles of clothes neatly stacked off to one side. "Are you sure?"

"Sit down, Sheila. We need to talk." Jamal got up and helped Sheila sit down in the only other chair that occupied the room that Jamal used when he talked to clients that happened to stop by. A look of forlorn was in his eyes, and Sheila couldn't help but feel the icy coolness in what he was about to say. "My business has suffered, and I can't see my way out. The attorney who I thought was going to represent us in a suit against Brenda Christianson turned me down. We don't have any real money coming in, and I don't think I can take much more of this."

Sheila looked at Jamal thoughtfully. "I didn't beg you to marry me. It was your very words that ensured me that you wanted to be with me for better or worse, although you were aware I had the virus. You were the one who whisked me off to Vegas with a suitcase already prepared with everything I needed for the trip, although my mind said I shouldn't go. You stood before the preacher...the justice of the peace, or whatever he was, *and* God and vowed *until death us do part* before putting the most gorgeous ring I've ever seen on my finger. I didn't ask you to, damn it. I didn't beg your ass to marry me."

"Sheila..."

"Wait, I'm not finished. You knew what you were getting into, Jamal. Now I'm thinking, maybe your business wasn't doing so well when you married me. Maybe you thought that there was money to be had and that Brenda Christianson was the answer from the git-go. You've been harping on it pretty good, although I haven't put up a fuss about it. You've been living here scot free like it's your right. What have you contributed to our well-being? Are you paying any mortgages anywhere else? These are questions I should've asked, but as you know I was too upset and sick to even give it a thought."

"You're barking up the wrong tree, Sheila, and frankly I'm getting a little pissed off. You aren't being fair and I'm hurt by what you've suggested. I've been there for you."

"Yeah, you've been here for me, but what was your real motive? I'm still getting disability from my job, and it has helped pay some of the bills. It isn't like we're destitute."

"And what happens when that runs out, which I'm sure it will any minute?"

"You're my husband the financial wizard. Surely, you ought to have a clue. You're the half of this family who's supposed to be the main provider."

"I'm your husband whose business has gone belly up. I'm leaving, Sheila. I'm done. I can't do anything else."

Sheila eyed Jamal, staring at him like she'd just witnessed a horrible tragedy. She seemed to contemplate what her ears had heard. With tears in her eyes, she shook her hand at him. "Gone, just like that, huh? You say it as if leaving is another event on the calendar. I thought you were different. I've thanked God over and over for sending me the perfect man; now look what I've got."

"No one is perfect, Sheila."

"Hell, I know that now. So, you want to walk? Well go. Walk. Get your shit and get the hell out. I don't need you." Sheila stood and began to shake. Her legs became weak and she fell where she stood.

"Sheila," Jamal cried out as he rushed to her. He scooped her limp body up in his arms, took her to their bedroom, and laid her on the bed. "I'm sorry, Sheila; I do love you." He kissed her wet cheek. Sheila's eyes began to flutter. When she opened them, and saw Jamal standing over her, she closed them and didn't say another word.

Jamal kneeled and brushed Sheila's arm with his hand. "I'm sorry, babe. I just can't do this anymore."

CHAPTER FORTY-NINE

Sheila lay on the bed listening to Jamal fumbling around in his office. After about a half-hour had expired, Jamal's silhouette enveloped the doorway. He had one suitcase in hand while the other toted his laptop. He sighed and pushed words from his mouth.

Shaking his head and then looking up to the ceiling, he offered the same lame sentiment. "I'm sorry, Sheila." Nothing else was forthcoming and he moved away from the room.

The front door creaked when Jamal opened it and she knew that this was truly goodbye. He came back into the house a few more times, carrying the contents of his belongings to the car. After a third trip, he stopped in and sat next to Sheila who was lying on the bed.

"I will stop by and check on you periodically. You can call me anytime, especially if you need me." Jamal let out a breath of air. "I do love you," he said, touching her arm. "I wish I was a better man."

Jamal waited for Sheila to say something, but she lay there, tuning him out. Her heart had sunk to a new low, and she didn't want to listen to his insincere mutterings that made her feel worse. After a few moments, Jamal removed himself from the bed and she cried when she heard the front door close for good.

The good feeling that Sheila had awakened with had vanished. She looked up at the ceiling and asked God why he had chosen her to teach a lesson. The tears came and went.

The sudden ringing of her cell phone woke her up. Sheila hadn't realized that two hours had passed. She rubbed her empty stomach that ached, reached for the phone, and hit the TALK button before the caller went away.

"Sheila, this is Phyllis."

Sheila looked at the number and couldn't believe that after all this time Phyllis had the audacity to call. Then she thought about it. "Did Jamal ask you to call me?"

There was hesitation in Phyllis' voice. "Well, kind of."

"Either he did or didn't, and I'll have to believe he did since I haven't heard from you in nearly a year."

"Sheila, I'm sorry."

"Please don't say you're sorry. I've heard enough of that for one day. You don't have to be polite or any of that stuff; your call is meaningless to me."

"You owed me that one. I've wanted to come by and see you, but I guess with everyone at the office talking negatively about what happened between you and Victor, I thought it best to distance myself."

"Okay, you've done that successfully. So…the reason for your call?"

"Look, Sheila, go ahead and be mad at me. Yes, Jamal called because he felt bad leaving you all alone."

"Damn, he hasn't been gone a good two hours, and

he's already put our business in the street. There's nothing you can do for me, Phyllis. I'm tired. Let's talk another time."

"If that's how you feel."

"That's how I feel." And Sheila hit the END button and threw the phone down on the bed. She shook her head at the thought of Jamal going behind her back and sharing their family woes with an ex-friend. How tacky. Sheila rose from the bed and pushed her way into the kitchen. She fumbled around with the bread wrapper until she could get a slice of bread out of it. She moved slowly to the toaster and dropped it in and waited for it to become toast. *What in the hell am I going to do now?*

CHAPTER FIFTY

The week had been a long one for Brenda, but tomorrow was a new day. She and John were finally going to the beach and she looked forward to getting away from Durham for a weekend. With Trevor's pending trial, her nerves were stressed to the gills. And there was also the unresolved issue between her and Mimi, which was taking more of her energy than she dared to admit. Only if Mimi hadn't come incorrect and been the friend she was supposed to be, maybe Brenda would've given her the four-one-one.

With a swipe of her hand, Brenda dismissed her wanderings about her friendship with Mimi and began to put the last few things in her luggage. A smile swooped across her face as she thought about her weekend with John.

Brenda zipped her luggage and sat it next to the wall and prepared for bed. As she scooped up a lump of cold cream to put on her face, her cell phone rang. Brenda quickly rinsed her hands and dashed for the phone. It could be only John.

She didn't recognize the number right away, but answered it. Brenda was surprised to hear Sheila's voice. It seemed as if she'd been crying.

"Hello, Mrs. Christianson. This is Sheila...Sheila Billops."

"Hi, Sheila, is everything all right? Your call is so...unexpected."

"I'm the last person you want to talk to, but I've been left with no choice. Jamal left me today. I had no one to talk to, and while this may sound strange coming from me, I couldn't think of anyone else to call. You were so nice to me the last time we spoke and I appreciate what you've done in allowing me to stay here. I'm sorry for rambling; I'm so down and..."

"Listen, I'm here if you need someone to talk to. I understand the predicament you're in, although I'm not sure I'm prepared to walk in your shoes."

"I'm sorry; I shouldn't have bothered you."

Brenda was silent for a moment. She was a psychologist for heaven's sake. Her degrees and training were for the purpose of helping people, and she had to look beyond the fact that Sheila was once Victor's mistress. Maybe God was trying to tell her something...show her something about compassion. That had to be it. Regardless of what anyone thought, she knew she had to help Sheila.

"You did the right thing by calling me. I know it's late, but I'm going to come over and see about you. I'm going out-of-town tomorrow, so I won't be able to come then. Can you hold on for a few? I can be there in a half hour."

"Mrs. Christianson, you don't have to do that..."

Brenda heard Sheila crying. "I'm on my way."

Brenda hung up the phone, slipped into a pair of denim jeans and a mint-green, knit top, and headed down the stairs. She put on her tan, wool coat and dashed into the garage and got in the car.

The moon illuminated the night. It was ten o'clock, and most people had settled down for the night. On the drive to Sheila's, Brenda did a lot of reflecting, a lot of soul searching—about her relationship with John, her friendship with Mimi, and the situation with Sheila that found her helping the woman who had an affair with her husband. All Brenda ever wanted in life was to be a good person—a good wife, mother, and a good citizen. This was her test. She had to be above the fray; she had to be the better person.

Before she knew it, she was in front of Sheila's condo. Brenda's only hope was that Sheila's nosey neighbor wasn't sitting behind a telescope canvassing the area. She wanted to slip into Sheila's place unannounced and do whatever it was she was supposed to do.

So far so good. Brenda practically ran from her car to the safety of Sheila's porch. She rang the doorbell and was surprised that Sheila answered almost immediately. When the door opened, Brenda's heart went out to Sheila.

"Hi," Sheila whispered. Sheila held the door open and closed it once Brenda was inside. Sheila was draped in a pink robe that was pulled tight against her very, thin frame.

"Hello," Brenda said in reply. She watched as Sheila, who was now a small shell of herself, walked slowly and sank into the overstuffed green chair. "When was the last time you ate?"

"I had a slice of toast this morning."

"You need to eat," Brenda said as she headed toward the kitchen. "You have anything else in here to eat besides bread?"

"A piece of toast is all I want."

Brenda came back into the living room and stood over Sheila. At first Brenda hesitated, and before she knew it she took Sheila's hand in hers. You need to eat something. You're weak and your body is craving food."

"I can't eat very much, Mrs. Christianson."

"Call me Brenda." Brenda patted Sheila's hands. "I'm going to do whatever I can to make you comfortable. I'll be right back and then we'll talk."

Relief showed on Sheila's face. "Thank you for coming, Brenda."

BRENDA HEADED BACK into Sheila's kitchen and stood in the middle of it, examining her immediate surroundings. She sighed as she noted that even for a sick woman, everything was orderly and in place. Victor was a neat freak and it only made sense that the women he was involved with would be the same. The more Brenda thought about it, the more pissed off she got. She had to let it go, as Victor was no longer part of the equation; she was there to help Sheila.

She rummaged around until she found a loaf of bread sitting in the refrigerator instead of the breadbox that was empty. Brenda plopped the bread into the toaster and then lifted the tea kettle off the stove. She filled it with water and put it on the stove to heat.

Amazed at herself, Brenda felt good about what she was doing. For months on end, she hated and despised the woman she now helped—her husband's mistress. Maybe it was that Sheila now had full-blown Aids, and in Brenda's mind Sheila still got the raw end of the deal. She snatched that thought from her brain and tried to allow only pleasant thoughts to enter.

The toast popped up and Brenda took the two slices and placed them on a saucer she found in the cabinet. Sheila had good taste in dinnerware. A few minutes later, the tea kettle sang, and Brenda poured hot water into a cup and dropped a bag of chamomile tea into it. Finding a serving tray, Brenda toted the toast and tea into the living room where she found Sheila asleep.

Sheila jerked up upon hearing Brenda's movements so close to her. "I fall asleep easily. Thank you for doing this."

Brenda sat the tray on Sheila's lap and held it for her. Sheila seemed so weak but ate and sipped as much as she could. Finally, Brenda took the tray away.

When Brenda returned, Sheila was staring into space. Brenda sat down on the couch and took Sheila's hand. "How can I help you?"

Water formed in Sheila's eyes. "Taking time out to see about me means a lot to me. Brenda, I'm scared. I haven't admitted that to anyone. I'm afraid of dying, and I don't want to die alone."

"Where is your family? Do you have any brothers or sisters who can come and help you?"

"My family lives in New York. I have one sister, who I haven't spoken to in years. Ours is a strange relationship, and she could care less if I live or die. My parents are both gone, but I have two brothers who are both in Saudi working for contractors. They're over there making that money."

"How did you end up in North Carolina?"

"Like a fool, I followed a boyfriend down here whose job transferred him to Raleigh. A year after we arrived, my boyfriend was no longer interested in keeping our relationship alive, and I was left to pick up the pieces. That's when I got the job at North Carolina Central University and I've been there ever since...well up until I had to go out on medical leave."

"Are you still on medical leave?"

"Yes, I'm receiving some money, but it's about to run out. I've about exhausted all my leave. I guess Jamal got frustrated about not having enough money to pay all our bills on top of the medical bills that were coming in. I hate myself. I was in denial when I first learned that I had the virus and didn't get the medicine that was prescribed."

"If I'm not being too nosey, what was Jamal doing to support you all? I'm not trying to be flippant about the fact that you all are living here for free, but having said that, surely Jamal was able to contribute to your well-being. After all, he is a working man."

"To tell you the truth, I don't know what Jamal was doing. I asked him that very question when he was on his way out."

"Something is wrong with that picture, Sheila. Somehow, I don't think Jamal has been on the up-and-up with you. I understand the mounting medical bills, but his overhead was next to nothing in my estimation. He wasn't paying rent. What man would move in with someone and not think he didn't have any responsibilities like taking care of his household?"

"I may be responsible for some of that thinking since he knew that Victor had paid for this condo. But that doesn't let him off the hook."

"No, he should've been moving you into a place that had no reminders of your former lover." Brenda bit her lip. She couldn't believe that flew out of her mouth. "He should've moved, you, his wife, into a place that was his and yours.

"Sheila, this doesn't come easy for me. While my marriage to Victor was in shambles, he was still my husband. We were married for nineteen years and had some pretty good times—even if I must reach way back to remember them. But that's beside the point. I loved him. I'm not totally sure why I'm helping you, but my conscience is eating at me. This may be a test of who I really am. As a psychologist, I swore to help people. So, I'm going to help you however I'm able. Are you ready to go to bed?"

Sheila looked thoughtfully at Brenda. "Thank you is all I can offer now. Thank you for listening. Yes, I'm ready to go to bed."

"I'll help you get there. I'm going to get a cleaning service and a meal service to help you, and I will stop by periodically. You have my number if you need me."

Sheila got up from the chair. Before she turned to walk toward her bedroom, she stopped in front of Brenda and gave her a hug. At first Brenda hesitated before hugging her back, but finally she put her arms around Sheila. Then she took Sheila by the hand, led her to the bedroom and tucked her in. *You can't get Aids from merely touching someone,* Brenda reasoned in her head. After all, God blessed her with a clean bill of health, and although she and Victor hadn't been with each other in a sexual way for months before he died, they lived in the same house and shared the same bed. Yes, this was a test and she was going to pass it with flying colors.

CHAPTER FIFTY-ONE

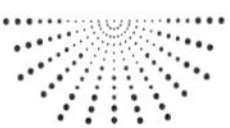

New York had become Mimi's city. She loved the flair of big city life—the shopping, the restaurants, the infamous hot dog stands, the Broadway shows, the fashion sense, the eclectic feel of the people who were New York, and more shopping. She'd been in town for almost a week and Minx had wined and dined her fabulously, while she charged up her credit cards that Raphael would never see, as her nice advance for inking a record deal would take care of her mischievous and frivolous spending. Anyway, you only live once.

She had been to the recording studio a couple of times; however, she was getting ready to learn that much of that free time she'd used to shop at Gucci, Neiman's and Sacs would soon be non-existent. Yohan had plans for Mimi Bailey. She was going to be in the recording studio morning, noon, and night—learning the music, preparing for publicity photos, managing her stage presence and learning what the whole record industry was all about. Azilet Records produced several chart-topping artists, and Mimi had been tapped to be their next sensation.

For the time being, Mimi enjoyed all the amenities at the Four Seasons Hotel where she was staying. It was almost like a mini vacation and not once had she thought about her fight with Brenda. In fact, she hadn't missed Brenda at all.

As she prepared to go downstairs and meet Minx for a leisurely lunch before going to the studio, her cell phone began to ring. She reached for her phone on the night-stand and smiled when she recognized Afrika's number. At first, she fought against answering it. Afrika might ruin her good mood with some gossip about Brenda since Afrika and Asia were roommates and shared everything. But she thought better of it, especially since she hadn't told Afrika that she was out of state having the time of her life.

Mimi pressed the TALK button. "Hi, sweetie, what's cooking?"

"Mommy, I've waited several days for you to call and tell me what happened between you and Mrs. Christianson."

"Look, Afrika. It's nothing you should worry yourself about. It's between me and Brenda. And when I'm ready to talk about it, if ever, I'll let you know."

"I'm coming over; we need a mother/daughter hashing out. Asia is my best friend, and I don't need my mother being viewed in a bad light."

"Oh, so what's the word on the street?"

"That you're jealous and went over to Mrs. Christianson's house on a pretense, while all the time you wanted to know if she was with Mr. Carroll. Jesus, Mom, you're not in high-school."

"There are two sides to every story."

"Well, what's yours?"

"Are you trying to get smart with me? I'm still your mother and can wear your butt out."

"Okay, Mommy, you can cut the dramatics. Please tell me your side of the story."

"The same as Brenda's." Mimi laughed.

"Mommy, you are not funny and I don't care for this side of your personality. Ms. Christianson is your best friend, and you're acting like a crazed woman who's after some man because someone else has him. You're married. Are you and Daddy not getting along?"

"Hold on one little minute. Why would you say something like that, Afrika?"

"Have you not been listening, Mother? Enough, I'm coming over now."

"Don't bother."

"What do you mean don't bother? Your issue is not with me."

"I'm in New York."

"New York? When did you go to New York? Who's with you?"

"Twenty questions. Jeez, Afrika, you're acting as if you've got me on a leash."

"Someone needs to. If I had a leash, I would've at least known that you were in New York. What if something happened to you and I didn't know where you were? What are you doing there anyway?"

"Working on my music for the album I'll be recording."

"Get out of here. For real, Mommy?"

"Yes, baby. Your mommy is going to be a recording artist. I feel so vibrant and alive."

"Mommy, remember you aren't a spring chicken. You can't go around acting like these young fools who trip on their new-found status and who for the first time in their lives have a little bit of pocket change and go out and buy ten cars and a mansion with the first check only to find out their contract was revoked the next day."

"Aren't you the smart one?"

"That's why I'm in school."

"Well, Mommy knows who she is; I'm a grown-ass woman who is intelligent, smart, bright and witty. And yes, I've been shopping and I think there may be a little somethin' somethin' for you in those shopping bags of mine, Ms. Afrika."

"In that case, shop on. But Mommy, you and Mrs. Christianson have to work out your differences. She's your best friend and she deserves to be happy. And I hope this recording contract and making this album doesn't go to your head. You've been acting weird—so not yourself lately. You need to chill."

There was a pause. Mimi couldn't believe that Afrika had checked her about her attitude. Maybe she was changing and she hadn't even realized it. She wasn't a snob and she had no right to be. But money does make you think differently. "I'll take a self-assessment," Mimi finally said. "Now, I've got to go. I'm on a tight schedule."

"All right, Mommy. Please think about what I said. I don't want to have to call Daddy on you."

"You do, and you'll be sorry."

"Do you still love Daddy?"

"Afrika! Of course, I love your daddy. He's the only man for me. I'll apologize to Brenda when I return. I was out of line; that I'll admit. All right, I've got to go. Talk to you soon."

Mimi hurried and ended the call. Her baby made a lot of sense. Now she was embarrassed that everyone knew she'd been an ass, although it was a small circle of people. As soon as she returned from New York, she would call Brenda.

Mimi's cell phone buzzed again. She swiftly picked it and answered it. “I'll be right down Minx.”

CHAPTER FIFTY-TWO

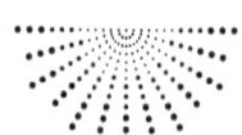

The waves slapped against the Myrtle Beach shoreline. The white foam glistened against the silhouette of Brenda's cappuccino-colored skin entwined with John's latte-color as they lay like beached whales on the large multi-colored beach towel. The sun, as little as it was, battled the breeze that seemed to have no effect on the lovers.

Leaning on his elbow, John raised his head and placed it on the back of his hand. His eyes cascaded over Brenda's body as she lay on her back with her eyes closed. John smiled as he recalled the tender moments they shared last evening. From the fiery kiss that set everything ablaze until the moment of total surrender, John was amazed at what a passionate lover Brenda was. She was soft and warm to the touch and offered herself so freely.

"Baby, let's get showered and dressed so I can take you out for a fabulous dinner," John said. "I've already made reservations at The Sea Captain's House."

Brenda didn't want to move. She felt so wonderful and free with the sound of the waves crashing against the shoreline. This was what she needed—a romantic getaway from all the drama she left back in Durham, even if only for a weekend. John had been warm and accommodating, and their lovemaking had become so potent that she never wanted to leave this man's arms. She breathed in the moist salt air and came back down to earth when she heard John call her name again.

"Come on, baby," he said softly. "I've got reservations for us at The Sea Captain's House, and I know you're famished."

Brenda turned her head slightly. "I wish I could stay here forever. This is what I've been craving for a good while—the two of us fancy free with no inhibitions. I feel on top of the world. This has been the most romantic weekend I've experienced…since forever, and we still have a day to go."

"Well, if you get up, I want to show you part three of this romantic weekend."

Brenda smiled and then slowly got up. She picked up her beach towel, clutched her hand in John's, and followed him to the room. In less than an hour, they were showered and dressed, ready to embark on the evening John had planned without Brenda's input.

They took a taxi to the restaurant. As soon as they entered the restaurant, they were shown to their seats with a view of the water.

"John, this is so wonderful. I can't believe how relaxed I am," Brenda said.

"For my special lady. I want you to enjoy this evening and always remember it as our special night."

Brenda smiled. "Why do I deserve you?"

"I should ask the same question? It doesn't matter; we're here together. Now let's choose a wine."

"White for me. Preferably a Chardonnay."

"I'll have the same. That's settled. I like it when we are on one accord."

The two lovers cruised their menus and were ready to order after giving their drink selection to their waiter. "For the lady, John said taking the lead, She Crap Soup."

"Excellent choice," the waiter said. "And for her meal?"

"She'll have the Long Bay Stuffed Flounder with a house salad, a loaded baked potato, and steamed broccoli."

"And for you, sir?"

"I'll have the Filet Mignon Neptune, a loaded baked potato, and broccoli. Baby, would you like a side order of oysters? I hear they're good."

The waiter smiled and cocked his head in Brenda's direction. "The oysters might make your night one to remember." Brenda laughed.

"No thank you. My night has already been one that I won't forget."

The waiter and John shared a laugh.

"All right then," the waiter said. "I'll get your order in right away. Enjoy your evening."

"Thank you," both Brenda and John said simultaneously. Brenda slapped John's hand.

"Why does everything have to be sexual to you?" Brenda asked with a smile.

"It isn't, however, when I'm with you I can't help myself. You're beautiful, baby, inside and out."

Brenda reached over and brushed John's face with the back of her hand. "I could be with you for the rest of my life. I've not felt this way about anyone in a long time. I know it's real, and it certainly isn't about the sex, although it's nice to know that I have a partner who can still throw down in the bedroom."

"Baby, that I can do and I won't miss a beat. I feel the same way, Brenda. I never saw this coming, but some things are worth the wait."

"I couldn't have said it better."

They sipped their wine and soon came their meal. It was apparent they enjoyed each item on their plate. The Sea Captain's House had won many awards to include Southern Living's Best Seafood Restaurant Reader's Choice Award. Brenda and John were satisfied, filled to the gills with the delectable food.

"Would you like dessert?" the waiter asked as he retrieved empty dishes from the table.

"No," Brenda said emphatically.

"Yes, I think we will have dessert. I would like a large slice of your Hummingbird Cake. We'll share." John winked at the waiter.

"One large slice of Hummingbird Cake coming up." And the waiter was gone.

"Okay, John, I let you order dinner for me, but who gave you the authority to override my decision not to have dessert? I'm full. I can't put another thing in my belly. I love that you're taking charge here, but I've got a say-so over what I put in my temple."

John smiled. "You're right, sweetie. I'm sorry; please forgive me. However, I would like for you this one time to share this piece of cake with me. It is so delicious, and I want this to be our special dessert on our special night that we've shared together."

"Smooth talk isn't going to change my mind."

Before Brenda could say another word, the cake was in front of them with two forks on either side of the plate. John smiled and picked up the fork on his side of the plate and began to eat little bites of the cake. "Come on, baby. Take a bite for me."

"Look at this big hunk of cake, John. You don't even need to be eating it. Where in the world are you going to put it? And it's lopsided."

"One bite. That's all I ask."

"Okay," Brenda said with a sigh of resignation. She picked up her fork and John swirled the plate around and pushed it in front of her. Brenda looked at him suspiciously. "What's up with you?"

"Eat one piece so we can go."

Brenda frowned and put her fork into the cake. "This is hard. My fork won't go through it."

"Let me see what you're talking about."

Brenda was disgusted. She put her fork down. John took his and poked in the same area where Brenda had placed her fork. John moved the fork around until the small object wrapped in Saran Wrap found its way out of the center of the cake. Brenda sat dumbfounded, not sure what to make of the object John had pulled from the dessert. "What is this?" Brenda asked searching John's face.

"In Durham, I asked you to marry me, and you said yes." Brenda clasped her hands to her face. "This is official." John scraped the cake residue from the plastic, unwrapped it, and uncovered a five-carat Marquise diamond. "Will you marry me?"

Like a bump on a log, Brenda sat in her seat amazed at the wonder of this man. Her eyes became large, round discs. She was speechless.

"Say yes," someone shouted, followed by another.

Brenda looked around at the faces who now gaped

back at her. Then she turned and looked at John. "Yes, yes, yes, I'll marry you."

The waiter came around and poured them a glass of wine on the house while other patrons got up and clapped for the couple. "Thank you for saying yes," John said with a grin. "For a moment, I was afraid you were going to turn me down. Girl, I don't know what I would've done if you had said no."

"You knew I wasn't going to say no, which is why you staged it in front of all these people. But, baby, this will be a night I'll always remember. Thank you, and I love you."

John placed the ring on Brenda's finger. "I love you, too. Now let's lose this place and make some beautiful music together. Check please!"

CHAPTER FIFTY-THREE

Mimi was on top of the world. She now had a single—a forerunner to her album that the producers had placed on schedule to be released at the beginning of the upcoming year. "Satisfied" was a hip, sultry number that dripped with sexual overtones and showcased Mimi's talent as a songstress. It was a little jazz and a little R&B.

Yohan Giles, the artistic director and mastermind behind Mimi's virtual success was pleased with the outcome of her single. Mimi was a fast learner with an apparent gift of song, and the likelihood that her album would be on time was not a far stretch.

Yohan walked up to Mimi and gave her a peck on the cheek. "You definitely got the pipes, girl," he said, as he checked Mimi out, his eyes roving and ingesting her beauty beyond the scope of his duties. It made Mimi uncomfortable, but she tried to dismiss it as company etiquette—whatever that meant.

"Thank you," Mimi said graciously, making no attempt to flirt. She might have read more into Yohan's gestures, but she wanted him to know from the jump, that she was a lady and while other artists may kiss and do other things to get to the top, she wasn't the one.

"Look, why don't I take you out to dinner tonight to celebrate?" Yohan asked.

Mimi looked from Minx, who'd been standing in the wings, to Yohan who had a mischievous grin on his face. "Why are you looking at Minx?" Yohan asked, catching Mimi's expression. "I'm the one who asked you to dinner. It's all business if that'll make you feel better."

Mimi gauged her words. "Well, sure, Mr. Giles. We've got to celebrate the success of my new single."

"And there will be many more. We are going to market you to the hilt. You can count your Grammys now."

That made Mimi smile. If Yohan had enough confidence that she was a marketable singer worth the money they were spending on her, who was she to discard his innocent gesture for dinner. "Can Minx join us?"

Yohan looked at Minx. "It would be best if this meeting was just between the two of us—company policy." Minx groaned. "As I said this is a business dinner, and while I understand that Minx is a good friend of yours, what happens at Azilet Records stays at Azilet Records."

"Okay. You don't mind do you, Minx?"

"Mimi, Mr. Giles, the director of your future, has spoken. I'll see you later." Minx moved from the wall he was perched on and left the building.

Mimi sighed. The last thing she wanted was a rift between her and Minx. He was responsible for making her new career happen. It was only a business dinner between her and Yohan. And when the check was paid, she'd go her way and he his—bottom line, she was going home alone.

MIMI STEPPED in front of the mirror and admired herself. She let her thick, black hair flow down to her shoulders that added a backdrop to her red-orange, form-fitting, lycra cocktail dress that hit an inch above her knees. On her feet, she wore a stunning pair of black stilettos with a red-orange patent leather panel that went around the outside perimeter of the shoe, crossing over the front in a swirl. Her make-up was flawless, her teeth whitened, with lips that matched her dress thanks to her neon-orange MAC lipstick.

With confidence, Mimi picked up her black clutch bag and walked toward the door. She stopped in her tracks, her heart sounding an alert about Minx. She hadn't spoken to him since he left the studio earlier in the day, and he was the last person she wanted to alienate.

Before Mimi reached the door handle, the telephone rang in the room. Maybe it was Minx, and they could sweep this afternoon's awkward moment under the rug. On the third ring, Mimi answered the phone.

"Ms. Bailey, your car is here," said the voice at the other end. "Your driver is waiting in the lobby."

"Thank you," Mimi said, disappointed that it wasn't Minx at the end of the line.

She proceeded downstairs and waved at the driver who escorted her to the limo. Mimi was amazed at what money and popularity could do.

The ride to the restaurant was in silence. The driver looked straight ahead and Mimi watched the bustling city roll by as the car whisked her to where she would be dining. It was in this moment of silence that she felt a twinge of guilt, more than she had felt before—her fight with Brenda, her shortness with Afrika, and her attitude in general. She put it all under her self-imposed microscope. Things didn't look good.

Her self-assessment had to wait. The driver stopped in front of the restaurant and came around to help her out of the limo. The driver waved his hand toward the restaurant and Mimi followed his direction.

Yohan was seated, investigating the menu when Mimi walked in. The aura of the restaurant had an old world feel with a touch of romanticism. She was escorted to the table where Yohan sat, he quite handsome in a black-and-white tweed jacket, red shirt, and black slacks. Mimi smiled in spite of herself that he was also wearing red.

When she neared, Yohan dropped the menu on the table and stared at Mimi as if she was a goddess…a mirage —a vision of something he had only dreamed about. He immediately stood to his feet and went around the table to pull Mimi's chair out for her to sit. He couldn't keep his eyes off her.

Mimi sat down, careful not to cause any undue attention. She smiled back at Yohan who had yet to utter a word. She watched as he smacked his lips together, took his eyes off her for a second, leaned back, and stared again.

"My, my, my," Yohan began, "you are fascinating to watch. You look radiant in that dress and every bit the star you are destined to be."

Mimi felt her eyes bat, although she hadn't done it intentionally. "Thank you. I wanted to be properly dressed for the occasion. You did say this was to be a celebration."

"And a celebration it is. What would you like to drink?"

"Uhh, I'd like a pomegranate martini, thank you."

"A 'tini' girl. I like a woman with class and style. Mimi you're going to go places that you've never dreamed of even in your wildest dreams. The sky is the limit. All you have to do is let me guide. Believe me, I'll only steer you in the right direction."

Mimi smiled. "You haven't any idea what my wildest dreams are, however, I'm ready for the ride. Singing has been my heart…my anthem ever since I can remember. There were things that kept me from pursuing my love for singing professionally in the earlier part of my life, but that's now water under the bridge. I guess you could say… that it's all about God's timing."

"Indeed, it is. Your voice is impeccable and if you want this like I believe you do, it's already a done deal."

Yohan signaled for the waiter who took their drink order. "I hope you don't mind me saying that you are wearing that dress. I like that you let your hair hang down to your shoulders. And it's the real stuff."

"You're very perceptive, Mr. Giles." Mimi kept her composure unsure of where the conversation was headed.

"How could I not? It's not every day that I'm sitting in front of a beautiful woman such as yourself. And please call me by my first name. We are going to be working together a lot; we're going to become very familiar with each other. I want you to be as comfortable as possible."

"Okay, Yohan, I got the message."

Mimi didn't feel familiar or comfortable in Yohan's presence. She'd wish that Minx could join them. Maybe then she could relax. She was going to drink only one martini in order to stay alert should Yohan try to change the celebration into something else.

"Your cocktails," the waiter said, sitting the drinks in front of Yohan and Mimi. "And, are you ready to order?"

"Yes," Yohan said, quickly. "We'll have the eight-ounce filet mignon with a baked potato and a mixed green salad. For an appetizer, I would like to order the sautéed mushrooms."

"Would you like bread with your meal?" the waiter asked.

"Yes, please," Yohan said in response.

"Very well. Your meal will be served shortly. I'll bring out the salads first."

"Thank you," Yohan said.

After the waiter had disappeared, Mimi took the liberty to speak up. "You ordered without asking me what I would like to eat, although I thought it was an excellent choice."

Yohan smiled. "I wanted to surprise you, and I hope you approve of the restaurant. I love the TriBeCa area. I heard you tell Minx the other day how much you enjoyed the filet mignon at the place you both dined earlier that day. I listen. I thought if filet mignon was an excellent choice when you and Minx had it, surely, you'd appreciate it here as Wolfgang Steakhouse is noted for their excellent steaks. I'm sure you'll feel the same once you've tasted it."

Mimi took a sip of her drink and smiled. "You amaze me, Yohan. You seem to be so in tune with your artists."

"That's what I do best. I'm paid to know everything about each one—what makes them tick and so on. And so, you know, I'm very in tune to what Mimi Bailey likes and don't like. Red with the hint of orange looks fabulous on you, I must say. You are a vibrant woman; it's part of your personality. Even in your singing, that vibrancy shines through. Just wait; those other so-called divas won't know what hit them when you emerge full-throttle on the scene."

Yohan picked up his glass of wine. "I'd like to make a toast." Mimi picked up what was left of her martini. "To Mimi…the new diva in town."

"I'll drink to that."

CHAPTER FIFTY-FOUR

Dinner was fabulous, just as Yohan predicted. Mimi wanted to pick her plate up and lick the remaining residue from it. It was that good. She had warmed to Yohan having now been in his presence for more than two-and-a-half hours. In between his taking a few phone calls and sending out an occasional text, her celebration dinner was a success. It didn't hurt that Yohan had conversation that she was drawn to and he didn't look half bad. Mimi found herself daydreaming.

"Where would you like to go next?" Yohan asked, drawing Mimi out of her daydream. "The night is still young, and I'm sure you haven't seen New York in its fullest."

Mimi pretended like she was looking at her watch that wasn't there. "Dinner was wonderful, but it's getting late and I need to get my beauty sleep. I have to get up early and prepare for another long day at the studio."

Yohan studied Mimi. "You're not trying to end our wonderful date because you're worried about what Minx would think."

"Oh, no," Mimi lied. Damn, it was as if Yohan could see right through her. "Not at all, although I didn't think this was a date. Minx isn't my keeper. Remember, I'm a married woman."

"Oh, yes, I had temporarily forgotten that. I will do my best to mind my manners, although, Mimi, you're making that task awfully hard."

"Well, I guess my answer is no. There's no place else that'd I'd like to go except for back to the hotel."

"Look, why don't we drive through New York…up to Harlem and have a nightcap. I promise not to keep you out late. I want you to be on top of your game when you're in the studio tomorrow."

Mimi was silent. "I shouldn't."

"Come on. I'm harmless as a flea. I'll get you back to the hotel at a decent time. One drink."

Mimi sighed. "Okay. One drink."

"Good. Give me a moment to call my driver so that he can come around and pick us up."

Mimi sat back and watched Yohan hit one button to summon the driver. She wondered what Minx was doing…what he might be thinking and wanted to change her mind about the nightcap. But before she could decide to do so, Yohan was up on his feet and escorting her out of the restaurant. The driver must've been nearby. When they exited the restaurant, the limo was parked out front.

They drove to Harlem with Yohan playing the efficient tour guide. Mimi could hear live jazz playing in the background as they entered the club, and immediately she felt at home and began to sway to the music.

They were ushered to a seat and Yohan ordered a pomegranate martini for Mimi and a Cognac for himself.

"I'm glad I decided to come," Mimi said at last. "Nice jazz."

"Do you want to sing?"

"Sing? Tonight…as in get up on the stage and…?"

"Yes, Mimi. I've pulled some of our talent right off this stage. You tell me what you'd like to sing, and I'll tell Rudy, the band leader and pianist and he'll hook you up."

"Yohan, what am I to say?"

"That you'll sing? You have arrived, baby, and you might as well give them a little bit of what you're about to give the entire world."

"Okay, I'll do it." Mimi whispered the name of the song to Yohan who got up and told the bandleader. Still watching Yohan, she got a chill down her back when he threw up his thumb to say it was a go. Mimi was thrilled.

After the next two songs, Rudy came to the mike and began to speak. "We have a special lady in the house tonight. I hear she has a voice that will break a window pane at the Empire State Building. She is one of Azilet's new recording artists, and you can say you heard her first —here at the Blue Note—before being introduced to the world. Mimi Bailey, come on up and sing for us."

There was a round of applause as Mimi moved from her seat to step onto the stage.

Rudy grinned. "Damn, and she's fine. Girl, you're wearing that red dress."

Mimi smiled and took the microphone when offered to her. "I was going to give you a peek at my new single that's coming out soon, but I want to do another number that I wrote entitled, "Free to Love." I'm going to start in a-cappella, and I hope the band will be able to pick it up and follow me. This song has sentimental value to me, and

I hope you like it. Mimi cleared her throat and began to sing.

I've watched my life float by like a tumbleweed in
the wind
Mirrors reflecting how my life wasn't supposed to
be...and then again
Secrets had me bound
But there was no one around...that I could tell, I
could tell.

I never thought the hurt and the pain of that day
would ever go away
I hadn't realized how many people I had betrayed
along the way
Because I refused to share the dark secret that
would've set me free
Free to love my man
Free to love my best friend
Free to love the best of myself

Mimi was lost in the song to the point she almost forgot she had an audience. She felt the words deep in her soul and immediately thought of Brenda. It was imperative that she make amends right away. When no one else is there, you can always count on a good friend...a best friend.

When Mimi came back down to earth and opened her eyes to the audience as she sang the final note, every patron was on their feet giving her a resounding applause. "Sing another song," an older gentleman shouted out. "That's what I call talent." The older gentleman dressed in a white-and-black pinstriped suit and wearing a white fedora approached Mimi and handed her a twenty-dollar bill. "And she's fine as hell. Baby, please sing us another song."

Mimi looked over at Yohan who gave her a nod. Mimi began to sing her new single and the crowd went wild. Yohan was the first person to his feet, and he stood, swayed to the music, and clapped his hands until Mimi returned to the table.

"You were off-the-chart, and no pun intended," Yohan said, giving Mimi a peck on the cheek as she moved to her seat. "They loved "Satisfied," and by the length of their standing ovation, you have a for sure hit on your hand. I liked your first song, also. You said you wrote it."

"Yes, I did. I wrote it for a special friend and our daughters."

"I think we should record it, which will also bill you as a writer. There are extra perks for being a songwriter."

"Are you for real, Yohan?"

"I can make a lot of things happen, Baby. Trust me. Aren't you glad you came?"

"I'm having the thrill of my life. Thanks, Yohan, for a wonderful evening."

"The pleasure is all mine. I guess it's time to get you home. I want you fresh in the morning so you can do what you did tonight."

Mimi smiled. "I'm ready when you are."

Yohan escorted Mimi to the limo that was parked in the parking lot of the club as small as it was. Mimi got in first with Yohan at her heels. Once inside, the driver took off. Yohan motioned for the driver to put up the partition.

Mimi jumped when Yohan patted her hand. "I didn't mean to frighten you, Mimi. I'm still on a cloud at the performance you gave tonight. Watching those people go crazy for you was music to my ears. You were sensational."

"Thank you again. I wouldn't be here without you.

Before Mimi knew what had happened Yohan reached over and kissed her. He slid a hand over her breast, and Mimi caught it before he had time to roam anywhere else.

"Yohan, I'm a married woman who loves her husband dearly."

"You mean to tell me that you and Minx have not slept together? He is considered a male slut in New York."

Mimi put space between her and Yohan. "Minx and I are good friends. In fact, he knows my husband. We were all friends in college."

"You didn't answer the question."

"No, Yohan, I haven't and have no plans to ever sleep with Minx. Ours is a platonic relationship, and I would like to keep ours a business one."

Yohan let his finger glide underneath Mimi's chin. She removed it and held his hand for a moment. "Yohan, I hope that getting this record deal doesn't entail me having to provide and special favors. I see the reality shows any confessions of those who want in the business, but that's not who I am. I will sing my lungs out for Azilet Records, but I'm not about to hop into bed with anyone for a deal."

"That's what I like about you, Mimi. You tell the truth no matter what the cost. Your benefit package doesn't include a rump in the hay with me. I'd be lying, however, if I didn't say that I would love to know what made Mimi tick and how you'd feel in my arms."

"You're bordering on disrespectful, Yohan. Again, I understand that this business can be downright dirty sometimes, but I'm not the one."

"Not now you aren't," Yohan whispered to himself. He

knocked on the glass. "Let's get the lady home. She has an early morning call at the studio."

The rest of the ride was met in silence. Mimi was glad she had stood her ground. She was there for the business and the business wasn't going to get her down, especially not down in the sheets with Yohan, regardless who he was and the power he wielded.

They pulled in front of the hotel and Yohan let Mimi out. "There's no need for you to go in with me," Mimi said. She waved at Yohan as he reentered the car and disappeared.

Mimi hummed as she entered the hotel. Despite Yohan's advances, the night had been amazing. She divorced Yohan's attempt to kiss her from her mind and let the words to "Free to Love" flow from her lips. As she moved through the lobby to the elevator, Mimi caught a glimpse of Minx out of the corner of her eyes. She stopped in her tracks, back tracked and walked over to where he was sitting.

"How long have you been sitting here?" Mimi asked Minx.

"Long enough to know that your dinner should've been over a long time ago. It's apparent your evening went well."

"It did. We lost track of time. Yohan took me to this nightclub in Harlem and I got a chance to sing my new single on stage. You should've heard the crowd, Minx."

Minx wasn't moved. He looked at his watch. "It's damn near eleven o'clock, Mimi. You have an early morning at the studio. "

"And you're not your sister's keeper. I didn't know that I had to report to you."

"I wonder what Raphael would think about his wife

gallivanting all over the city with some record producer? I don't think the Colonel would like it all. In fact, and I can bet your bottom dollar that you haven't even told Raphael that you're in New York."

"He's fighting a deadly war, Minx. My being in New York is the last thing on his mind. It's late, and I need to get my beauty rest. Listen, sweetheart, you don't have to worry about me."

"Oh really? It's like that is it?"

Mimi grabbed her bag and headed for the elevator. She turned when Minx grabbed her arm. "Watch yourself around Yohan. He's going to want you to give up the goods sooner or later."

"Funny, he said you were the slut."

"Believe what you want, Mimi. I'm the only person in this town that has your back. You wouldn't even be here if it wasn't for me. Remember that."

"Sounds like your jealous," Mimi shot back.

"Sister, I've already had you. Don't make me have to break Raphael's heart and tell him how you came to me when you guys had that big, blow-out after he walked out on you for what was it...a week?"

"You wouldn't, Minx. That was a mistake and never should've happened. It happened only once and God knows that it was innocent enough and it didn't mean anything."

"You enjoyed it. I enjoyed it. True, it might have been innocent enough, but Raphael doesn't ever need to know that. Hmmm?"

"I thought you were my friend, Minx. I love you like a brother, and I would never do anything to hurt you. I laid the law down to Yohan tonight. I told him that I didn't roll like those wannabe girls that would do anything to get into the industry."

"So, he did try and come on to you."

"I didn't say that, Minx."

"So, what are you saying, Mimi? I'm going to say this once. Watch your back. This is an industry that will eat you up and spit you out like watermelon seeds at a watermelon eating contest if you're not careful. I'm out, but I'll be waiting here in the lobby first thing in the morning to see you to the studio."

Mimi watched as Minx walked off.

CHAPTER FIFTY-FIVE

Minx was waiting in the lobby of the hotel as he said he would. Normally, Mimi would have received a phone call from Minx to let her know he was ready and waiting. Mimi was met with a cool reception, the tension between them still very evident.

"Are we going to have breakfast before we go?" Mimi asked in her attempt to be cordial and break the ice between her and Minx.

"I'll wait if you want to eat." He looked at his watch. "We only have forty-five minutes before you need to be at the studio."

"Minx…"

"Yeah…"

"Minx, let's repair this rift between us. We've been friends forever, and I'm not going to do anything to jeopardize my marriage, my integrity, and certainly not my friendship with you. I really did lay down the law to Yohan. I'm here to sing and make records. That's it."

Minx looked into Mimi's eyes. "How can I stay mad at you? I'll admit that I was a little jealous, but that's because

I know Yohan, and I'm a little over-protective of my little sister.

"Look, Mimi, I'm sorry what I said last night about us...us having that one indiscretion. That's what it was... one indiscretion. I've never lusted for you; I've always been happy that my boy, Raphael, was taking care of his main squeeze. I know beyond a shadow of a doubt that the two of you were made for each other and will love each other until the end of time. I'm afraid that Yohan may be setting you up...trying to twist your brain, manipulate you so that you'd fall into his clutches all for the sake of making records."

"I'm a big girl, Minx. I've been faithful to Raphael our whole married life, except for that one time with you."

"And your secret will be safe with me."

"You know I hurt Raphael awfully bad last year."

"What are you talking about, Mimi?"

"Afrika isn't his biological daughter."

Minx' expression was one of surprise and then he looked at Mimi suspiciously. "Well, she's not mine. You were good and pregnant when I met you. You didn't trick my boy, did you?"

"Yes. No, although I never told him that I was pregnant when I met him. I was about two months pregnant when I came to Hampton. I was raped by my best friend's fiancé."

"And you never told Raphael?"

"Not until Afrika went to college in Durham, North Carolina. It was the place where I was raped. And who would've thought that my daughter would become best friends with my best friend's daughter? I hadn't seen Brenda in nineteen years, and yes, she had married the rapist. He found out I was in town and all hell broke loose. And eventually Raphael found out. Secrets are bad, but I'd like our secret to stay that way."

"You have my word on it. I'll never tell. Now let's get to that studio. I'll spring for lunch unless Yohan has other plans. Just watch your back, baby girl."

"Minx, I know you'll have my back. I'm glad we had this talk. I can't afford to lose another good friend."

"Now what are you talking about?"

"That's another story and it's too long to tell."

It was all business in the studio. Yohan went over the day's assignment with Mimi and carried on like nothing had happened the prior evening. Yohan dismissed Minx—the self-appointed bodyguard to Ms. Mimi Bailey—but bodyguard or no bodyguard, Yohan had every intention of getting under his new number one star's skirt. And Yohan would relish the moment when it happened; in his mind, he knew she'd be delicious.

He couldn't take his mind away from the curve of her hips and how she swayed them when she walked. Even though Mimi was in her late thirties, bordering on forty, she still had the look. Her breasts were always arched nicely in her clothes and he just loved the sassy way she would throw her body into everything she did, especially when she was singing. There was going to be a single and an album, and while getting there, he was going to make her sing in the keys of c, f, and g. He could taste it.

CHAPTER FIFTY-SIX

Brenda couldn't wait to call Asia and her sisters to tell them the good news. She knew they would be excited for her, now that she'd found real happiness. They hated the ground Victor walked on.

She and John basked in the glory of their weekend and arrived back in Durham late Sunday night. Brenda kept looking at her beautiful ring and wished she could share her excitement with her best friend. What would Mimi say when she found out about her engagement to John? Would she hate her? Would she even speak to her again? Brenda looked at her ring again. She hadn't heard from Mimi in almost a week, and now Brenda was going to put an end to this division between them.

Her cell phone rang. Brenda picked it up and looked at the caller-ID. It was Sheila. She wasn't in the mood to deal with her right now, but she had promised to do whatever she could. Against her better judgment, Brenda answered the call.

"Brenda?" said the feeble voice.

"Sheila, what's wrong?"

"Brenda, would you take me to the hospital? I'm having a hard time breathing. Sorry to bother you."

"No bother. I'll be right over. Make sure I'm able to get into the house."

"I'll…I'll go right now and unlock it."

"Okay. I'm on my way."

Brenda hadn't anticipated that Sheila would be calling so soon. Her good news had to wait. She rushed up the stairs and grabbed her purse and then headed back down and out of the door. Hopefully she would return in time to meet with her two o'clock client.

THE DOOR to Sheila's condo was unlocked when Brenda arrived. She knocked softly then pushed the door open. The foyer and living room were dark. She moved forward, stopped, and gasped when she saw Sheila's frail frame lying face down on the couch. Brenda inched forward, afraid of what she might find. She touched Sheila's wrist and found a faint pulse.

Brenda pulled out her cell and called nine-one-one. "Hurry," Brenda said, giving the dispatcher the address. "I'm at the home of a friend who has Aids and she's barely breathing."

"Stay on the line, ma'am. I'm dispatching an ambulance to that address."

Brenda stayed with the dispatcher until the ambulance arrived at Sheila's condo. They moved swiftly, first taking her vital signs and then swiftly putting her on a gurney. "We're taking her to Durham Regional Hospital."

"I'll be right behind you."

Brenda followed the gurney as they placed Sheila in

the ambulance. "Hey, Ms. Lady, where are they taking Ms. Sheila?" Ms. Pomeroy asked from her usual lookout on her balcony.

"To the hospital. She's very ill."

"What about her husband?"

"What about him?" Brenda hollered back.

"Aren't you going to let him know? He has every right to know what's happened to his wife."

"If you're so concerned, why don't you call and tell him yourself? Now, I've got to go, if you don't mind."

"Don't use that tone of voice with me, Ms. Lady. I'm old enough to whip your behind."

"Try it. Now mind your own business." Brenda tuned out anything else that Ms. Pomeroy said and walked swiftly to her car. She got in and drove away.

Sheila was immediately moved to a triage room upon arrival at the hospital. The Emergency Room seemed chaotic as doctors and nurses alike were moving in a tail-wind. Brenda watched as a legion of doctors piled into the one room before one weary doctor after another nurse filed out one by one.

"My name is Brenda Christianson," Brenda said to the receptionist. "I was the one who called nine-one-one for Mrs. Billops. Is she going to be all right?"

"Are you a relative?"

"No, I'm a friend. Mrs. Billops called me to come and take her to the hospital. I found her unconscious when I arrived at her house."

"Hello, I'm Dr. Oliver." He offered his hand to Brenda as he walked up to her upon hearing her ask about Sheila. "Are you a relative of Mrs. Billops?"

"No, I'm a friend. She called and asked me to come

and take her to the hospital. She was finding it hard to breath."

Dr. Oliver lowered his head. "I'm sorry Miss…"

"Mrs. Brenda Christianson."

"Are you the psychologist, Brenda Christianson?"

"Yes, I am. Sheila Billops used to be the secretary to my husband before he passed away last year."

"Oh, yes. I read about it in the paper. Sorry for your loss."

"Thank you. And what were you saying about Sheila?"

"I'm sorry, Mrs. Christianson. Mrs. Billops went into cardiac arrest. She didn't make it."

"Oh my God," Brenda said, clutching her chest. "Please tell me it isn't so."

"I wish I could tell you different. There will be an autopsy to determine the actual cause of death. If you will stay around, the police will come and take a statement from you."

"She had Aids…full-blown Aids. I can't believe that it took her this fast. She was still alive when we left her condo."

"For some, the disease hits harder and faster than others. Do you know if she was taking her meds?"

"That I don't know. Her husband may know."

"Is her husband around?"

"They recently separated. Sheila had asked for my help when he suddenly decided to leave her. I'm sure his number is listed in her cell phone. I'll go back to the house and get it."

Before Brenda could say another word, Jamal rushed up to her. "Where's Sheila? What are you doing here?"

"Are you Sheila's husband?" Dr. Oliver asked giving Jamal a cursory glance.

"Yes, sir. Where can I find my wife?"

Dr. Oliver exhaled. "I'm sorry, Mr. Billops. Your wife expired several minutes ago."

"Expired? Do you mean expired as in dead?"

Dr. Oliver looked at Brenda. "I'm sorry, Mr. Billops. Please follow me and I'll take you to see her before she's taken away."

Jamal looked at the doctor and then back at Brenda, waving his hand in her face. "It's all your fault."

"Maybe if you'd been with your wife instead of leaving her to die alone, she'd still be alive. I came when she called me." Brenda turned and walked away.

CHAPTER FIFTY-SEVEN

Sheila's death weighed heavy on Brenda's heart. She hadn't completely forgiven Sheila for her transgressions with Victor, but for some odd reason she felt a connection. Maybe it was the psychologist that had conditioned her to search for the truth—the where, what, and why of it all. Brenda couldn't shake the feeling that maybe if she hadn't been so hard-hearted, she might have been able to save Sheila—at least extend her life.

The problem with her thinking was that it was all too late. Sheila was dead, possibly caused by the deadly virus that Victor had inflicted upon her. A cold chill came over Brenda as she recalled Sheila's call for help. Sheila wasn't Brenda's problem. However, in the end, she was glad that she had put aside her anger long enough to be the Good Samaritan.

Tears streaked Brenda's face. She drove away from the hospital and headed for home. The more she thought about Sheila, the more the tears dripped down her face. Brenda wasn't sure where this sympathy for someone she had despised came from, but it said something about the person she was to most people, and that was she had a good heart and would help almost anyone.

Now home, Brenda opened the garage and drove the car inside. She sat a moment and let the rest of her tears fall. When she was finished, Brenda sighed, got out of the car, and went inside.

Brenda slumped onto the couch in the family room. Out of nowhere, Beyoncé rushed in and jumped on her lap. Brenda brushed and hugged her beloved Beyoncé to her chest, grateful that there was something warm she could hold on to.

Slumber took over and Brenda fell into a deep sleep. Her mind pushed her to revisit Sheila in her comatose state. The vision was vivid as she recaptured Sheila slumped over on the couch in her pink robe, her body all but limp as the paramedics took her vitals and tried to awaken her. She saw Jamal rush into the hospital with his nasty disposition, as if he wasn't responsible for having abandoned Sheila at a worst time. Then her dream conjured up Victor who held Sheila in a naked embrace, showering her with kisses.

Brenda shook as she tried to break out of her dream and come into the present. She gasped as she forced her eyes open, looking around but glad that she was in a familiar place. Even Beyoncé had gone about her way, probably curled up in a corner taking a nap of her own.

Brenda reached for her iPhone. Without wasting time, she punched in a speed-dial number and waited for the phone to ring. On the second ring, she heard her voice.

"Mimi, this is Brenda."

"Hey, Brenda, I've been meaning to call you."

"I've wanted to call you, too. But the reason I'm calling is that Sheila is dead."

"Sheila? You mean the Sheila that worked in Victor's office that has Aids, Sheila?"

"Yes, Mimi." Brenda began to cry. "She called and asked me to take her to the hospital, and when I got to the condo, she was unconscious."

"Oh my God, Brenda. Where was her husband?"

"They're separated."

"You mean he walked out on her while she was ill?"

Brenda sighed. "Yes, that's what I mean. I just left the hospital. I feel so helpless."

"Brenda, it wasn't your fault. Many people would look at you and ask why you were helping her in the first place. She's the woman who had an affair with your husband."

"That's true, however, for some reason I had to help Sheila. Inside, that woman was a kind heart believe it or not. I'm sure Victor entrapped her with his charm and gifts, and she fell for it like so many others."

"But she knew he was married."

"I guess. Right now, I need my friend. Can you come over?"

"I'm not at home right now. I'm in New York?"

"New York? What are you doing in New York?"

"I'm recording. I've finished my first single and I'm preparing for my album."

"Wow. I didn't know."

"Look, Brenda, I'm going to take a flight home tomorrow night. When I get home, we'll talk. I miss my best friend, too, and I want to apologize face-to-face about my recent behavior."

"I apologize to you for not saying anything about John. I wasn't sure how you would feel about the two of us getting together."

"You don't owe me an apology. Look, let's talk later.

I'm in the middle of a session and I've got to go. I'll be there for whatever you need."

"Thanks, Mimi. That's all I can ask for. I need my best friend, too."

MIMI WAS happy to hear Brenda's voice, although the message she delivered wasn't a happy one. Mimi was in the throes of experiencing the best time of her life, and she wanted to share it with Brenda. They had been friends forever and a man certainly wasn't going to be the catalyst to sever a thirty-year friendship.

The tracks for "Free to Love" were done. Mimi really liked the arrangement Azilet Records had come up with. Best of all, she would retain all the rights to the song, which was a great feeling.

She and Minx had ironed out their differences and were now in harmony. But Minx kept guard over her like a bloodhound. She also noted that he had words with Howard Austin, the co-owner of Azilet. Mimi was sure Yohan had gotten the message, as his manner had been nothing but professional ever since.

Yohan approached Mimi and gave her a peck on the cheek with Minx looking on. "It's a wrap for today. I've got another artist I need to work with. Your single is due to hit the airways in a few weeks, and you should be ecstatic. I'll be working on getting you some gigs on some of the morning shows like *Good Morning America, The Today Show, Kelly and Ryan,* and most definitely *Jimmy Kimmel Live.* You're on your way. If you keep working these songs like you've been doing, it won't be long before your album drops. It's some ways off but not as far as you might think.

Also, you need to get an agent, not that fake wannabe in the corner over there."

Mimi dismissed Yohan's remark about Minx. Her relationship to Minx was none of his or anyone else's concern. "Thanks, Yohan," Mimi said politely. "I only want to do my best and make Azilet Records happy. This has been a long time in coming."

"So, what does your boyfriend over there think?" Yohan asked, pointing in Minx's direction.

"I believe he's proud of me. Right, Minx?"

Minx nodded his head. "You ready to blow this joint?"

"Yeah," Mimi said in response, her eyes dancing and showcasing all her teeth.

"Well, let's go."

"Early morning," Yohan said behind them. "I heard you needed to catch an early flight home. If you nail this next song, that won't be a problem."

"Thanks, Yohan. I'm going to do my best." Mimi put her arms through Minx's arm and left the studio.

"Mimi, I'm not fond of Yohan."

"You've said that a hundred times."

Minx ignored Mimi's comment. "He's done some scrupulous stuff in his day and has a reputation of being a player. These record execs don't always play by the rules, and I won't stand by if they mess with you. I ain't having it."

"Let's enjoy the rest of our day. I'm not thinking about Yohan, and if he knows what's good for him, he won't step to Mimi Bailey. I've got this."

"Mimi, these guys can be ruthless. They are rich and throw their power around like it was pocket change. One day you're a star, but mess with them, you can be in a back alley licking your wounds."

"Why are you trying to scare me, Minx?"

"It's not that I'm trying to scare you. I want you to realize that this industry is not a game to be taken lightly. You must know how to play it. All I'm doing, sweetie, is looking out for your welfare...your best interest. I'm sure Raphael will thank me for that."

"I hear you."

"I hope so. Trust me when I say that I know what I'm talking about."

"I trust your judgment. Now enough of this talk; let's have lunch."

"It's damn near four o'clock. How about dinner and a movie?"

"Sounds like fun to me. I'm glad you're here in New York to see about me. I'm going to call Raphael and tell him that you took good care of me."

"You may want to keep it to yourself. Although Raphael is my boy, he's a jealous Negro that don't like other Negros hanging around his woman."

"Is that because he knows how you are?"

Minx looked at Mimi and smiled. "I guess you might say that's it. My brother trusts me only so far."

"I'll have to tell my husband when the time is right that you've been nothing but a gentleman and a scholar."

Minx laughed for the first time in a long time. "Girl, he isn't going to believe one word of that. Raphael's name for me was always Dog and sometimes it was Dirty Dog."

Mimi laughed. "Minx, you're so funny. Well, let's enjoy our dinner and a movie. Tomorrow, I'll be heading back to Durham. Yohan said I should start back in about a week."

"As you know, I'm your New York connection. I'll be here when you need me."

CHAPTER FIFTY-EIGHT

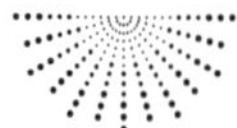

Mimi drove straight from the airport to Brenda's house. Upon her arrival, she noticed John's car in the driveway. It only made sense that John would be there to console Brenda, after all they were now a couple. And she hadn't warned Brenda that she was coming.

She willed her childish jealousy to a back seat in her brain and moved toward the door. She was going to give John and Brenda her blessing. Her mission was to console Brenda and to help her in any way she could.

Mimi rang the doorbell. Brenda opened the door with a look of apprehension on her face. "Mimi, John is here."

"Girl, I see his car in the driveway. He is your man; he's entitled to be here if that's where you want him to be. Give me a hug."

Brenda reached up and hugged Mimi, and Mimi hugged her back. Mimi followed Brenda into the family room where John sat watching television. He got up when Mimi entered.

"Hi, Mimi, I hear you have good news."

"Wow, news travels fast. How are you doing, John?"

"Great."

Mimi watched as Brenda took her place next to John on the couch. They looked so right together. Brenda was dressed in a beautiful gold-colored caftan and John wore blue jeans and a white polo shirt with Nike running shoes on his feet. She sat in one of the leather chairs opposite them.

"How was your flight?" Brenda asked, making small talk.

"Fine as flights go. I was anxious to get home. You seemed very distraught over Sheila's death, which is why I came straight over from the airport."

"I appreciate you coming. It was hard for me." Brenda let out a long breath. "Mimi, before I go on, I have something I want to share with you."

Mimi looked from Brenda to John. She didn't have a clue as to what Brenda was about to say. "It's not bad news, is it?"

"Quite the contrary," John jumped in to say.

Brenda took back the controls. "Ahh, John and I are engaged." Brenda extended her finger and Mimi covered her mouth when she saw the beautiful five-carat, white-gold, Marquise diamond engagement ring sitting high on Brenda's finger. She couldn't believe she failed to notice it when she first came in.

"Congratulations, guys!" Mimi said with forced enthusiasm. She jumped out of her chair and hugged both Brenda and John. "I'm happy for you. For a moment there, you scared me. I wasn't ready for any more sad news. I'm surprised Afrika didn't tell me."

"Asia doesn't know yet," Brenda said. "I'm going to have a small dinner party, and I've invited Asia and Afrika, so that I can tell them my good news. You're also welcome to come."

"Don't you want this to be a private affair with just the two of you and Asia? I promise not to tell Afrika until after you've told Asia."

"The two girls of ours are stuck like glue—how you and I used to be. I consider Afrika to be one of my daughters; she's always here."

There was a twinge of jealousy, but Mimi didn't let on. It was true that as close as she and Afrika were that she had neglected her recently. That had to change. Becoming a recording artist was one thing, but family always came first. She was going to call Afrika first thing when she got home and invite her to have a hot meal with her mother. If Asia wanted to tag along, she was welcome to do so.

Snap, snap went Brenda's fingers. "Are you all right, Mimi? You seem so far away."

"I'm ingesting your good news. This is a total surprise." Mimi stared at the two of them. "I'm really happy for you," she said as her head bobbed up and down. "I hope you don't mind if I skip your dinner party."

There was a moment of silence. "I'd really love for you to be there," Brenda insisted.

"That should be a special time for you and your immediate family. We can get together later and talk. What's going to happen with Sheila?"

"That's another matter. I was going to offer to help pay for services, but I haven't heard anything from Jamal. I'll wait. I've got enough on my plate with Trevor's case coming to trial."

"When will that be?"

"Mid-August."

"That's soon. I pray everything goes well."

"Me too, Mimi. I need some good news. With both Evelyn and Sheila dying, it cut so close to home. If it wasn't for the good news from the Health Department, I'd be a nervous wreck."

"Count your blessings, girl. Well, I'm going to go home now. Sorry for the interruption."

"Mimi, you don't have to go," John said.

"Yes, I do. I'm tired. I've had a grueling week in New York, but it was all worth it."

"My best friend is going to be a music icon," Brenda said. "You've got the talent."

"Thanks, Brenda. I appreciate it." Mimi got up and retrieved her purse. "Good night, and congratulations again."

"Are you okay, Mimi?" Brenda asked with concern in her voice.

"Why wouldn't I be? Walk me to the door and watch me get in my car so that no one puts the snatch to me."

"Why don't I do one better and walk you to your car?" John offered.

Mimi turned her head and looked at John. "I'll be all right. You take care of Brenda."

"I'm going to walk out with you anyway and don't fight me on this."

"Suit yourself. Bye, Brenda. Love you."

"Love you back."

John escorted Mimi to her car in silence. When they stopped in front of the car, John turned Mimi around. "Why are you acting like a jealous girlfriend? Can't you be happy for us? That woman has nothing but love for you."

"I'm not jealous, John. I'm a happily married woman. You know that."

"I want to believe what you say, but your actions say otherwise."

"Don't misinterpret what's not there, John. I love Raphael. Okay, part of me was jealous, as I realized our time had truly passed. It wasn't that I wanted you. I was in love with the illusion that my first true love would be by my side whenever I needed him."

"Is that fair? You were using me like one of your trinkets...one of your bangles that you pick up when it fits your purpose...when you want some special adornment for your arm. I'm better than that."

"Not quite like that, John."

"I got the picture, Mimi. Take your bangles off; I'm in love with Brenda for keeps."

"I can see that, John, and I'm truly happy for you. Good night."

JOHN OPENED and held the door for Mimi until she was safely inside. He watched as she drove away without even a cursory glance back. At another time and space, he would've gladly taken Mimi in his arms and made love to her. Even when he saw her for the first time after she had disappeared into thin air nineteen years earlier, leaving him alone and hurt, he wanted her. John had allowed his male intuitiveness to get in the way of clear thinking even after Mimi told him she was married. Mimi was partly to blame because she teased him, but then the big, bad wolf Colonel came home when Afrika was shot by Victor and all that changed.

John was now in love with Brenda. Mimi was past tense. For the first time in a long time, he was truly happy. When Mimi's taillights were no longer visible, John walked back into the house so that he could wrap his arms around the only woman he cared about.

CHAPTER FIFTY-NINE

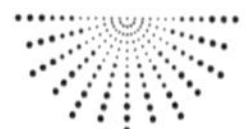

So much had happened in a week. Asia was now the recipient of the news that she and John were engaged. Brenda laughed to herself when she registered Asia's reaction, which was hesitant and nonchalant. In the end, Brenda convinced Asia that she wasn't on the rebound and that John was her true soul mate.

Sheila's funeral was grander than anyone could've imagined. Many of North Carolina Central University's staff came out in support of her. Sprays of flowers and plants filled the church, and the testimonials painted Sheila as a loving and wonderful colleague, although not one soul came around to see about her when she really needed a friend. Jamal must have come into some money. He acted like he was king for a day, sporting a brand-new suit that Brenda was sure cost more than two or three-hundred dollars. Jamal never asked Brenda for any help. In fact, Brenda had to track him down to get information about the funeral. She and Mimi surmised that Jamal had been waiting for Sheila to die. He'd get his.

She and Mimi had made amends, although Mimi

seemed reserved when she was around her. Brenda wanted to believe that it was due to Mimi being caught up in producing her album that was going to put her on the map. Mimi was back in New York and whatever was bothering her, Brenda wasn't going to waste any more time worrying about it. All her time would be devoted to Trevor's defense and her man. She loved John more than anyone knew. She was truly free to love.

CHAPTER SIXTY

Press kits promoting Azilet Records' new recording artist littered television's mainstream circuit. Yohan was overwhelmed with the schedule of appearances he had already garnered for Mimi's debut. Her single, "Satisfied" had only been out a week and already two-hundred and fifty-thousand copies had been sold—something unheard of for a relatively new artist. "Satisfied" received airplay in every major and local city across the U.S., and the timing of Mimi's appearances on daytime's premier news shows would certainly put Mimi in contention for a Grammy.

Photo shoots and a music video further promoting Mimi's single were on track. Mimi couldn't believe the grueling schedule that was before her, but she didn't mind. If she wanted to succeed in the industry, and indeed she did, there was no time for whining. Mimi was going to give it all she had.

Mimi couldn't believe that tomorrow she would be a guest on *Good Morning America* and after that fly out to California for a stint on *Jimmy Kimmel Live.* Mimi loved all the attention she was getting—the flowers, candy, and personal gifts from Yohan who had been on his best behavior, but remained grounded knowing all could end at the snap of a finger.

Today, Minx was going to take her around to look for a small apartment to rent while she stayed in New York. She had been in the city for more than a month and was tired of hotel living. Finding a spot away from all the hustle and bustle of hotel life and always bumping into people she didn't know would afford her to live a more private life, such as it was, now that her song and the face behind it were becoming a noticeable commodity. Mimi wondered if this was the life she really wanted—all the glitz and glamour and having to be beautiful twenty-four seven for the public.

For a moment, Mimi allowed herself to crawl back to Durham. She smiled at the thought that Brenda and John were not only an item, they were in love and engaged to be married. They'd moved on without her; they'd become best friends. And Mimi felt abandoned. That's why New York was where she wanted to be at the present time, and her busy schedule kept her mind occupied.

Mimi jumped at the sound of the telephone ringing in her room.

"Hey, Mimi, I'm downstairs."

"Okay, Minx, I'll be right down. I don't understand why you won't come up to the room."

"Do you really want me to answer that question?"

"It wasn't a question, but I don't think I want to know the answer if indeed you perceived it as one. Anyway, I want you to have a key to my room in case of an emergency."

"All right, if you insist. Now bring yourself on down

here. I've got several places to show you; I'm sure you're going to love them. With the advance you received, it's affordable."

"Okay. See you in a minute."

She was blessed to have someone in her corner, looking out for her welfare. She also appreciated how he respected her space and hadn't once tried to hit on her, even though he was a good friend of Raphael's. Mimi brushed her hand over the lycra-knit surface of her sundress that dropped to a low V and grabbed the curvature of her breasts. The dress had splatters of an orange and gold design on a pink background and hit two inches above her knee. Her manicured toenails were painted orange and accented the pink, sling-back sandal that helped make her dress sizzle.

MIMI WAS anxious to see the apartments that Minx selected to show her. When she reached the lobby, he had the day's paper in his lap, pouring over the contents of whatever he was reading. Although Mimi was attracted to bald men, she loved Minx's dreads. When he was in casual dress, he looked so Neapolitan, and when he was dressed in one of his rich two-piece suits, he looked like cake tasted—uhm, uhm good.

Minx looked up from the paper when Mimi walked up. He gave her the once over and seemed to approve. "I like your dress."

"It's compliments of one of my shopping sprees."

Minx took another look. "My car is in the garage; I'll go and get it. Wait outside."

Mimi put on her shades and waited at the entrance of

the hotel for Minx. She smiled when he pulled up in his shiny, black Benz. It began to dawn on her that she would no longer be obscure but a celebrity. At that moment, that was how she felt—like a celebrity.

Hopping into the car, Mimi couldn't resist palming the smooth, buttery, leather interior. She was sitting in the lap of luxury at its best. Minx hid behind his shades, and they looked like a celebrity couple headed for the Hamptons.

"I see you like my ride," Minx joked, giving Mimi a light fist pound on her knee.

"Very nice. Turn on the radio."

Minx hit a button and the radio was blaring. "Girl, listen to that. That's the introduction to your song. You have arrived."

"Yes!" Mimi screamed. "Woke up early this morning...on top of the world, lying next to my baby feeling satisfied. Last night he wrapped me...in the well of his arms. Made love to me and I'm feeling so, so satisfied."

"You're singing that song, girl."

"Shhh, Minx. Let me finish singing. Can you believe they are playing my song for all of New York?"

"Yes, I can. Now sing."

"With love like that you can't ignore the passion that's between us. He's the man for me and I can truly see that our love is gonna last. Satisfied, satisfied, satisfied, yeah, yeah, yeah, yeah; I'm so, so, satisfied."

CHAPTER SIXTY-ONE

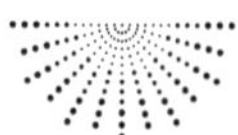

Minx inched his way through the streets of Manhattan, finally able to navigate his way out of the snarl of traffic. Mimi popped her fingers to the music still excited about hearing her voice on the airways. The July sun beamed through the car windows and warmed Mimi's heart the more.

"You better get that," Minx said, as Mimi ignored her cell phone whose ring was almost louder than the music.

"They can wait; I'm feeling satisfied," Mimi said, as she laughed at her attempt to signify about her song.

"It must be important. They aren't letting up."

Mimi looked at the caller ID. "It's my baby. I've got to get this." Minx turned the volume down on the radio. "Hey, Afrika, how's my baby doing?"

"Mommy, I heard you on the radio. You sound so good."

"You mean they are playing my single in Raleigh? Yes. How did it sound?"

"Mommy, you did it; you were rocking it. I had no idea your voice could sound so smooth on the radio. I'm on a campaign right now to get all of my friends to download it to their iPods."

"You are so sweet. I love you."

"Oh, I got a letter from Daddy. He's ready to come home. He lost two of his soldiers."

"Oh, that's terrible. I worry about him all the time. I hope he comes home soon. How do you think he's going to feel about your mother being a star?"

"Daddy was always down with your singing. He may not care about you running all over the country, but I'm sure he'll be cool with it when you bring home that big bank account. Why don't you send him a video message singing your new hit?"

"That's a plan. I haven't talked to him in a couple of weeks. I've been busy. I'm going to work on that video tonight. Right now, I'm out shopping for a place to live while I'm in New York."

"How long are you planning on staying out there? Aren't you almost finished recording your album?"

"It takes time, Afrika. I'm tired of living out of a hotel room, and I hope to get something I can lease for at least a year so that while I'm in New York, I can rest my head in the comfort of my own place."

"That sounds cool, Mommy. Maybe I can come and visit on one of my breaks."

"I would love that, baby. Do you want to come next week?"

"Mommy, school starts in a few weeks. I really need to get ready for that. Asia and I are going to stay in the apartment and live off campus. I'm going to get a job so I can help out with the rent."

"I've lost track of time. Of course, you've got to get ready for school. I don't think it's a good idea for you to work. I want you to concentrate on your studies. I'll help you with your half of the rent."

"No, Mommy. I'm going to work and pay my fair share. My studies are going to be fine. I promise I won't let nothing interfere. Oh, in case you forgot, Trevor's trial is about to start. You may want to give Mrs. Christianson a call."

"Afrika, you've always been my conscience. I haven't seemed like a good friend to Brenda lately…"

"Mommy, she understands that you're recording. She's happy for you."

Mimi smiled. She didn't want to say to Afrika that she'd been selfish when it came to Brenda because she was still a wee bit jealous of her and John. But in truth, she had a record that was on its way to the top and she'd been very busy working on the other songs that were to go on her album. "I'll call her. I've got to run now, sweetheart. I'll come home next week to help you get everything straight for school."

"Okay. Keep doing your thing, Mommy. Love you."

"Love you, too. Bye."

Minx looked over at Mimi when she had finished her phone call. "Beautiful."

"What are you talking about?"

"Your relationship with your daughter. You seem so in tune with her."

"Minx, my daughter is everything to me. Raphael and I have given her all the best tools to be a successful young lady, and she hasn't proven us wrong. She received good grades in her first year in college, despite the setback when she was shot and had to take time to recover."

"Shot?"

"Yes, her biological father tried to kill her. He tried

everything within his power to get rid of me and Afrika so that his wife, my best friend, wouldn't find out that he had raped me and fathered a child. He didn't know anything about Afrika until we returned to Durham, against my better judgment, but Afrika wanted to go to school there."

"Damn. So, you mean to say that the son-of-a-bitch tried to kill his own child?"

"Yeah, that's what I mean. After I told Raphael, he came home on the first thing smoking and took charge. He almost got himself killed at the hands of that crazy man."

"As crazy as Raphael is, it's hard to believe he'd let any man put his hands on him. I always said the military was the best place for him."

"He went crazy all right. Nobody was going to harm his daughter and get away with it. One of these days, I'm going to write a novel about my life and all that's happened. Anyway, Victor, my daughter's biological father was killed by his son. His trial is coming up soon, and I need to go and support his mother."

"Dang, baby, you've been through a lot."

"It hasn't been easy. I betrayed a lot of people along the way, keeping my secret from people I thought it would harm. I felt so bad that I hadn't shared with Raphael that I had been raped and was carrying that baby when I met him. He was furious when he found out, but because of our love for each other, we've survived the worst of it. Sometimes I wonder if he really forgave me."

"I'm sure you worry is in vain. That man loves you, and you know it. Okay, we're at our first stop. Let's redirect our energies and find you a place to stay."

"I'm ready."

CHAPTER SIXTY-TWO

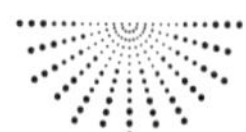

Excitement about having a place of her own thrilled Mimi to no end. She wasn't exactly ready to pay the cost to live in Manhattan, although there wasn't anything keeping her from looking elsewhere, however, the feel it gave her to live on the edge of the city made her redirect her thinking. After all, she had a million dollars at her disposal.

She and Minx viewed three studios and several one and two-bedroom apartments. The prices ranged from twenty-six hundred dollars to three-thousand dollars a month for a studio and from the low three-thousand for a one-bedroom apartment to seven-thousand dollars for a two-bedroom apartment. She'd fare better if she chose to go to Secaucus, New Jersey, but she liked the sound of New York as a residence.

"So, did you see any place you want to call home?" Minx asked. "All of this running around has made a brother hungry."

"It would be more prudent to get a little studio in

Jersey, but without a car, I'd rather take a place in the city where I have easy access to everything."

"Sounds like you've at least settled on the area. Now you've got to decide on the place. I saw you eyeing that cute number at 5th Avenue and 31st Street."

"I liked Tower 31. I can get a studio and lease the place for six months or a year if they'd let me."

"It was very nice. Easy for me to stop by and scoop you up every now and then for dinner and a movie."

Mimi laughed. "You are so smooth. I didn't see that coming."

"I didn't mean to scare you. Just letting you know I'm there for you."

"Okay, Minx. I'm going to make an offer at the Tower. I'm ready for privacy. Before we go to lunch, I need to stop by the hotel for a minute."

"Sounds good to me. Oh, oh, there's your song again, Mimi. Let me turn it up."

"Woke up early this morning...on top of the world, lying next to my baby feeling satisfied…yeah, yeah, yeah."

MIMI SECURED a temporary residence in New York and felt like she could now get lost in her new sanctuary. When she had to deal with the real world, she'd fly back to Durham and catch up on the hum-drum lives of her best friend and her new fiancé and make sure that Afrika had what she needed.

Minx pulled into the guest drop-off spot at the hotel. "How long are you going to be?" he asked Mimi.

"A few minutes. I'm going to change my clothes and

put on something a little warmer since we'll probably be in the night air."

"I'll park and wait for you at the bar. Don't take too long."

Minx parked his car, went into the hotel, and sat at the bar. He ordered a gin and tonic and sipped while he waited for Mimi to return. In the meantime, he watched all the fascinating people who popped in and out of the hotel, some of whom he recognized.

Out of the corner of his eyes, he thought he saw Yohan ease by him. Minx jumped from his seat and rushed to see where Yohan was going. Yohan stopped at the elevators and waited for one to open. "What in the hell is Yohan doing here?" Minx asked out loud.

Minx scratched his head and continued to nurse his drink as he watched Yohan get in the next available elevator. Minx checked his watch and decided to give Mimi a few more minutes to show herself. Parking himself in one of the plush seats in the lobby, Minx waited while time ticked away.

THE KNOCK on the door startled Mimi. Before she gave it a second thought, she reached for the door handle and pulled it open. "So, you changed your mind about waiting downstairs," Mimi said, her back turned to the door as she picked up a pair of linen pants off the bed.

"So, this is how you and Minx roll."

Startled, Mimi jumped and turned around at the sound of his voice. "What are you doing here, Yohan?"

"Would you like for me to help you out of your dress?"

"No thank you. And for your information, Minx is downstairs waiting for me to come down any moment. If I don't show up soon, he'll be up here."

"And I'm afraid of your boyfriend."

"He's not my boyfriend."

"Well then, there's nothing to worry about. I stopped by to congratulate you. Your new single is number one on the charts."

"What!" Mimi exclaimed, letting her guard down. "Are you serious, Yohan?"

Yohan advanced and placed the bottle of wine he'd been carrying on the desk. "You, Mimi, are number one—our new star."

"I can't believe it." Mimi fell into Yohan's outstretched arms to give him a hug. Before Mimi could push away, Yohan pulled her all the way into his arms and kissed her full force on the lips. And as if some kind of centrifugal force guided Yohan's hands, he cupped her buttocks and squeezed tight. Mimi tried to pull away, but Yohan held her, pushing his body up against hers. He grabbed the zipper on the back of her dress and pulled it the rest of the way down and with one swift flick of his wrist, yanked the dress off her shoulders and then let it slide to the floor.

"Leave me alone and get the hell out of here!" Mimi shouted.

Yohan covered Mimi's mouth with one hand and picked her up with the other and threw her on the bed. With all that she had, Mimi pounded Yohan's chest, but he seemed oblivious to it. He pulled her legs apart and fell on top of her, grinding his body into hers. Yohan put his mouth on hers in an attempt to keep her quiet and with his hands he tore off her bra and began to squeeze her nipples until they were erect. Mimi tossed and turned but couldn't move Yohan off her. Then he took her nipples one at a time and suckled them while Mimi continued to kick and thrash about, and then he raised up to pull down the zipper to his pants.

"Help!" Mimi screamed. "Help me somebody." Yohan slapped her in the face. "Help me," she whimpered.

Yohan kissed Mimi's lips, allowing his tongue to travel down her neck, and she fought him tooth and nail. Tired of the fight, Yohan lifted his body up slightly and slid his pants and boxers down over his hips and pushed Mimi's legs further apart. Just as Yohan tried to enter her, he yelled and fell back.

Minx kicked Yohan in the side until he fell to the floor. With the pointed toe of his shoe, Minx kicked Yohan again and took his heel and drop kicked him in the back until he lay flat on the floor panting, the carpet smothering his face. Mimi grabbed her chest, while mascara traveled down her face.

"Help me," Mimi whispered. She reached out one hand to Minx, while covering her breasts with the other. Minx sat on the bed next to her, pulled the comforter around her, and put his arm around her shoulders.

"It's all right, Mimi. I've got you. I'm going to throw this scum of the earth out of the room."

Panting, Mimi looked up at Minx. "How did you know?"

"I saw him come through the lobby, but I wasn't sure. When I saw him enter the elevator, I gave you ten minutes to come down. If you hadn't exited that elevator when the ten minutes had expired, I was going up. I remembered I had the extra room key, and I figured this might be the emergency."

"Thank you, Minx. I owe you."

"You don't owe me anything. I'm glad that I waited for you inside instead of sitting in the car."

Yohan began to stir.

"Put your damn pants on," Minx said, giving Yohan a swift kick on his naked butt.

"There's a price you pay for being number one," Yohan said in a raspy voice. "You're going to pay for this one."

"If this single is all I do," Mimi shouted at Yohan shaking her hand at him, "I'll be satisfied. I'm not going to compromise my life and that of my family to make a record. It isn't worth it. I won't sell my soul to have a hit, and no amount of money will change my mind."

"Well consider yourself a one-hit wonder," Yohan said, as he finally got up from the floor and pulled up his pants. "You weren't that good anyway."

"Think again," Minx said. "I can call the cops now. Attempted rape wouldn't look good on your resume. Howard Austin won't take too kindly to one of his artists being mistreated, especially by his partner. Howard and I go way back, and if Mimi's album gets messed up in the fray, your tail won't see the light of day."

"You don't scare me, Minx. Your girlfriend's time is short at Azilet Records."

"That may be, but there will be somebody else to pick her up. Now get your sorry ass out of this room, and don't you ever come near or touch Mimi again. Next time, I'll kill you."

Yohan snatched his bottle of wine off the dresser. He looked back at Mimi. "You probably couldn't please me anyhow." He hobbled out of the room.

"You bastard," Mimi screamed after him. After the door closed behind Yohan, Mimi looked up at Minx. "I'm going to call the police and have him arrested. Years ago, I made the same mistake and nineteen years later the rapist tried to kill my daughter. I'm through, Minx. I can't do this."

"What about your career, Mimi? It's just getting started."

"I have a husband and a daughter who love me. I've conquered my dream, Minx. Now it's time to go home and take care of my family. I'm cancelling the contract on that studio."

"You have a million-dollar advance."

"Wow, was it really worth it? I'll give the money back if I have to or honor my commitment so long as Yohan is out of the picture. Give me the phone. I've got to make this call."

CHAPTER SIXTY-THREE

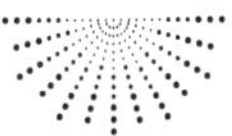

Brenda paused in front of the mirror as she put the finishing touches on her face. She wore her lightweight, brown-tweed, wool suit and a burnt-orange chiffon blouse underneath the jacket with a collar that Brenda tied into a nice bow. Today was the first day of Trevor's trial and her nerves were on edge.

John had been her rock of Gibraltar, and she wouldn't have made it if he hadn't been by her side. Attorney Reynaldo Aziza assured Brenda that everything was under control and that he was going to present the best defense for Trevor. Although Brenda made several visits to the prison to see Trevor who seemed to be in somewhat good spirits, it didn't make what she knew lay ahead any easier to endure.

Brenda picked up her MAC Cosmo lipstick and colored her lips. Still looking at herself in the mirror, she thought back to Michael Jackson's trial and how his mother, Katherine, was at the courthouse every day in support of her son. It had been a media circus covered by local and national news, and Brenda was sure that the international media may have been caught up in the celebrity of it all as well. But Trevor had killed someone—his father, and he was being tried for Murder I. Michael, on the other hand, was tried for child molestation, although the brutal battle he faced in court was surely as painful for his mother as what Brenda was about to go through.

The doorbell rang. Brenda heard Asia's voice as she opened the door to let John in. They were going to the courthouse as a unified group in support of each other.

"I'll be right down," Brenda shouted. She picked up her brown, gator bag and looked around the room...the room she once shared with her husband, whose death was the central focus of their son's trial. The more Brenda thought about it, she wanted to pull Victor from the grave and spit on him, curse his name, and slap him back down to his final resting place. If he hadn't been a fornicating, slithering snake-in-the grass his ass would still be in the land of the living and Trevor would be beginning his first year of college. That wouldn't happen for Trevor, even if he was exonerated. If Trevor's verdict turns out to be self-defense, he still killed a man, and no college would accept him onto their campus.

John was standing at the bottom of the stairs like a dutiful soon-to-be husband when Brenda finally exited her room and began her descent down the stairs. "Hey, baby," she said softly, trying to keep the tears at bay that threatened to disturb her make-up.

"Hey, yourself. You look like you're dressed to root for the winner."

"Trevor is going to win," Brenda said softly, looking

from John to Asia who stood quietly by. "I believe in Aziza, and I feel good about his course of action. I hate that Trevor has to endure this at all. Is Afrika coming?"

"She's with her mother," Asia said.

"You mean in New York?"

"No, Mrs. Bailey is in Durham. She came home suddenly, and Afrika has been mum about things, although whatever it is, she seems pretty upset about it. Something happened in New York is all I could gather from the brief conversation Afrika had with me. She's been staying with her mother for the past few nights."

"Her single came out," John interjected. "I have to say it's pretty hot."

"I think it's on the way to the top," Brenda added. "Well, Mimi isn't our priority today; Trevor is." Brenda sighed. "If you all are ready, I'm ready to go."

"I want to say a little pray for Trevor, if you don't mind," Asia said. The trio locked arms and Asia asked God to oversee the trial and allow Trevor to come home.

THE COURTROOM WAS FULL, much to Brenda's surprise. She recognized some of Victor's colleagues. They were probably there to be nosey so they could run back and spread the court proceedings all over North Carolina Central University's campus. Brenda refused to lock eyes with any one of them, especially the women, as anyone could've been Victor's mistress at one time or another. And then Brenda's face glowed when she saw her sisters march in, and she motioned for them to come and sit by her.

The back door of the courtroom opened and the bailiff escorted Trevor to his seat. He was dressed in a charcoal gray suit that Brenda had brought over for him to wear to the trial. His feet and hands were still shackled but were relaxed once he sat comfortably next to his attorney. Aziza seemed to reassure Trevor that he was prepared to do battle—of course the ultimate goal to see him freed from prison. Reynaldo Aziza was suited down in a whispering-blue piece of fabric that had to come from one of the best men's dress shops in the city. He looked like power and Brenda hoped he would wield it.

"All rise," said the bailiff, "The Honorable Judge Andrew Builder presiding." The judge, a rather pudgy man, slow dragged to his seat.

Judge Builder was an older African-American man who'd sat on the bench for more than thirty years. Brenda recalled meeting him and his wife at several civic functions, and he seemed nice enough. However, he gave no clue to how he felt about the case before him, neither looking at Trevor or the sequestered jury, although it was hard to ascertain anything through the lenses of his large, horned-rimmed glasses. Prosecuting Attorney, Nola White, the lead attorney for the State, sat smug in her seat confident that the verdict had already been decided in her favor. But it wouldn't be until later in the week when Aziza presented his defense that Nola and her team would have a true picture of what they were up against.

The judge woke up the crowd with the sound of his gavel and addressed the jury before he turned the questioning over to the prosecution who presented the obvious. Trevor had killed Victor. There was no denying that as Trevor had confessed to as much.

Nola White brought up several key experts or what

they called witnesses for the prosecution who reported that Trevor had killed Victor with a thirty-two caliber gun that belonged to a close friend of his mother's, Mrs. Setrine "Mimi" Bailey, who was at the hospital with her daughter at the time of the murder. The reporting detective stated that Trevor had gun residue on his hands; that Trevor confessed to killing his father, Mr. Victor Christianson; and that Trevor had motive for killing his father, which was none other than pure unadulterated hate due to what he'd learned about his father's adulterous affairs.

Brenda watched the jury as they stared her son down, some writing notes on pieces of paper they had in their laps. And she watched as the prosecution showed each member of the jury the crime scene photos—Victor lying in a pool of blood in Mimi's Lexus, with several wounds to his chest.

Trevor leaned his head on his hands and wouldn't look in the jury's direction. Aziza whispered something in his ear, and Trevor sat up straight and appeared to only look straight ahead. Off in one corner, a sketch artist was busily sketching a charcoal likeness of Trevor in what appeared to be his moment of distress.

Aziza didn't make any objections to the prosecutions statements at first as Nola simply stated the case as she believed it to be, but Aziza became unglued when the prosecution suggested that Trevor was a thug due to his association with Freddie whose mother was a known junkie. When Trevor saw his father and Freddie's mother together, Trevor lost it and blew Victor away.

"Objection, your honor, this is fabrication at its best. The prosecution is trying to sway the jury without the benefit of the truth. The detective has no knowledge as to why Trevor was there in the first place; he's merely speculating."

"Objection sustained. Please strike the question," Judge Builder said.

And that was the end of the first day.

CHAPTER SIXTY-FOUR

Day two of the trial was a blur for Brenda. They—she, John, Asia, and Brenda's sisters, Mable and Tracey—sat through another day of expert witnesses for the prosecution that included a fingerprint expert, a psychologist, the coroner, and the police officer who was one of the first responders to the crime scene. Trevor sat in his seat staring straight ahead without any movement. In late afternoon, the prosecution finally rested its case.

It was time for the defense and Attorney Reynaldo Aziza, dressed in a charcoal-grey, pinstripe Armani suit and a pair of polished, grey Stacy Adams on his feet, stepped before the jury and addressed them. His good looks, the product of his Puerto Rican and African-American heritage, made the female jurors swoon. Brenda watched how they stared when Aziza stood in front of them, looking as if they were vying for his attention. Even Nola White's crossed legs got a little excited when Aziza eclipsed her view of the jury, which she didn't seem to mind at all.

Aziza began by stating that the burden of proof was on

the State to prove that his client, Trevor Christianson, killed Victor Christianson in cold blood. Aziza stated that the State hadn't proved it beyond a shadow of a doubt and that he would prove otherwise. Aziza further stated that he had several witnesses to Victor Christianson's character—the kind of man he'd become—a liar, rapist, adulterer, an attempted murderer, and to some the scum of the earth. He had many affairs with other women outside of his marriage to Brenda Christianson.

"Several key witnesses are no longer with us as they are now deceased having contracted the Aids virus from Victor Christianson, and we, the defense will show that his careless and wayward acts of infidelity were the cause of their deaths. We will show that Victor Christianson provoked his murder and that his death was an act of self-defense.

"Judge Builder, I would like to ask for a recess until tomorrow morning so that we can have a fresh start with my battery of witnesses."

Judge Builder looked over the top of his glasses at Aziza. He picked up his gavel and brought it down with a thud. "So, granted. We will resume testimony tomorrow at eight a.m. sharp!" *Rap, rap.*

Brenda liked Reynaldo Aziza's style. He cut to the chase and didn't waste time on theorizing, just gave the facts plain and simple. And it was the plain and simple facts of the case the prosecution had yet to see.

CHAPTER SIXTY-FIVE

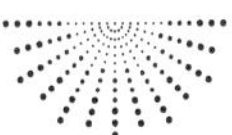

The trial had now entered its third day, and Attorney Reynaldo Aziza presented his case for the defense. Trevor sat at attention, waiting for Aziza to work his magic. The courtroom was packed—a full house with standing room only, and Brenda saw him smile, almost flirting with justice.

The noise level in the courtroom died after the jury took their seats and the bailiff stood off to one side in his imposing manner. "All rise, The Honorable Judge Andrew Builder presiding."

Judge Builder pushed his way to his seat as he had done the previous two days and rapped the gavel on the desk to begin the proceedings. He pushed his glasses down on the bridge of his nose, as he eyed the day's material sitting on his desk. Judge Builder sat back as Aziza stood up.

"I'd like to call as my first witness Setrine 'Mimi' Bailey," Reynaldo said, waiting for Mimi to come down the aisle so he could escort her to her seat.

Brenda jerked her head around and was overcome with

emotion as Mimi marched to the stand, swore to tell the truth, and nothing but the truth. Brenda drew her hand to her chest elated that her best friend was a witness for the defense. Whispered conversations could be heard throughout the courtroom, some recognizing Mimi as the singer of that sensational new single entitled "Satisfied."

Rap, rap, rap, went Judge Builder's gavel. The whispers subsided and the crowd waited for the questions that would be asked of the first witness.

"Mrs. Bailey, what is your relationship to the Christianson family?"

"Brenda Christianson is my best friend," Mimi stated matter-of-fact. She looked in Brenda's direction and gave her a big smile. "We've been best friends since junior high school."

"So, it seemed to be a natural course of action that you both went to the same college upon graduation from high school."

"Yes, we were inseparable."

Nola White, dressed in a black and white suit and black pumps, jumped to her feet. "I object, Your Honor. What does this witness' relationship with the deceases' wife some twenty years ago have to do with Victor Christianson's murder?"

"I'm getting there," Aziza said. "It is very relevant."

"Overruled. Aziza, let's take the shortcut to where it's relevant," Judge Builder said. "I don't plan to be here all day."

"Yes, Your Honor. Mrs. Bailey, is it not true that twenty years ago Victor Christianson raped you in a college dorm and as a result a child was conceived?"

Mimi sighed. She put her head down. Brenda could tell Mimi was reliving the day all over again. "Yes, Victor

Christianson raped me. I didn't tell Brenda because I was ashamed and I wasn't sure how she would react if I told her."

"What did you do instead?"

"I withdrew from school without telling anyone. It wasn't until my daughter wanted to go to the college I attended nineteen years prior where that awful thing happened to me did I return to Durham, North Carolina."

"And did you let your daughter attend the college where you still have those awful memories?"

"I did everything I could to discourage her from wanting to go to NCCU, but she was a very persistent young lady, and I opted to let her go."

"What happened once your daughter entered college at NCCU?"

"She met and became friends with my best friend's daughter, although I didn't know it at the time. When I first saw Asia Christianson, I knew right away that she was Victor's daughter; she looked so much like my own. And when Victor found out I was in town, he harassed and threatened me and told me to get out of town or else."

"Why was it imperative that you leave town?"

"He was married to my best friend, and he knew that if Brenda and I had any contact, the truth of my daughter's conception might come out, although he had nothing to fear from me. I had every intention of carrying my secret to the grave."

"Mrs. Bailey, you didn't leave Durham. What happened since you didn't heed Victor Christianson's warnings…threats?"

"He tried to kill my daughter—our daughter." There was a gasp from the crowd. "He shot her in the back and she was in the hospital for over a month."

There was another loud gasp and roar from the crowd. "Victor also tried to kill my husband on the night that he was killed. My husband had gone to the Christianson's home in search of Victor to confront him about what he had done to our daughter. Victor wasn't home, and when Raphael, my husband, got back into the car, Victor was hiding inside. Victor ordered my husband to drive while he pointed a gun at his head."

"Where is your husband now?"

"He is in Afghanistan serving his country."

"We appreciate what he's doing for our country, as well as all the men and women in the armed forces. Can you tell me whose gun Victor was holding against your husband's head, Mrs. Bailey?"

"It was my gun. It was in my car as protection from Victor. I have a permit to carry it."

"So, what happened to your husband the night Victor was murdered?"

"My husband was hijacked. Victor had him to drive to a housing project in Durham. When Raphael got an opportunity to escape he did. He called me and told me what happened and asked that I pick him up. Raphael was unaware of what happened to Victor after he ran."

"Thank you, Mrs. Bailey. That will be all for now."

"Ms. White, will there be any cross-examination of this witness?"

Nola White stood up and approached the box where Mimi sat. "Yes, Your Honor." Nola sized Mimi up. "Mrs. Bailey, do you make it a habit of carrying a gun in your car?"

"No. I'd just purchased it and had picked it up that very day. I didn't have time to take it into the house, as I was in a hurry to be with my daughter who was in the hospital."

"So, it's safe to say that Victor's murder might not have occurred if that gun hadn't been in the car."

"I can't answer that Ms. White," Mimi said with anger in her eyes. "It wasn't my gun Victor used when he shot my daughter, his biological daughter, in the back."

"That's all," Nola said and returned to her seat.

"You may step down," Judge Builder said.

Mimi managed a smile for Brenda when she passed her on the way to her seat. She was visibly upset.

"Your next witness?" Judge Builder asked.

"I'd like to call Afrika Bailey to the stand," Aziza said.

Reynaldo asked Afrika about the day she was shot by Victor and when she realized that he was her biological father. "I hated him," Afrika cried, looking in Asia's direction then quickly away as the tears fell in torrents at the memory of what Victor had done to her.

"One more question, Ms. Bailey," Reynaldo said. "Once you learned that Victor Christianson was your father, how did you feel?"

"I felt betrayed by my mother and hated him even more because he tried to kill me. What kind of person attempts to kill their own child? And then I learned that he had children by other women that weren't by Mrs. Christianson. There was no way that I could ever call him my father."

"That's all, Ms. Bailey," Aziza said.

"You may step down, dear," the judge instructed. "I hope this line of questioning will in some way be helpful to your defense. At the present, I don't see it." Nola White exposed all her pearly white teeth, ejecting a smile that crawled the width of her face.

"It will, Your Honor. I'm establishing that more than Trevor Christianson had a motive to kill Victor Christianson."

"And your next witness?"

"I'd like to call Virginia Green to the stand," Aziza said.

A tall, lanky, brown woman, with glistening legs that were stuck in a five-inch pair of stilettos that hiked the already short dress up even further, sashayed down the aisle. She raised her hand and swore to tell the truth, nothing but the truth, so help her God before climbing the six-inch step up to the witness box. Reynaldo asked her about her relationship with the deceased Victor Christianson and about the hideaways, cruises, condos, jewelry, furs, and clothes he bought for her during their three-year tryst. Ms. Green was followed by ten other former mistresses of Victor, who all told a semblance of the same story of how a married Victor had wined and dined them, made love to them, bought them designer shoes, purses, and clothes and how they didn't have to want for anything until Victor got tired and was on to his next conquest.

Brenda was disgusted and didn't want to sit through another detail of Victor-the-slut's encounters with his whores. In fact, at that moment, she wanted to stab Reynaldo with a fork, as he seemed to derive pleasure from making these women divulge their appetite for Victor and all he did for them. It was bad enough that Ms. Prosecutor, Nola White, raised more than twenty objections that were overruled by the judge. She wanted to puke. Her sisters, Mable and Tracey, reached over and rubbed her back, hoping to assuage some of the pain the testimonies had created. "Get to the point," Brenda said under her breath.

"As our last witness," Reynaldo said, pacing the floor and taking his time in announcing the name of the next witness, "I'd like to call Freddie Slater to the stand." For the first time, Trevor turned his head to see Freddie walk down the aisle, almost as if this was the first time he was interested in what was going on with his case.

CHAPTER SIXTY-SIX

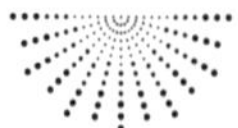

Freddie took his time coming down front. Trevor began to squirm in his seat as he watched Freddie go through the ritual of being sworn in. A thin veil of sweat began to cover Trevor's face as he stared at Freddie who had yet to give Trevor a cursory glance.

The fear on Freddie's face was so transparent that Aziza stopped to ask him if he was all right. Freddie fidgeted in his seat and couldn't seem to keep still. His eyes danced around the courtroom but still failed to make contact with Trevor's. The prying eyes of the jury seemed to wait heartlessly, like a school of carnivorous Piranha fish set to eat their prey. Freddie hadn't attended the trial the previous two days and seemed uncomfortable at his place on the witness stand. His brother, Zavion, was also in the courtroom, and Freddie locked eyes on him for comfort.

Asia turned around in her seat and spotted Zavion who was sitting next to his girlfriend. He looked past Asia, and she turned back around and stared straight ahead.

"Mr. Slater, please tell the court what your relationship is to the defendant," Reynaldo Aziza began.

Freddie sighed and put his hands underneath his chin. He looked up at Aziza and then away. And for the first time, he looked at Trevor. "Trevor and I went to the same high school. We both played basketball and began to hang out."

"So, you and Trevor had a good relationship—you were boys as they say…good friends?"

"Yes, we were good friends."

"Have you ever been to Trevor's house?"

"Yes."

"Did you ever meet Victor Christianson on any of the occasions that you were at Trevor's house?"

"No, Victor was never home during the times I was there. I've only been to Trevor's house maybe four times."

"I noticed that you called Mr. Christianson by his first name...as if he's familiar to you. Had you ever met Mr. Christianson prior to you and Trevor becoming friends?"

"Yes, briefly, but I never knew he was Trevor's father. In fact, I never even linked or gave it a thought that Trevor might be related to Mr. Christianson."

"May I ask how do you know Mr. Christianson?"

"I really didn't know him. He and…and my momma were seeing each other. I found out when I became a teenager that he was my biological father. He was just a man that was in and out of Momma's life, but he was never in my life."

"So, you didn't really have a relationship with your father."

"I don't have a father. My grandma raised me. My momma was a drug addict and the man who my momma said was my father didn't acknowledge me."

"What do you know about your mother and Mr. Christianson's relationship?"

"She said he was her boyfriend. He'd give her money for drugs and other stuff. He also treated her bad. He was mean to her, and sometimes she'd come to my grandma's house after he'd beat her up. But my momma would go back to him. She said she loved him, although he used her only for sex. He was Momma's cash flow for the drugs she craved. I wanted a father, but I wouldn't pick Victor Christianson to be it. If he was my father, why didn't he take me to the park or come to my pee-wee basketball and baseball games and spend time with me? Do you want to know why? Because he was a sorry ass son-of-a-bitch and didn't give a damn about me."

There was rumbling in the courtroom, and the transcriptionist recorded every word.

"Okay, son. Let's not resort to name calling. We understand how you feel," Aziza said.

"Do you? Do you really, sir? You weren't there when my momma was high on drugs and people would come and tell my grandma that she was lying out in the street. You weren't there during the few times she visited my brother and me and was so pissy drunk that she'd vomit on my grandma's carpet, fall asleep in the middle of the floor, and all we wanted was for her to go home. But I loved her."

"Where is your mother now?"

Freddie rolled his eyes and stared at Aziza as the tears began to form.

"Answer the question, son," Judge Builder admonished.

Freddie wiped the tears that crept down his face with

the back of his hand. His nostrils flared. "She's dead. She died of Aids."

"Did you know that Mr. Christianson also had Aids?"

"Not until I read it in the papers."

"Mr. Slater, let's go to the night Mr. Christianson was murdered. You and your good friend, Trevor, took a ride out to your mother's house. Am I correct?"

"Yes."

"Tell me, why did you go to your mother's house that evening?"

"My momma called me and said she needed some money. I told her that I didn't have a lot, but she insisted that she needed it and asked me to bring it to her."

"Being the dutiful son that you are, although your mother wasn't always the mother you needed her to be, you took her what money you had in your pocket."

"Yes, sir, I did."

"Objection, Your Honor," Nola White said, standing to her feet. "What does this line of questioning have to do with the defendant killing his father?"

"Your Honor, if I can continue with my questioning of this witness, I will show the court how it ties in."

"Objection overruled; let's get to the point, counselor," Judge Builder said.

"When you arrived at your mother's house, tell the court what happened."

With his fingers pressed together, Freddie brought them to the edge of his mouth. He had a vacant look on his face, and he took a chance and looked in Trevor's direction. All eyes were on Freddie as the courtroom observers waited to hear his answer.

"Trevor rode out with me to Momma's. She was in a halfway good mood once she saw that I had money in my hand. I gave her a hug and we hung out for a few minutes. Just as we were getting ready to leave, we heard a commotion outside.

"We peeped through the curtain in the front room and saw these two guys arguing. Then suddenly one of the men—the tall one—swiped at the other man knocking him down, and the tall man took off running. The other man got up, picked something off the ground, and headed toward my momma's house. I recognized him as my momma's so-called boyfriend. And he had a gun in his hand.

"He stormed through the front door without knocking and started cussing at my momma. She cussed back and told him to get his sorry ass out of her house unless he was dropping off some money. Victor Christianson called my momma every name in the book, and I won't repeat what he said. They were loud and cussed each other to high heaven. All of a sudden, Mr. Christianson saw Trevor."

"What happened then?"

"He asked Trevor what he was doing there. I asked Trevor if he knew Victor, and he said he was his father.

"Then my momma got mad and Victor slapped her. Then he started waving the gun in her face and told her that if she didn't shut up, he was going to pull the trigger and blow her brains out. My momma agitated that man, but I wasn't going to allow him to hit my momma again."

"So, what happened, Freddie? What happened after Mr. Christianson said he was going to kill your mother?"

"I was mad as hell, and then he hit her again because my momma wouldn't shut up. I grabbed the gun and pointed it at him."

"So, you were holding the gun...not Trevor?"

Freddie peered out into the audience in search of his brother, Zavion. There was definite tension on Freddie's face. He sat there without answering.

"Please answer the question, Freddie," Aziza encouraged.

Freddie let out a loud sigh. "Yes, I was holding the gun." There was a gasp from the crowd.

"Where was Trevor during all of this?"

"He was watching but I could tell he was angry at his father."

"And then what happened?" Aziza pushed.

"I cocked the gun and told Victor that I was going to blow his brains out if he hit my momma again. And Victor tried to charge me, and out of nowhere, Trevor tried to take the gun away from me, but it went off. I left the gun dangling in Trevor's hands. And we stood there and watched Victor fall to the floor." The crowd gasped and the sketch artist's hand was moving feverishly.

Trevor turned slightly and looked at his mother. Brenda had cupped her hands to her face and began to cry out loud. And then a frustrated Nola White jumped to her feet again.

"What is Aziza trying to pull here? This witness is not on trial; Trevor Christianson is."

"Hush, Ms. White," Judge Builder said. "I want to hear the rest of this. Continue Aziza. I'm not quite sure I like where this is going."

"Thank you, Your Honor," Aziza said. And Nola sat down frustrated, scribbling something on her legal pad.

"And when Victor Christianson fell to the floor what happened next?"

"Trevor was still holding the gun and my momma was

screaming and yelling to get him...Victor out of the house."

"Was he dead?"

"He didn't move and blood was oozing out. Whether he was or wasn't, Momma wanted him out of her house. She got a blanket and we dragged him to the car that was out front. Trevor didn't want to help, but Momma kept screaming so he finally helped me put Victor in the car. I think my momma had a clear moment because she threw me some gloves and told me to put them on. I drove the car to the railroad tracks, ditched it, and walked back to my momma's house. Trevor was traumatized."

"I'm going to ask this question as delicately as I can. Did you pull the trigger on the gun that killed Victor Christianson?"

Freddie went mum. He sat and stared into space and began to rock back and forth. Then he broke down. "I'm sorry, Trevor," Freddie said, as his body shook when he released the pent-up tension. He laid his arms on the wooden ledge that surrounded the witness stand and dropped his head on the top of his arms. Freddie's torso moved up and down in rapid succession as he cried out loud in the open courtroom. Even Aziza couldn't console him. Nola White sat back in her chair, along with her team, and watched as Freddie dismantled the State's case.

"Why didn't you tell the police what you told us this afternoon?"

Freddie lifted his head. "I was scared and since Trevor confessed, I wasn't going to say anything."

Judge Builder rapped his gavel on the podium. "This case has certainly taken a dramatic turn. Considering the testimony that was witnessed by this court, I remand Mr. Freddie Slater into the hands of the Sheriff's Office of

Durham County where he will be held over for trial. This case is dismissed. Mr. Trevor Christianson, you are free to go with time served." The judge rapped the gavel again, dismissed the jury, and left his post with his black robe only a blur. There was nothing left for the jury to debate.

Brenda was up on her feet as well as Asia, John, Mable, Tracey and other well-wishers. Brenda raised her hand high, thanking God for this victory. She had her moment of praise and then rushed to where Trevor stood next to Aziza who had his arm wrapped around her son's neck.

"Thank you, Reynaldo. I had faith in you, and this is a blessed day," Brenda said, giving him a great big hug.

"I told you I'd get the job done."

"You did it, although I'm curious to know if you've had an inkling for some time that Freddie was the actual killer."

Reynaldo blinked his eyes and shook his head discretely. This wasn't the time or the place to discuss the piece of evidence that unraveled the case.

Brenda hugged Trevor who couldn't believe his good fortune. He hugged his mother and cried tears of joy. Soon the whole clan joined them in celebration. "Thank You Lord for this day. I will always trust You," Brenda said out loud.

In the midst of their rejoicing, Brenda jerked her head around when she felt the tap on her shoulders. There stood Mimi, her best friend, and her daughter, Afrika. Mimi pulled Brenda to her and gave her a big hug and then did the same to Trevor. "God is good," Mimi said.

"After Trevor is processed out, I'm going to take everyone out to eat," John interjected as well-wishers continued to embrace Brenda and Trevor.

"You better have some deep pockets," Brenda's sister, Mable, said. "I'm famished after all of this."

"American Express, Visa, or Mastercard will take care of it," John replied. "I don't leave home without it." Everyone laughed.

Asia and Afrika hugged each other, grateful for Trevor's release and happy that they could move on with life. Asia whispered something in Afrika's ear, and they both turned around and looked out into the crowd that was dispersing. The subject of their discussion, Zavion, was nowhere to be seen. It was almost as if he had simply vanished into thin air.

CHAPTER SIXTY-SEVEN

It was a happy, jovial crowd. They filed into Maggiano's restaurant eight persons deep, still reminiscing about the outcome of Trevor's trial. Reynaldo decided not to join them as he had another commitment. Brenda's sister, Mabel, was the most animated as she re-enacted the scene of all the women who paraded down the aisle in four and five-inch heels to share their brief encounter with Victor.

"Did y'all see all of Victor's whores sashay down the aisle to the witness box like they were on a stroll?" Mable started in once the group had been seated. The ladies keeled over from laughter, while John and Trevor looked on.

"You're a mess, Mable," Brenda put in, choking on her own spit as she tried to control her laughter. "But that's exactly what they looked like. I mean to tell you they got those weaves tight for their day in court, though."

"They probably bought brand new suits and dresses for the occasion, too," Tracey added. "I don't understand what all of them hoes saw in Victor." Mable, Tracey, and Mimi doubled over with laughter.

Brenda noticed that the girls and Trevor weren't enjoying the little scenario that was playing out before them. "Are you guys all right?" Brenda asked, more so to Trevor than to Asia and Afrika.

Trevor didn't say a word. Asia reached over and rubbed Trevor's back.

"Let's talk about something else," Brenda said, quickly changing the subject. She tapped John on the arm.

"I still hated him," Trevor said, his anger evident and transparent. "He deserved to die."

"Trevor," Brenda said, getting up from the table. "Your dad was a lot of things, but we don't wish death upon anyone regardless. You reap what you sow, and unfortunately, he got his."

"He disrespected you, Mom. He was a cheater, a liar, and a wannabe pimp. I was there and saw how he treated Freddie's mother even though she wasn't much to talk about."

"Why did you confess to the murder, Trevor? We could've avoided this whole ordeal as it concerned you."

"I was partly to blame. I did try to get the gun away from Freddie when it went off. I was traumatized, I guess. You weren't there when the bullet hit him and he fell to the ground. Blood was coming out of him, and I didn't do anything to help him."

Everyone at the table was mum, sitting on the edge of their seats. John got up and stood next to Brenda who put her arms around her son and held him from the rear. "Trevor, you're free to move on with your life now. You've been exonerated. You don't have to go back to that awful place ever again," Brenda said.

"We'll go to counseling with you, Trevor," Asia said. "You have your big sister to lean on for whatever you need." Asia hit Afrika in the arm. "In fact, you have two big sisters and we'll both be there for you."

"She's right, Trevor," Afrika interjected. She reached over Asia and squeezed Trevor's arm. "We've got you."

For the first time in the past twenty minutes, Trevor's countenance seemed to change. He looked up at his mother. "Thanks for believing in me, Mom."

"Baby, my faith in God is what pulled me through… what pulled this family through."

Trevor smiled and then he looked at Mimi. "Mrs. Bailey, I heard you have a dope song out."

Mimi's smile traveled clear across her face. "Wow, Trevor. Dope, for real?"

"I heard it on the radio, and I couldn't believe that my mother's best friend was doing it up. You sound as good, if not better than Beyoncé."

Everyone clapped for Mimi. "Thank you, Trevor. That was the nicest thing anyone could have said to me. Unfortunately, I don't think I'm cut out for the life of a superstar. You have to sacrifice too much for what you get." Tears began to fall from Mimi's eyes.

"What happened in New York, Mimi?" Brenda asked.

Mimi looked up and tried to compose herself. "Nothing."

Brenda watched Mimi thoughtfully. "We need to talk."

"There's nothing to talk about. Excuse me; I need to go and powder my nose. Afrika, order me a white wine when the waitress comes to take our order."

"I'll go with you, Mommy," Afrika said. Mimi waved her away and left to go to the restroom by herself.

Brenda got up from her seat. "I'm going to see about my friend. Something is definitely wrong." Brenda saw the frustration in Afrika's eyes and knew she was right. She headed for the restroom and when she stepped in, she could hear someone crying. She moved to the front of the stall where the noise came from. "Mimi, it's me, Brenda. What's wrong, baby? What happened?"

Mimi didn't say anything and Brenda pushed the door to the stall. It was locked. "Mimi, open the door." After a few minutes, Mimi unlocked the door and came out.

Mimi surveyed the empty room and began to speak. "I was raped…well, it was more of an attempted rape."

"Mimi, no. Who did this to you?"

"A record producer who was supposed to guide my career. Brenda, it seems that to survive in the entertainment industry, you must sell your soul and that includes having sex with god-awful people, doing drugs, and all kinds of things. I'm not cut out for that, and I'll be damned if I'll sacrifice my life with my family for a song."

"I hear you, girl. Good for you; I'm so proud of you for taking that stance. So, are you going to abandon the idea of singing professionally?"

"For now, I am. I did complete an album, but I'm not sure what's going to happen with it after leaving New York abruptly and calling off some scheduled commitments. However, I did something I should've done when I was raped the first time. I called the police and had Yohan—that's the record producer—arrested. No more hiding and no more secrets. I couldn't tell you when I first came home. It wasn't fair; you were dealing with your own trials. I'm so happy for Trevor." Mimi put her arms around Brenda, hugged her, and wouldn't let go.

"You know," Brenda began, continuing to hold Mimi

in an embrace, "you can start your own record label. Everybody is doing it."

"I haven't a clue about the business except for exercising my chops. All I want to do is sing."

Brenda moved back. "You can record "Free to Love" and we can pool our monies together and get it produced."

Mimi smiled. "You would do that for me, sis?"

"Yes, of course. That song tells our story—yours, mine, John's, Trevor's, Asia's, and Afrika's. Think about it, Mimi."

"I will." Mimi held her head down. "I sang it in a nightclub several weeks back. I led and the pianist followed and gave it a nice melody. I'll think about it. In fact, I can't; Azilet already recorded it and now has the rights to it, although I still have rights to the song as its author."

"Well, we'll re-record it."

Suddenly the door to the restroom flew open. In walked Afrika, Asia, Mable, and Tracey. "The cavalry, headed by John Carroll, sent us women in to see what was going on," Mabel said. The group laughed. "Y'all all right?"

"Yes, we're fine, Mable," Mimi said, giving the group a smile. "We're fine. Let's order up some food since John Carroll is paying."

"I second that," Brenda said. She hugged Mimi and the group single filed out of the restroom and back to their seats.

The conversation was lively once everyone ordered their food and drink and filled their palates. "I'd like to make a toast," John said. "Everybody pick up your glass of whatever you're drinking." Everyone lifted their glasses. "To family," John continued. "May it always be blessed."

"Yes," said Mable followed by everyone else.

"You really love my mother, don't you?" Trevor asked John with a serious look on his face.

"I really do. And very soon, we're going to the courthouse and have a civil wedding. There's no need to prolong what is supposed to be."

Mimi smiled.

"I approve," Trevor said. "Any man who would take time to come to the prison with my mother to see about me deserves my respect."

"Thank you, Trevor." John was overcome.

"That was so sweet of you to say, baby," Brenda said. "We want you all to be there when we say our 'I do's."

"I'll be there," Mimi chimed in. "I'm happy for the two of you."

"That means a lot, Mimi," Brenda said. "It means a lot."

Everyone's head turned when Mimi's smartphone began to ring. "I'm sorry guys. I meant to turn it off." When Mimi pulled the phone out of her purse, she saw Minx's number in the caller-ID. "I need to get this. Hi, there."

"Hey, Mimi, how are you doing?"

"Much better. In fact, we're having a fabulous lunch. Brenda's son, Trevor, was acquitted today, and we're at a restaurant celebrating."

"That's good news. I won't keep you, but I have some good news for you."

Mimi sighed. "I can't possibly think of anything it could be."

"Sit still. You're going to like this. Howard Austin called me today."

"What did he want?"

"Don't try and steal my thunder."

"Well, you're taking too long to say what it is."

"Okay, Ms. Impatient. You were nominated for a Grammy as best new artist."

"What?" Mimi screamed.

"Wait. Your single "Satisfied" was also nominated for best R&B song, along with Mary J. Blige, Kelly Rowland, and Rihanna."

"Oh my God!" Mimi moved the phone away from her mouth. "I've been nominated for two Grammy's."

Everyone screamed and gave Mimi hi-fives.

"Sorry, Minx. I couldn't hold that news in. Thank you for making my day. What am I going to do?" Mimi looked over at Brenda who mouthed the word, *sing.*

"Mimi, I've been thinking. Let me be your manager. Let me manage your career. I won't let anyone hurt you ever again."

"Minx, I don't know what to say. I have to talk it over with Raphael first. He and Afrika are my priority. I'm sure he'd want to see me realize my dream, but I want to do things differently. I'll get back with you on that."

"That's fair enough. Raphael is my man, too. And I recognize what you're saying. But in the meantime, girl, get your best dress and best hair on. We're going to the Grammy's."

"This has been a day for good news. I've got to go now. We're celebrating Trevor."

"We're celebrating life," Brenda said. "I think this calls for another toast."

"Gotta go," Minx. "Will talk with you later. Thanks for the wonderful news. I'll include you in our toast."

"Okay, Mimi. You're on your way. I'll talk with you later."

Mimi couldn't erase the smile from her face. "You did it, Mommy. My mom is a superstar," Afrika said, raising her fist. "I'm so proud of you."

CHAPTER SIXTY-EIGHT

There was glam everywhere. Wall-to-wall fans were there in massive numbers to observe their favorite recording artist. Last night at the Beverly Hills Hilton at the party for the stars was more than Mimi had imagined, but this was the moment Mimi had always dreamed of. This very afternoon, she felt like she was still dreaming. Her stretch limousine waited its turn in the lengthy line of limos that transported iconic entertainers from all over the globe.

Her limo pulled to the curb, and the dutiful doorman opened the doors to the vehicle and escorted her out so that she could embrace the red carpet. On her arm was her husband, Raphael, who had recently returned from Afghanistan on his way to retirement. Mimi's faithful manager, Minx, and her daughter, Afrika, stayed to one side, enjoying the moment for her. As if she always belonged, Mimi and Raphael graced the red carpet, she in a red Haute Couture gown by Christian Lacroix and Raphael in a gray tux by Yves Saint Laurent. Mimi waved as they floated past the fans and participated in interviews with Ryan Seacrest and several others. She was in seventh heaven, and no one could take this day…this moment away from her. Although Mimi was now a star in her own right, she couldn't believe how star struck she was as she gawked at the likes of Alisha Keyes, Beyoncé, Rihanna, Chris Brown, Usher and others as they floated down the red carpet.

Mimi smiled when she saw her name and that of her husband, manger, and daughter taped to seats in the second row. This thing was real, and for the first time she really believed.

The night got underway with Jimmy Kimmel playing host. He told a basket full of jokes, but the night belonged to the artists, songwriters, and producers. Mimi was overwhelmed as the categories were named and the winning artist came up and received their Grammy. And then the announcement was made for song of the year. It was an honor to be nominated and if she didn't win, that would be all right, too. Her fingers were intertwined with Raphael's, his with Afrika's, and Afrika's with Minx's.

Kanye West and Jill Scott were on stage to announce the winner. They did a cute little slap-stick number between them and then Jill announced the nominees. Then Kanye took his time opening the envelope with the name of the winner. Finally, he said, "And the winner for Song of the Year…can I get a drum roll please…is Mimi Bailey for "Satisfied."

There was a thunderous applause in the building. Stunned, Mimi was unable to pry herself away from her seat. Raphael whispered something in her ear, and she jumped to her feet and covered her face. She couldn't believe that her name had been called. Then suddenly returning to earth, she moved out into the aisle and almost ran to the stage where she received her first Grammy from Kanye and Jill who gave her kudos.

Mimi turned and looked out into the audience as she hugged her Grammy tight. "Wow," were her first words. "God is good. I've dreamt about receiving a Grammy when I was a little girl, singing in my mother's kitchen. This is such a good, good feeling. I want to thank the Academy; my record label, Azilet Records; my manager, Minx Gordon; my producer, Howard Austin; my wonderful husband, Raphael, and my beautiful daughter, Afrika, for being the wind beneath my wings. I wouldn't be here today if it weren't for these people. They've been my rock and my guiding light as I embarked on this venture late in my life." There were some snickers. "But I did it. I want to especially thank the fans for supporting me and making this moment, right here and right now, come true. Thank you and I love you."

The audience stood to their feet and gave Mimi a round of applause. Even after she left the stage and was being interviewed backstage, she couldn't believe how surreal it all was. The night was perfect and she wouldn't have had it any other way.

CHAPTER SIXTY-NINE

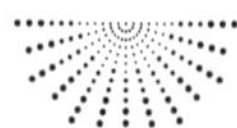

Trevor lay across the bed in the comfort of his bedroom. He stared up at the ceiling and watched as the fan twirled round and round. It was only yesterday that he had been confined to a space one-fourth the size of his bedroom. The difference was that he didn't have the luxury of getting up and moving about when he tired of staring at the ceiling.

Images of Freddie ran across his mind. He couldn't shake the fact that not once had Freddie come to see him while he was in the hell hole, and to add insult to injury, he had the nerve to get up on the stand and say he let Trevor take the rap. He felt sorry for Freddie, as he was a victim of the same circumstance. Damn, they were half-brothers. There was some remorse at how it all went down. Bottom line, Freddie let him take the rap instead of owning up to his part from the get-go.

But he was free now and ready to move forward with his life. Maybe he would continue to play basketball, but he wasn't sure. Trevor would make up his mind when it was time for him to go to college.

Right now, he had a wedding to attend. He was escorting his mother to City Hall to claim as her husband the man who truly loved her. Trevor smiled. The Christianson's were going to be all right.

AND SHE LOOKED like an angel with her family gathered all around. Brenda was beautiful in her simple white dress, white shoes, and white clutch. Her man was gorgeous in all white. And when the Justice of the Peace announced that they were man and wife, there was pandemonium in the court house, so much so, they were asked to leave the premises or be arrested. It was a joyful day.

BOOK DISCUSSION

FOOD FOR THOUGHT:

The knowledge of HIV hit the nation like a ton of bricks when it came on the scene in the mid-1980's and continued to soar in the 1990's and beyond. While you don't hear about many incidents of it broadcast on the news as before, it's still a deadly disease, especially in its full-blown element, Aids. I look at Magic Johnson, who contracted the virus over twenty-years ago, who's still going strong and seems to have overcome the full impact of the disease. Money to pay for high-priced drugs and Jesus has surely been in his favor.

In *Free to Love,* Brenda Christianson has a dilemma. Her now deceased husband, Victor Christianson, had the Aids virus and gave it to several women he'd been with outside of his marriage. While Brenda's marriage hadn't been wholesome for some time, there was still the fear that she might have the Aids virus. In the first scene, she travels to a clinic to be tested.

Free to Love suggests that there may be good news in

Brenda's future, although the title has several significant meanings. Question: If you suddenly become aware that someone you love may have contracted HIV but was given a clean bill of health, would you continue to see them, as well as enter into a sexual relationship with that person?

ABOUT THE AUTHOR

Suzetta Perkins is the author of *Behind the Veil; A Love So Deep; Ex-Terminator: Life After Marriage, Deja vu; Nothing Stays the Same; Betrayed; In My Rearview Mirror; At the End of the Day; Silver Bullets; Hollywood Skye; Two Down: The Inconvenient Truth* and a contributing author of *My Soul to His Spirit.* She is also the co-author of *The Adventures of Grammy and Sammy,* a booked she penned with granddaughter, Samayya.

A native of Oakland, California, Suzetta resides in Fayetteville, North Carolina. Suzetta is the co-founder and president of the Sistahs Book Club and Secretary of the University at Fayetteville State University. She is a member of New Visions Writing Group and resident Author of Chosen Pen Writers Group. Suzetta Perkins is also on the Board of Directors of the Fayetteville State University Friends of the Library.

For more information, you can contact Suzetta Perkins as follows:

www.suzettaperkins.com

nubianqe2@aol.com

Made in the USA
Columbia, SC
10 December 2020